To

Enjoy

THE CATALYST

Love Dad

STEPHEN C. LAWLEY

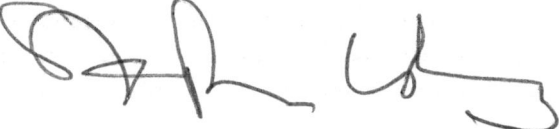

CONTENTS

PROLOGUE

THE PRESENT DAY

Tilumba Island, 50 miles NW of Malé

The air was warm and humid, typical of a tropical climate. It was the kind of day that only the stunning Maldives could offer. A gentle breeze lightly rustled the fronds of the palm trees surrounding the small beach. The sand was pristine and white, contrasting against the vibrant greenery and turquoise waters. A black hermit crab scuttled from under a fallen trunk into the fringe of the glistening waters in search of some relief from the oppressive heat. The white terns skimmed the water's surface, feeding on the plentiful food supply as they plummeted into waters just outside the coral reef.

Smoke still curled gently from the wood fire on the sand. The remains of charred white fish were untouched, along with fragments of yams. A black wild pig cautiously approached the prone form lying on the beach. Its black prickly nose twitched as it nuzzled into the still-warm body.

There was no movement.

There wouldn't be, and indeed there couldn't be. The man had been dead for four hours.

Already the black ants were investigating the small black hole in the centre of the forehead.

The hole was ringed by dried blood encrusted on its very rim.

In a week, all that would be left of the corpse would be bleached bones, as the other occupants of the island feasted.

PART-1

BEGINNINGS

CHAPTER – 1

CLERKENWELL UNIVERSITY, LONDON

By 2022, the university experience in England had evolved into a two-tier system, with a notable difference from the days of grants and means tests in the 1970s. Those who needed to work after graduation made sure to only take out small loans. As for the fortunate students with substantial financial support from their parents, they didn't worry about passing or failing as much. Many of them already had job opportunities lined up in the city upon graduation, regardless of whether they received a first-class or second-class degree.

Obtaining their degrees was effortless for them since their parents had paid for costly tutoring that guaranteed their desired final grades.

Apart from that, despite the Government's attempts at social engineering, aimed at discriminating against the public school system, most other students still landed up in the universities that had been created between the late 60s and the late 90s.

Clerkenwell University was one of the new interlopers.

Its sprawling campus never managed to meet the achievements of its illustrious neighbour, Imperial College. The chemistry department was in the centre of the smallest building, which was an independent research laboratory that carried out experimental work on nylon polymers in the 1930s.

The chemistry laboratory was undergoing dramatic change, but three departments were still stranded in the early '60s. The

5

inorganic laboratory was the most run-down. It was situated at the far end of the Chemistry faculty, due to be pulled down at the end of the academic year to make way for a new atomic physics laboratory. Chemistry in its purest sense would no longer be taught at Clerkenwell.

Inside the dimly lit laboratory, two students were beavering away chasing an elusive result.

'Shit!' Paul said, as he dropped the test tube on the floor. It smashed into myriads of tiny glass shards. The hydrochloric acid had boiled over and burnt his fingers.

Paul looked around the laboratory in dismay. Years of neglect had transformed a once-leading-edge laboratory into a dirty hovel. Tattered frayed curtains, browning from sunlight and chemical spills, covered cracked, filthy windows.

This year's chemistry intake was down to just 12 students, and he was finding it intensely boring. He had only taken up the subject because of his father. He had been on the verge of quitting, but then three events changed his mind: the death of his sister in suspicious circumstances, the untimely death of his father of cancer, and then being recruited by a PhD student to support a bizarre, fruitless project on fossil fuel alternatives.

Paul suspected that the three events were related. He was convinced that his father had been killed because he had been involved in similar research.

He bent down and swept the fragments into a dustbin, then emptied the contents into the bin in the centre of the laboratory.

Paul was a gangling, average–looking 22–year–old student with blond hair, bluish eyes, and fair, slightly pock-marked skin. He glanced across at Alicia O'Garra, the 30-year-old PhD student from the southern USA, though she had clearly inherited her looks from Irish ancestry. Alicia had joined Dougie on the project directly from the US. She had been part of the US team, which had far more resources and money. Paul wasn't completely sure how the two teams were working together, but, for the moment, there was intense cooperation, as it was thought a possible breakthrough was imminent.

She had a flat in Hampstead.

Paul had a dingy bed-sit in Kilburn.

Nevertheless, despite these jealousy pangs towards her lifestyle, she was an extremely attractive woman and Paul was working out whether he could find the courage to ask her out. He looked at her again; she was very quiet, and he was not sure how she would take it.

Paul had been permanently miserable since Christmas after losing his first real girlfriend. He had dithered for over six months and now there were only six weeks left in the term.

His thoughts turned to the man who had burdened him with this project at the beginning of the year. All the heads of department had canvassed him, but it had been a two-hour chat with Dougie that had convinced Paul of the project's incredibly exciting potential. Although Paul was still heartbroken after the loss of his father, he had agreed to join the team.

Dougie Fields, a Cambridge chemistry scholar, had convinced him to work on a research project that could revolutionise the petrochemical industry. Dougie was extremely enthusiastic, and his energy had initially rubbed off on Paul but in couple of months it started to get a bit too much.

He did not mind working in a laboratory until 8 pm. every night as long as it served its purpose and gave the results they were hoping for.

Also, since Dougie had returned from a recent trip to Canada, he had been strangely quiet and withdrawn, which was also not helping Paul's mood.

Paul had met Dougie at the end of his second year, barely a year after the death of his father. He had been on the verge of quitting university for good and just escaping for a year – maybe going on a worldwide trek.

On that particular evening, he had gone to a chemistry social in the main university building, mainly because there was nothing much else to do; at least it was a few drinks to try and liven up his mood. As Paul entered the university bar, the loud chatter and an Oasis song filled the crowded space. He made his way through the crowd to the cordoned off area at the end of the room, where students were gathered holding wine glasses of different colours and variously sized beer bottles.

Paul strolled to the nearby table and snagged a bottle of Moonwalker beer, one of the latest craft beers from a nearby brewery. It was there that he struck up a conversation with Dougie. The two spent a couple hours at the social, discussing Dougie's exciting new discovery. He had been experimenting with a catalyst for several months now, and it showed great potential. Combining unstable metals, he referred to it as a 'metallate'.

A metallate, though totally inert to any other chemical, would convert water and air to pure ethanol or methane at room temperature.

Dougie had almost limitless funding from the oil and chemical industry, which clearly realised its importance.

'That importance being,' Dougie had enthused, 'ethanol has

a higher-octane rating than Petrol and its by-products are far less poisonous. Also, in this climate crisis, the beauty of this is that it is greenhouse-gas-negative, so it removes them from the atmosphere.'

'How?' Paul asked.

'It's obvious,' Dougie had said, sounding exasperated. He started waving his arms around and scrawling on pieces of paper. 'It's like a sausage machine, except you put water and carbon dioxide in one end, in the middle it becomes alcohol which you burn as fuel, and then at the other end, out comes carbon dioxide and water, except if we decide to make it into methane or ethane then it actually absorbs them.'

He explained that metallate was the holy grail of the industry – literally the most important chemical ever to be manufactured.

Paul questioned him about all the other supposed alternative fuels such as hydrogen (too dangerous' said Dougie with a wave of his right hand), and biofuels ('excellent' but they are only going to reduce carbon emissions by 10% at best'). So, it came back to ethanol, methane or ethane as the most attractive options.

Paul continued, 'Surely wind power or solar power will become the key power sources and all cars within 10 years will be at the worst hybrid or all electric?'

Dougie looked down at the floor and furrowed his brow. 'The oil industry and car manufacturers are so protectionist that they would never allow the cars to be transformed that way. This is particularly the case in the US, with their desire to resurrect the so-called "Rust Belt". And in any case, it will not solve the carbon crisis, given the way that China and India are still growing. So it really does come back to metallates.'

Paul nodded continually while listening to Dougie's passionate explanation. When he finished, Paul said, 'OK, let's get started.'

The major problem they faced was that these catalysts were so expensive and incredibly unstable. (One gram of the stuff was 50 times more expensive than a gallon of petrol!) The only way for them to become a viable proposition was to make them reusable over 10,000 times, which was incredibly difficult to achieve.

Dougie was always full of enthusiasm when he spoke about this subject, and he dreamed of one day making a breakthrough in his research. After coming back from his trip to Canada, he seemed distant and detached. Dougie had been very enthusiastic when he left for Canada halfway through the final year's first semester; there had been promising developments in their research. But upon his return, he seemed anxious and highly tense. Paul couldn't quite figure out why, but it seemed like something catastrophic had happened during his trip, reading between the lines.

Paul glanced across the room to Alicia; it was obvious that she wasn't nearer to any sort of success either.

However, there was something peculiar in her views.

Sometimes she seemed in favour of the project, but sometimes so aggressively against it, it was unreal.

'Hey Alicia!' Paul shouted above the whirr of the machinery and the bubbling test tubes. 'How are the nickel compounds going?'

'No good,' she said sounding frustrated, 'No good at all!'

Since Dougie's return from Canada, he had not really given any support. Whatever had happened in Canada had obviously been truly traumatic. After a pause, Alicia shouted, 'Can you help me, Paul? I just need you to hold this tube while I pour in the acid.'

'Sure. Let me put down this phial.'

Alicia placed it carefully on the wooden tube holder in front of her. 'What's the problem?' Paul asked. He sauntered over, nearly stumbling over disused racks of glass beakers.

'I can't get this to dissolve.' she said, with a tinge of frustration. Paul examined the contents of the test tube and squinted to look at the bottom of the tube, he stretched out his left gloved hand and she placed it carefully into his palm.

Paul couldn't focus, his gaze constantly shifting as he tried not to stare down Alicia's blouse while she handed him the test tube. Paul's fingertips burned as he gripped the red-hot tube, despite the protective asbestos-lined glove. Suddenly, it slipped from his grasp and fell into the sink, shattering into countless shards in a matter of seconds. It was the second test tube he had dropped within ten minutes.

Brown slurry stained the sink; on top of the deposit Paul had left earlier.

'Paul, you are so clumsy,' Alicia said. 'These cost a fortune!' She glared angrily.

'I'm sorry,' Paul exclaimed, That tube was so hot it was impossible to hold,' he said as he washed his hands under cold water. Then, he just blurted it out: 'Alicia I am really sorry, but my mind is elsewhere.' 'I have been meaning to ask you for a long time.'

'Go on?' She raised her eyebrows.

'Perhaps we could go for a drink sometime?' Paul struggled to get the words out through his tightly pressed lips.

Her eyebrows closed to a slight frown and then her lips curled into a faint smile.

'When?'

'Well, now', Paul said allowing himself to breathe.

'Alright then,' she said in a casual voice.

CHAPTER – 2

LATER THAT DAY

Clerkenwell University

Dougie sat in the taxi and watched the raindrops streak down the window. He glanced at his watch and saw it was 9:00 pm. The laboratory should be empty by now, so he planned to take his usual tour of the chemistry building when he arrived. His mind wandered back to the tough day he had just endured, along with thoughts about his disastrous trip to Canada that he couldn't seem to shake off. He shuddered as he remembered arriving earlier that day in a black cab outside the executive offices located in the upscale area of Mayfair called Hays Mews. Despite having signed in at the front desk many times before, it felt like they didn't even recognise him. Once again, he went through the routine of signing in before being grilled by Rhys Williams, the Executive VP of Shetland Petroleum, who was sponsoring their research project. Apart from the very many questions about Canada and all the complications that were likely to ensue, Rhys quickly moved on to all the justifications for the continued research. 'How is Paul getting on; he is your prodigy after all?' asked Rhys intently.

Dougie didn't answer immediately, except to nod briefly and mumble, 'OK, I guess,' He continued, 'He is very curious about Canada; at some stage, I am going to have to tell him about it.'

Rhys inclined his head in agreement. 'Well, that can wait

until you get back from America, it sounds like our American cousins may have had a breakthrough.'

He read the briefing document that he had prepared the previous week before he had heard from America. 'This doesn't mean much until I get the full story and the more complete picture from the US.'

'I agree wholeheartedly,' Rhys nodded.

'Let's hope it is more successful than your recent efforts.' Rhys then went into his normal diatribe.

Dougie did not need to be reminded by Rhys (as he was continually) that the success of this would lead to a product bigger than most of the combined GDPs of Western Europe. There would be no more dependence on OPEC or states in political turmoil for the supply or non-supply of oil or a huge increase in price.

Dougie pondered his situation. He was a university PhD student and a very poor PhD student. If they could just find a solution, a solution they had so nearly unearthed all those years earlier, it was worth so much money. More money than he could even dream possible.

He could buy decent clothes. He could move out of his bed-sit into a semi-reasonable one-bedroom flat, maybe somewhere near the Angel Islington.

He remembered the expectation in Rhys's eyes. He knew that Rhys was desperate, too. But now, the initial hope of the last few months was gone, and Dougie could see that hope was being replaced with exasperation.

He now knew that Rhys would not be able to afford further research; he believed the funding would run out in about six more months. *Well never mind. He would face up to Rhys in a few weeks, hopefully with some better news.* He comforted himself with this thought and a wave of optimism swept over him for a moment.

In a couple of weeks, he was flying to the USA to meet his counterpart in California, Tom Dingwall. Dougie had been in contact with Tom several times while they were both working on the Catalyst. This would mark their first in-person meeting since Canada's visit.

Tom had accepted the offer to work on the Catalyst, but with a different approach thanks to his connection with Sean O'Paul, whom he had met in Canada. Despite conducting all of his research under extreme pressure and temperature conditions, Tom was not making any significant progress. However, his funding source appeared to be more understanding of his difficulties. Fortunately, Tom still had ample funds from Houston Oil, the second-largest producer in America and the 20th-largest company in the world. When they spoke, Tom seemed enthusiastic and even mentioned the possibility of sharing knowledge.

'Maybe that's where we see the progress,' Dougie said with a heavy emphasis on the word 'progress'.

'That will be ten quid mate!' said the taxi driver, in the typical jolly but condescending manner they tended to use.

Dougie woke up with a start; he must have dozed off. The taxi driver had spent the whole ride talking about his favourite football team (apparently, everyone in the London taxi trade was a West Ham supporter) and then switched to discussing climate change as if he were an expert on the matter. This topic was closely tied to Dougie's chosen career path, so he tried to contribute some of his own thoughts, but the all-knowing driver brushed them off as unrealistic fantasies.

He opened the cab door, which was annoyingly stuck and pulled himself out of the black leather seat and onto the wet pavement.

As he stood in front of the laboratory, his eyes scanned the building. The once grand structure was now in a state of disrepair; black paint flaked off its metal window frames and contrasted starkly against the smog-stained red brick walls. Pages from today's Evening Standard newspaper fluttered by, along with crumpled candy wrappers that eventually settled on the damp sidewalks or clung to green trash cans.

It was a pity that after just over 40 years, the university would be shutting down this summer. Clerkenwell had once been a leading institution for research laboratories and had played a crucial role in the development of newer universities in the 1980s. However, it was now facing its demise, collapsing only 45 years after its establishment. With government regulations tightening, only the top-performing institutions were receiving external funding, leaving no room for struggling schools like Clerkenwell to continue operating.

Dougie pushed gently against the entrance and slipped inside. He thought about using the lift but decided to get some exercise and walked around the corner to the steps around the rear of the building. Trudging slowly up the stairs to the third-floor Chemistry laboratory, Dougie had time to reflect on the extraordinary events of the previous few months.

He finally arrived at the laboratory door, pulling out his key and fumbling to insert it into the lock. With a slow turn, he entered the pitch-black room. The darkness seemed almost unsettling to him. "Strange," he thought with concern on his face. Suddenly, Dougie jumped and turned around, convinced that someone had just stepped back into the shadows behind him. But there was no sound, and he couldn't see anyone there.

He thought he had left the lights on earlier, but no one had been expected back this evening, and certainly not this late!

'Oh well, maybe Paul and Alicia had come back after all to complete the final experiments,' he thought ruffling his black slicked-back hair. Dougie lit a cigarette and tossed the stil- lit match into the white laboratory sink where Alicia and Paul had stood barely an hour earlier. He noticed a faint whoosh and flames flickered over the liquid and brown sediment in the sink. The brown sediment glistened in the half-light with a distinct smell of hydrocarbons.

He wondered why the sediment had been left in the basin and why no one had tried harder to wash it away.Dougie glanced around and found a small test tube in the rack above the chipped sink. He took a small sample of the sediment with a sterile spatula, placed it neatly in the test tube and resolved to look at it later.

A sudden thought made him turn back. Since her arrival, he had never completely trusted Alicia. Paul was fine even though he had reservations at first, but there was something distinctly suspicious about her. He walked over to her work area, not knowing exactly what he was looking for, but he knew that he might find something.

Slowly, he opened the drawer just underneath the sink area. Underneath, there were several shrivelled, brown-edged pieces of jottings, interspersed with a lot of correspondence from America. Dougie noticed that they were all unsigned. The postmarks on the letters were from the greater Atlanta area, catching his attention. As he read through them, one name stood out to him: Rhys. Why was Rhys mentioned? How did this person know that Rhys was funding him? It wasn't a major detail, just a passing mention of the funding. Curiosity piqued, he continued browsing through the papers and couldn't help but feel unsettled by the tone of the words. It seemed as if Alicia was gathering evidence to discredit him.

'Why?' he wondered.

Words like 'waste of funding' and 'wrong directions' had been doubly underlined in red ink. Dougie carefully folded a piece of the correspondence and thrust it into his pocket. He rearranged the rest of the papers to appear that they had not been disturbed. The papers would be examined along with the remnants in the test tube. It was clear that he needed to speak with the two of them tomorrow morning, especially Alicia. The question of how he could do that without raising suspicion lingered in his mind. A sudden thought crossed his mind, causing his brow to furrow even more. Was Paul also at fault? He was even beginning to wonder if Rhys's decision to agree to a joint project with the USA was foolish or maybe even dangerous, particularly with this very strange additional party now involved.

The research appeared to be facing opposition from external sources. He cleared his throat in his usual manner before walking away from the building. As he descended the stairs, his mind returned to the incidents that had taken place in Canada.

CHAPTER – 3

A LITTLE RECAP

Dougie was born Douglas David Earnest Fields.

His father was a well renowned nuclear physicist on the global lecture circuit and his mother was an internationally acclaimed opera singer. Both expected a great deal from their son. However, because of his parents' globetrotting, Dougie spent most of his childhood in boarding schools and saw very little of either of them.

Boarding school had been a difficult experience for him. His introspective and contemplative nature made him a prime target for bullies. As a result, Dougie kept to himself and refused to respond to the barrage of taunts.

When he was 15, he began to take a firm interest in two topics, 'The effect of carbon on global warming' and 'Inorganic chemistry'. The rare earth elements fascinated him and filled the void left by lack of friends. He took great pleasure in naming them ,

Lanthanum
Cerium
Praseodymium
Neodymium
Promethium
Samarium
Europium
Gadolinium
Terbium

Dysprosium

Holmium

Erbium

Thulium

Ytterbium

Lutetium

Scandium

Yttrium

Although he did not believe in all the dire predictions of global warming, he saw that the trend was definitely almost unstoppable. He strongly felt that rare metals could influence carbon emissions in some way, but he was unsure how this could be achieved.

His obsession with the subject led him to consistently rank as the top student in chemistry from the ages of 15 to 18. Not only did he excel in this field, but he also possessed all-round academic ability and was a guaranteed success for university. It was no surprise, as his father had also attended Cambridge after excelling in science. Like his father, Dougie was expected to follow in his footsteps. When the time came, he applied to all colleges specializing in inorganic chemistry and with his predicted grades of 4 'A*' levels, he was confident he would at least secure an interview. In early October, before his 'A' level exams the following summer, he received a letter inviting him to an interview at King's College, Cambridge. He passed the interview with ease and, after getting his results, secured a place at Cambridge University.

Dougie was both excited and nervous as he made his way to Cambridge for his first year of university. He had always dreamed of following in his father's footsteps and attending Cambridge, and now that dream was becoming a reality.

As he arrived on campus, Dougie quickly settled into his dorm room. He was pleasantly surprised to find out that his roommate, Dave, was also studying in the science department. Dave was doing Environmental Science, and the two quickly bonded over their shared interest in the subject.

Over the next few weeks, Dougie and Dave became inseparable. They spent long hours discussing their classes and their research projects. Dougie was particularly intrigued by the work Dave was doing with renewable energy sources and environmental conservation.

By the end of the first year, they got to know each other better. Dougie learned that Dave came from a small town on the coast of Scotland. His family had always been heavily involved in environmental activism, which had sparked Dave's passion for the subject. They were both eager for their second year when they would have the opportunity to study rare metals with the renowned professor George Carruthers.

CHAPTER – 4

THE UNPLANNED ADVENTURE

After a hard year of work at the university, Dougie and Dave decided to embark on a few weeks' travel on Eurorail. The first leg of their trip was in Paris. They were staying a mile from the Place de la Madeleine, in the 8th arrondissement in a lively bar area with plenty of nightlife and reasonably priced restaurants.

After initially getting off at the wrong stop on the Metro they finally found themselves outside the small bed and breakfast.

'This looks alright,' Dougie said confidently. 'Yes, it's perfect.'

Their small bedroom had two single beds, a large antique chest and a small upright wardrobe. Brownish-stained net curtains covered shutters that had been left open to get air in, on an oppressively hot early August night.

The shutters themselves could also have done with a coat of new paint, as shreds of the previous colour were still clinging to the now exposed wood.

They glanced at each other and without saying anything, they both agreed that they should get out into Paris nightlife as soon as possible.

Stepping out into the night air, they strolled along the cobbled path between the narrow buildings and soon enough came across the bar which they had passed on the way to the B&B.

It was rather exotically called Bar Pygmalion.

Inside Dougie and Dave could see a lot of activity with French waiters with trays loaded with glasses of different coloured wines raised above their heads. The waiters weaved among the throng before finding the right table, where they unloaded their substantial plates of steaming food and selections of wine.

Dougie nodded towards a small table tucked away in the corner. 'That will do Dave,' Dougie said.

After having two glasses of red wine later, Dougie and Dave left the bar, albeit a little unsteadily, and wended their way across the square to a bistro which they had spotted earlier. Inside, there were a couple of empty tables in the corner; the waiter shrugged his shoulders and pointed rather vaguely at them. It was a typical bistro, with red checked tablecloths, a burning candle in a wine bottle in the middle of the table and cutlery in a small receptacle on the side.

Two hours later, after enjoying a wonderful French steak washed down with a bottle of house red, it was time to make their way back to the hotel.

'That really was a great start,' Dougie said with some sincerity.

It was not until 10 am the next day that they both awoke and were only just in time for breakfast. Breakfast consisted of pain au chocolat, and a baguette with copious amounts of coffee. It was sufficient, though, and both felt sated as they strolled out into the already scorching sun under a perfect blue azure sky. Out of their entire trip, this was the only part they had prearranged. Being there for just one day meant that every detail had to be carefully thought out and organised.

Ultimately, it was decided that they would start their day by visiting the Eiffel Tower in the morning before the lines became too long. Next, a stop at the Louvre Museum to see the famous Mona Lisa painting. A late lunch at one of the museum's restaurants would be followed by a leisurely walk down the Champs Elysée to admire the stunning Arc de Triomphe. They planned to end the day by exploring the bars and nightlife around the controversial Pigalle red light district.

Dougie was very disappointed with the Mona Lisa; it was so small and so heavily guarded that he could barely see it. Dave wasn't keen on the Eiffel Tower, although very impressed with the views. He hadn't realised how bad he was with heights. They agreed that, if they never saw another plate of French bread and cheese, they would be extremely happy, but they both loved the Champs Elysée.

It had been an enjoyable, full day until a strange thing happened as they sat enjoying their last bottle of French red wine in a cosy bar in the Pigalle district.

Dougie stared into the distance beyond the red velvet chairs and dimmed lanterns in the corner of the bar. He looked once and then again at the small table in the alcove, where two men in white T-shirts seemed to be in deep conversation.

One of the men's faces was reflected in the light of the lantern.

Dougie leaned towards Dave, trying not to look too conspicuous.

'Isn't he the chemistry professor from college: you know, the one who is always smoking a pipe and mumbling to himself as he walks around the campus?'

Dave instinctively turned round.

'Don't,' Dougie implored.

But it was too late; they had been spotted; the man stood up from the table and walked straight towards them.

'Is there a problem? ' he said.

Dougie looked him in the eye and paused.

'You're Professor Carruthers, aren't you?' he said.

'Who are you?' Carruthers said with a puzzled expression.

'I am Dougie Fields, I am going to be a student in one of your lectures next year; in fact, it is one of my favourite subjects.'

Carruthers frowned. 'And what subject is that Dougie, if I may ask?'

'The Rare Metals course,' Dougie said. Carruthers suddenly looked panicked.

'Don't even say that word, particularly here.' He jerked his head back towards the corner he had just vacated, where his companion, with his back to Dougie, remained motionless.

'OK, I was just excited,' said Dougie.

'Well don't mention that subject again,' said Carruthers, as he stormed off back to his companion.

They both just sat in silence for a while and then, in very hushed tones, resumed their conversation.

'What the heck was all that about?' said Dave. Dougie shrugged his shoulders.

They continued chatting, and sipping their wine until there was a sudden disturbance at Carruthers' table. Both men raised their voices before Carruthers' companion rose abruptly and stormed out of the restaurant. As he brushed past them, Dougie glimpsed his face, which expressed both fear and anger. He slammed the door behind him, and, after a few seconds, the restaurant's patrons resumed their conversations. Dougie stared at the now motionless back of Carruthers.

'What's he doing now?' said Dave in a whisper.

'Nothing,' Dougie whispered back. 'Let's look at tomorrow's schedule.'

Dave retrieved the schedule from the back pocket of his jeans.

'Well, it's an early start again, then Amsterdam by mid-morning,' he said. 'Two nights there before we go to Berlin,' he continued.

As Dave was about to reveal their next day's plan, Carruthers abruptly stood up and manoeuvred through the tables, heading towards the exit. Dougie quickly averted his gaze, hoping to avoid any potential conversation. However, Carruthers stopped by their table and whispered, 'Don't say a word. If anyone asks, you didn't see me here,' before striding out of the restaurant with determination. 'What a weird night,' said Dave. 'Probably we should head back to the hotel?'

'Yes, let's do that,' said Dougie.

The following morning, they took a cab to the station. The checkout had been easy, although there was some dispute about an extra lodging charge. Neither of them mentioned the incident the night before.

They were early for the train. After a short walk, they came across a small coffee opposite the newsagent.

It wasn't until they started to sup the coffee that Dougie caught a glimpse of the headlines in one of the newspapers.

It was just one word: 'Meutre'. Underneath was a picture of a clean-shaven man too indistinct to recognise from where they were seated.

'What does "Meutre" mean, Dave?' Dougie said.

'Murder, I think.'

He picked the newspaper to have a better look.

Dave translated the article, 'It says that he was an American tourist and was a frequent visitor to Paris.'

'It's him,' Dougie said, with a tremor in his voice. 'Who?' Dave said.

'The guy at Carruthers' table, I would recognise him anywhere, those huge bushy eyebrows, the scar on his left cheek and in particular those green eyes,'

Dave read on and stopped, 'Oh my God. It happened just round the corner from the restaurant we were in.'

Dougie stared again at the headline and whispered quietly, 'What shall we do?'

Dave pondered for a moment, 'I think the best thing would be to ignore it for now.' He continued, 'If we get involved, we could get stuck here for weeks and we really don't know anything except we thought we saw them together, it doesn't prove a thing .'

'Also, it talks about one of his colleagues helping the police, and that could well be Carruthers.'

'I guess so,' said Dougie.

'C'mon Dougie, let's get on the train and we can chat about it later.'

Of course, in the coming days, they did nothing of the sort as European city after European city came and went.

After some carefree experiences in Amsterdam, Prague, Vienna and Berlin, they arrived late at night in Budapest. A few hours later, Dougie received a message that was to cut short their fun.

The phone gave a bleep for an incoming text. He glanced at his watch.

'Please meet me in Nice tomorrow, it is very urgent, and I can explain everything about Paris C. PS: I have sent cash to the American Express office in Budapest.'

'Dave, wake up! I have just received this really weird text.'

'Go back to sleep Dougie, it's way too early.' Dave stirred.

'No, no, you got to read it; it's from Carruthers, I think.'

'Give me the phone.' Dave sat up instantly.

He paused. 'It doesn't make any sense at all Dougie. How did he get your number, and also how did he know we were in Budapest?'

Dougie paused and thought for a moment before responding, 'My phone number is listed in our university student records. There can't be too many people named Dougie in his class for next year.' He added, 'But I have no idea how he knew I was in Budapest.' After another brief pause, he continued, 'Wait a minute, what if he called the emergency number that's listed, my parents' contact details, and explained that he was from Cambridge and needed to urgently get hold of me?'

Dougie dialled his home number. 'I am so sorry Mum, but can you just let me know if anyone from Cambridge has called in the last couple of days trying to get hold of me?'

'I don't know,' she paused. 'Oh, just a minute, there was a weird call yesterday. Let me think, yes, he wanted to know your location, he had an urgent package for you. I hope you don't mind me disclosing this information to him; he was very persistent in obtaining it.'

'No, it's not a problem. Mum, that answers what I needed to know; thank you so much.'

Dougie turned to Dave, 'I guess you heard all that. '

'Yup I did, but it has messed up our holiday big time.'

'It should be alright Dave, if we can get to Nice today, we can still spend a couple of extra days there and then still get back on schedule.'

'I am not so sure,' Dave raised his eyebrows in exasperation, 'Well, let's get to the AMEX office when it opens in a few hours and see what this is all about.'

At nine o'clock, they were waiting patiently for the doors to open in the central Budapest AMEX office.

The officer slid open the bolts and glared at them both.

'Are you American, it is always the Americans who are so keen.'

'No English.'

'OK... come in, what can I do for you two gentlemen, please?'

Dougie jumped in first, 'Do you have a package addressed to Dougie Fields please?'

'Let me look?'

He thumbed through a full tray of identical-looking envelopes, 'Ah yes, here we go Mr. Fields, here it is.'

Dougie grabbed the outstretched envelope and, with a polite thank you, turned and headed for the door.

He tore open the top of the envelope and inside was a considerable quantity of Hungarian currency and an even larger quantity of Euros. There were also two first-class plane tickets to Nice for later that day.

Dougie glanced at his phone and realised it was only a couple of hours before the flight.

'We better get a taxi, Dave; otherwise, we stand a risk of missing the flight. 'OK,' Dave flagged one of the numerous taxis circling the tourists on the quayside.

Using some of Carruthers' cash, Dougie peeled off a few more notes in preparation for the taxi fare.

The 30-minute journey to the airport seemed to take forever. Rush hour in Budapest was very much like any other European City.

Before boarding the flight, they browsed the duty-free goods before settling on a very expensive couple of bottles of vintage wine and a 25-year-old bottle of single malt Scotch each. Smiling, and clutching their goods they headed for the Magyar airlines first class lounge.

Dave smiled as he pressed the buzzer which gained them immediate entry. A smartly dressed Magyar Airlines employee, whose name badge said Martin, asked, 'Gentlemen, can I have your names please?'

Dougie answered for them both, 'Dougie Fields and Dave Williams'

'Ah yes, Mr Fields, I have a message for you.' the man said in crisp, perfect English.

He thrust a brown envelope into Dougie's outstretched palm.

Dougie glanced at Dave, 'I bet this is Carruthers making sure we are on the plane!'

And indeed, it was the message was very curt and precise. 'Hilton Hotel, Main Reception. Nice, 8.30 pm.' Nothing further was discussed until they were about to land at the Nice airport.

'What do you think is going to happen, Dougie, and why all the weird behaviour?'

'I don't know, but we will find out soon enough,' he replied. There was a bump as the plane landed rather hard on the Nice runway and, within moments, the cabin staff had announced their arrival at Nice airport.

CHAPTER – 5

THE MYSTERY BEGINS

Walking through customs, Dave saw a smartly dressed chauffeur holding up a board with Dougie's name on it. They followed him to a large black Mercedes parked just outside the main car park. The chauffeur was uncommunicative, with just a couple or so brief sentences the entire journey.

'My name is Stephane, I am taking you to the Hilton. There you will check into your prepaid rooms. Afterwards, you will meet Mr Carruthers as agreed.'

The Hilton in Nice was one of the more exclusive in the chain, and its rooms were palatial. Dave lay on his bed for a few minutes just before they were due to go down and must have dozed off for a few moments until he was startled awake by an urgent knock on the bedroom door.

'Dave, we have got to get downstairs now, Carruthers will be waiting for us.'

'OK, he said lazily, 'let's go.'

The main reception downstairs was empty except for a loud American complaining about the size of his bathroom. They looked at each other. Suddenly, there was a shrill tone from the front desk phone, which the receptionist answered within two rings.

'Yes,' she said before looking around. 'There are two young men by the concierge desk.'

The unknown caller must have asked something as the receptionist gestured towards both of them.

Dougie picked up the handset and held it firmly to his right ear.

A hushed voice asked, 'Is that Dougie Fields?'

'Yes,' answered Dougie.

'This is Professor Carruthers, but I guess you already know that. I believe I am being followed so I can't meet you there.' He continued, 'There is a small bar, Le Bon Chance, very close by; turn right out of the hotel and then immediately right again. The bar is noisy but safe. See you there in ten minutes.'

With that, the call ended, and Dougie hung up the phone. He turned to Dave with a sense of urgency.

'We have to leave immediately.'

They quickly followed the route they had been instructed to take.

'This is it, Dave, Le Bon Chance.'

It was very similar to the bar in Paris a week or so earlier: just as chaotic, except much smaller.

Dave looked around. 'I can't see him, but I am not sure I would recognise him in any case.'

Dougie peered through the clouds of smoke; in the corner by the outside bar was a man wearing a baseball cap pulled over his eyes with his hand raised.

'There he is, Dave.' They made their way through the crowd to get to his table.

Carruthers proffered a handshake to both of them.

'I am sorry about all the secrecy; it's been an insane two or three weeks.'

Before Carruthers could say anything, Dougie began to speak, but Carruthers raised his hand for silence.

'Let me explain everything first; there will be plenty of time for questions later. Let's start with that night in Paris; the guy you saw me with is… was… an eminent professor, Jean de Clerc; His specialty was in rare metals, and he was intrigued by the significant advancements in their use as catalysts. In particular, he was interested in catalysts that could theoretically change water and air into new types of petrocarbons. He was discussing with me that night the possibility of Cambridge University funding his research as, understandably, he was getting a lot of resistance from the oil industry. In fact, he had told me confidentially that there had been some threats to his life and the lives of his immediate family. So when you approached me, I was wary and hesitant to engage with you.'

Carruthers paused and then lowered his voice and continued.

'I explained to him that research grants were hard to come by at the moment, but when I returned to England, I would approach both the university and also some other potential partners. I also explained that some of the smaller oil companies in England, unlike France, did have some interest in research into alternatives to oil and petrocarbons. Our conversation did, however, get a little heated; as he insisted, I was trying to hide things from him. That was when he left in a hurry, and you probably heard the expletives.'

Carruthers paused again as though he had thought of something else but shook his head briskly and finished his story.

'I asked you not to say anything before I left because I was still seething, and I apologise for being somewhat brusque. As you know, it was at least half an hour between Professor de Clerc's leaving and my subsequent departure.'

Carruthers drew breath again and continued.

'When I left the restaurant, I jumped in a taxi which was conveniently parked outside and headed back to my hotel. This was later corroborated by several people, including the hotel receptionist, the waiting staff in the restaurant and the barman at the hotel, where I had a number of nightcaps. Jean de Clerc's murder was timed while I was either in the taxi or at the hotel bar.'

Carruthers paused. 'Now you may ask, why all the secrecy?'

Dougie and Dave both nodded vigorously.

He continued, 'Well, since that incident, I, too, have been receiving many threats. All of them have been related to my conversations with de Clerc, and now, to be frank, I am a little frightened and getting paranoid. Any questions now?'

Dougie stepped in first: 'Only one question really sir; why us?'

'That's a bit more difficult to explain. When you introduced yourself to me as students from Cambridge University, I felt relieved. After verifying with the university, I was grateful to have someone I could confide in and share this information with in case of any unforeseen circumstances. Basically, I am going to take a year off and head off to Canada. I have a small ranch near Calgary, and I just need to get away. I need you to be my eyes and ears back at Cambridge University, where there may be a lot of questions and inquisitive people. I will give you an email address, which I will access once a week. All I need you to do is report anything unusual and/or any approaches from any individual, no matter how insignificant it may seem at the time.'

Dougie and Dave looked at each other and shrugged: 'Yes, that's fine, Sir.'

Carruthers replied, 'Please call me George, and thank you for doing this; it takes a load of my mind.'

Carruthers's shoulders eased downwards.

'One last thing, you can keep all that cash I gave you of course; however, I would suggest that you purchase a laptop for the sole purpose of contact with me,' he paused and removed a sheet of paper from the back pocket of his jeans. Carefully unfolding the paper, it showed a model of a computer and underneath an email address that was just a number of digits and special symbols.

'I suggest you memorise this email and don't write it down anywhere.' Dougie nodded. 'Great, well with that I am going to leave you; the next communication you will hear from me will be from Canada. I will text you your login details, probably in about four weeks. Good luck next year.' With that, Carruthers got up and left.

They looked at each other; it was Dougie who spoke first.

'Well, that was really weird.' He paused, 'Why did he pick on us? To be honest, I think it was just a coincidence that we happened to be in that bar that night; don't you think that was the reason?' said, Dave said rubbing his chin.

'Yes maybe.'

It was very dark at the bar now; as they glanced around it, was certainly a lot quieter.

'What a night, Dave,'

It was well after 2 am when they ended back at the room, and slumber soon followed.

The following day, sometime after eleven in the morning, they sat down to breakfast and had a lengthy discussion. They ultimately decided not to rush back to England right away. Instead, Dougie wanted to spend a few more days in Brussels before returning home.

Dave couldn't help but ask, 'What do you think that was all about?'

Dougie replied, I believe we met a man who was extremely frightened. He and his family were likely threatened by someone or something unknown. It must have been a terrible experience for him to take a year off and leave behind what he clearly loves.'

He paused and then continued, 'In any case, I think he has also become a little paranoid since his colleague was murdered. Maybe he blames himself partially for his death. You know, if he had stayed with him and then they had left together, maybe it would never have happened.'

Dave nodded in agreement: 'I don't think we 'll have him next year, and I also doubt if he will come back for the final year, but we will see.'

CHAPTER – 6

BACK IN ENGLAND

After a few busy days in Belgium, the journey home had been uneventful. Dougie was lying in his bed at his new lodgings in Cambridge, wondering whether it had all been a dream—or a nightmare.

Dougie had been right about the second year. The work was dull, and although the subject was interesting, the work had become far more mathematical than conceptual. He had always hated that area in the first year, so this year was no different. At least there were always the weekends to look forward to when he and Dave could find some pleasant watering hole in town or sometimes further afield.

They had agreed to invest some of Carruthers' cash in a small car and ended up with a two-seater Mazda sports car. It was a little old-fashioned in shape, but it was a great little run around.

Every weekend, as agreed, they sent a one-line email to Carruthers. They would only respond to the requests if asked, but there were never more than one- or two-word answers, either All OK? or Everything good?

As the weeks turned into months, and then terms, the end of the year came upon them before they knew it. Christmas and Easter had passed without either of them returning home, which made time fly by even faster. They both found exams fairly simple and managed to achieve their desired grades: a 2:1 for Dave and a first for Dougie. They now only had one more year left before graduating. With the summer approaching, they both decided to go their separate ways for various reasons. Dougie had even landed a job at a local chemical factory for the summer. As the school year came to an end, they said goodbye with a warm hug and a promise to see each other again in September.

That should have been the end of it at least until their final year. However, everything changed when Dougie received a strange message in late July.

While he was at work on the product testing line, Dougie glanced at his phone and noticed a message from an unknown caller.

All it said was, 'The Barge, 8.00pm, tonight, urgent. G.'

Dougie knew the Barge well, it was always busy and particularly on a Thursday, (which was today). He made the not unreasonable assumption that G was Carruthers.

Dougie thought for a moment and wondered if it was a possible trap.

But then again, how could it possibly be a trap when it was in such a public place?

CHAPTER - 7

THE BARGE, 8.00 PM

The sun was still shining bright when Dougie reached the Barge, and it was packed with tourists as expected in the summer months. Dougie peered around to look for Carruthers, but there was no sign of him. He looked again towards the fence and saw a middle-aged man carrying a small green rucksack who was gesticulating wildly at him.

Dougie quickly glanced behind him to make sure the man wasn't mistaking him for someone else. When he looked back, the man was still waving urgently. Dougie hesitantly walked over to where the man was waiting and grabbed a pint from the outdoor bar on his way. As the man approached Dougie , he looked furtively from one side to the other still clutching his green rucksack.

'Are you Dougie Fields?' he asked without introducing himself.

'Yes,' said Dougie rather defensively, 'And who are you anways?'

'You don't need to know this Dougie, just that I am a messenger from C.' 'Is that Carruthers,' said Dougie, getting more impatient as the conversation continued.

'I cannot say,' the man replied.

He opened the rucksack and took out a small package in a clear plastic folder.

Dougie could see a small memory stick and an old-fashioned mobile handset.

'This is for you Dougie, dial 121 for a message on the phone and open up the information on the memory stick.' He paused, 'This will explain everything.'

With that, the unknown man turned away and headed back down the river path.

Dougie looked at the package and almost threw it into the river but then steadied himself. He gulped his pint and headed back along the river in the opposite direction to the man with the rucksack listening to the message on the way. It was Carruthers. He referred to the memory stick and then asked him to confirm by text to another number that he had read the instructions and clearly understood them. It then asked him to dispose of the phone. Dougie grinned to himself; he had half expected it to say the phone would self destruct in 30 seconds as per the *Mission Impossible* films.

Arriving back at his lodgings in Cambridge, Dougie opened up his laptop and inserted the memory stick. There was only one file on the stick. He read through the document, which was a matter of fact, with several steps he had to follow. It was clear that Carruthers was not going to return until the final semester the following year, he talked about unfinished business in Canada in an introduction to the document.

Dougie printed off the document and read through the instructions once again.

(1) Confirm by text you have read this message and then destroy the handset.

(2) Remove all records of the email address on ALL devices used.

(3) My successor at Cambridge, who will be delivering my lectures next year is not to be trusted. Therefore, do not under any circumstances pass on information about my present or future whereabouts.

(4) The following is a code for a safety deposit box at the local branch of Coutts. Please memorise and do not keep any record of the number. Inside the box are some details on the progress I have made on rare metal catalysts research.

This should only be opened if anything happens to me. All being well this will not have to be touched until next April, when I intend to return to England.

(5) In case of absolute emergency please contact this number.

Keep safe,
C

Dougie sat down and wondered what to do, and when to go to open the box.

Oh well, he thought to himself, let's see what the final year will bring.

CHAPTER - 8

FINAL YEAR AT CAMBRIDGE

Dougie was relieved when Dave returned to Cambridge; he had missed his company and the friend to drink with. He was itching to tell Dave about the communication with Carruthers but decided to wait until that evening when they had settled in and were having a drink at one of their regular haunts.

It was around 7.00 pm when they had settled in for a pint at the Plough and Thatcher when Dougie went through all the communication he had received from Carruthers the previous week. Dave listened to everything Dougie said and then went silent for a while. He leaned forward and said quietly so no one could overhear.

'He is in trouble, Dougie; I seriously believe that he thinks that his life is in danger.'

'But why me, Dave? Why does he always come back to me and no one else?'

'Maybe it all comes down to that Paris encounter and he felt he could trust us from then on.'

Dougie shook his head. 'No, it has got to be something else, Dave,' he continued, 'Surely he can trust his family in Canada?'

'Obviously not, Dougie, otherwise you would not have received that communication.'

Dougie paused for a moment, 'Just a thought: what if something has happened to a member of his family?'

'Don't be ridiculous,' Dave replied. 'He would surely have said something in the communication.'

'Well, you never know and there is a very easy way to find out.'

Dave raised his eyebrows, expecting an answer.

'Well, what would that be?' he said when he didn't receive an immediate reply.

'Let's use Google to get some answers,' Dougie said.

'Hmm let's start by looking at unexplained deaths in Canada,' he said, without any real conviction.

Sure enough, that search bought up over 1,000 names. 'OK!' said Dougie, 'let's narrow it down a bit, shall we?'

Dougie typed in- *Unexplained deaths in Canada in the last two months.*

This was a little bit more rewarding; it brought up only 40 names. He scrolled down the list carefully looking at each one. It took thirty minutes and he had almost given up.

Dave looked at him and said, 'What are you exactly looking for Dougie?' 'Well just any name with same surname as Carruthers,'

Dave laughed out loud and then said. 'Do you honestly think that someone is going to use his real name under any circumstances?'

Dougie nodded 'Well it is possible, isn't it?' he said, looking rather glum.

'Let me have a look at that list.'

Dougie passed over the phone and Dave scanned through the first few names.

'You're right, there doesn't appear to be a match.' He paused, 'Ah wait a minute, what's this?' Dave said. 'Look at the last one on the list,' as he read.

'The wife and eldest daughter of English Cambridge professor John Carruthers were involved in a tragic boating accident. The accident happened near the town of Kingston, Ontario. The eldest daughter was killed instantly, while Jeannette Carruthers remains in a critical condition in the nearby hospital. A witness told the local police that the boat appeared to lose control and flipped overthrowing both occupants into the water. Jeannette made it to the shore but fell unconscious soon after, while Lisa died at the scene.'

Dave looked at Dougie; 'Maybe George is his second name, and he preferred using that?'

Dougie nodded.

'Yes, I guess you are right; it can't be anyone else, and it would also explain the cloak and dagger approach.' He paused.

'In particular, I think this is why he has chosen me. Look at it this way. His daughter has been killed in very suspicious circumstances. Next, he has decided to stay at least six months longer in Canada, probably to get to the bottom of what happened. Also, he is not very likely to leave his wife when she is still in a coma. On top of that he does not trust his replacement at all and has asked me to avoid contact at all costs. Yes, it is all slipping into place.'

After the revelations from the pub night, Dougie found it difficult to sleep for a few nights. He knew he needed to pull himself together as lectures were about to start, and the new professor, replacement of Carruthers, was set to give the first lecture of the day. Dougie had done some research on the new professor and found nothing dubious or suspicious in their background. The new professor's name was James Flowers, age 34 years, graduated from Imperial College and then took a PhD in the role of rare metals in treating medical conditions. He became a junior lecturer at the college for three years before moving to Cambridge as a deputy head of department in Inorganic Chemistry. He is married with two daughters aged two and four.

It was a wet autumn afternoon as Dougie headed towards the lecture, which was to be held in the main Chemistry building in the college. James Flowers was already waiting for his students as Dougie entered the room and headed towards the backbenches as he normally did. Dougie looked at him and noticed a typical lecturer's dress code: brown checked trousers, a careworn leather jacket with a flowery shirt just showing above the jacket lapels. His appearance matched his clothing; he had a straggly beard with a droopy moustache. His hair was brushed back away from his forehead to display a pair of brown framed glasses, behind which were two piercing blue eyes, which seemed to track your movements around the room.

James started speaking with a loud, clear voice, introducing himself. He went on to describe what he intended to cover in the two terms he was likely to be with the group. He explained, as Dougie already knew, that Carruthers would be unlikely to join them until the Spring term.

'My intention is to cover the role of rare metals in treating certain medical conditions such as epilepsy and even some types of cancer. I will not be covering their role as a catalyst as I believe that a lot of the theories and the science behind them are not worthy of exploring as a final year Chemistry subject.' He paused: 'Any questions?'

Dougie was going to put his hand up but to thought better of it. Instead, one of the women raised their hand.

'Yes, what is your question...?'

'My name is Veronica, and my question relates to Mr Carruthers.'

'Yes, go on,' said Flowers, a bit irritably.

'When I read the prospectus for this year, Mr Flowers, it clearly stated that we would be studying the role of rare metals as catalysts and not as medicinal cures, why has this changed?'

'There are several reasons but the main two are that firstly, I have very little knowledge of rare metal catalysts. Secondly, out of all the experts in this field, there are only a handful who have enough knowledge to give even one lecture. And out of those, there may only be five who could go as far as giving 10 or 20 lectures. Carruthers is undoubtedly one of them, and while it's not guaranteed, he will most likely not be here for the final term.' Flowers paused, 'Does that answer your question?'

Veronica nodded and sat down.

'OK, let's get started then,' Flowers said.

For the next hour he droned on, talking about a subject that Dougie had little or no interest in whatsoever.

The semester went past very quickly and soon it had reached Christmas. Dave and Dougie had little time at weekends as both were concentrated on achieving the highest grades possible.

After the last lecture before the short Christmas break, Dougie realised that he had left his notes in the lecture theatre and went back to retrieve them. Flowers was still sitting at the front desk and initially didn't notice Dougie's re-entry into the theatre. However, he noticed him as he was about to leave.

'You are Dougie; Dougie Fields, aren't you?'

Dougie nodded, wondering what was coming next. 'Have you got a minute please?' said Flowers.

'Sure,' said Dougie.

'I think you may be able to guess what I want to talk about; it's about Carruthers, I was told that you may have been in contact?'

'No, what makes you think that?' Dougie replied.

Flowers softened his voice, but it seemed to carry more threat. 'OK, but if you do hear from him, I need you to tell me immediately. It is extremely important, is that clear!'

Dougie nodded and after a brief pause, asked, 'But why is it so important?'

'Let's just say that some of the university research sponsors need to get hold of him, I believe it is a funding problem,' said Flowers bluntly.

'OK, I will let you know if I hear anything, was there anything else?' 'No! See you next year.'

Dougie turned away and headed back to the flat. As he walked, he thought about Flowers' words; although they were not especially sinister, he had sensed a veiled threat. He decided not to mention anything to Dave. There was no point in worrying him just before Christmas.

CHAPTER – 9

THE UNEXPECTED VISITOR

Christmas had come and gone, and now there was only one more full term of lectures before they broke for Finals preparation in early May.

It was on a cold, wet March morning that Dougie received a call on his mobile that would change his life.

'Is that Dougie Fields?'

'Yes,' he answered quietly.'

The female voice continued, 'It's the College office; you have a guest; can you come across immediately?'

'Who is it please?'

'I am sorry he wouldn't say, just that it is urgent.'

'OK, I will be over right away.'

Dougie stepped out from his flat wondering who it could be at this time of the morning.

The rain was slanting in almost horizontally straight into his face and felt icy cold. Swirls of debris whipped across the street, accentuating the mood of impending disaster. A few minutes later, Dougie found himself outside the main office and pushed the door open.

In a way, it was no surprise to see a very dishevelled George Carruthers sitting in the corner. He was wearing a grey raincoat, still damp from the rain that was pounding the glass windows in the office.

Carruthers smiled sheepishly at Dougie, 'I bet you didn't expect to see me again!'

'Well to be honest, I did have my suspicions.' Dougie said with a slight grin lingering on his face.

Carruthers smiled back and said, 'Shall we grab a coffee across the road? If we run, we won't get too wet.'

Soon they found themselves in a favourite student coffee shop The Second Cup. After finding an empty corner, they spoke in hushed tones to ensure their conversation was not overheard by the few customers present. All of them were students, bemoaning their lack of funds.

Carruthers started, 'I guess you know something about what happened in the last 18 months?'

Dougie nodded with a glum expression. 'I found out that your daughter was killed, and your wife was in a coma, though I don't know what has happened recently?'

'Well Dougie, I won't ask how you found out that information, but I guess that is the power of the internet!' he continued, 'My wife has fully recovered thankfully, but obviously is extremely upset. She blames herself but cannot fully recall the events of that fateful day.'

He leaned forward.

'There is something extremely suspicious about how a boat in tranquil calm water can suddenly flip over, but I guess I will never know.'

He continued, 'I am returning for your final seven lectures and will be discussing the role of rare metals in the creation of catalysts, and in particular catalysts that can break the hydrogen/oxygen link in water and the carbon/oxygen bond. This will only be theoretical in the lectures; however, I can tell you that research is underway to explore this possibility.'

'Where do I fit in then?' asked Dougie.

'There are several ways, Dougie. I have looked at your predicted grade and you are a nailed-on certainty for a first-class honours' degree. What I would like to offer you therefore is a chance to study further in Canada, and I have cleared this through the Head of Department, Brian Vickers, a PhD in Rare Metal Catalysts. This will be jointly funded by the University and by Shetland Petroleum. Shetland have invested a lot of money and are expecting results quickly.'

Dougie raised his hand to interject.

'I have nearly finished, Dougie; on top of this, I have an opportunity for you to earn £100,000 tax-free in the summer. There is a camp in Canada, which is trying to accelerate the catalyst process and will also give you a big head start in your PhD.'

Carruthers paused. 'Any questions?'

'Yes,' replied Dougie, 'What's the catch? Paying £100,000 for a piece of research, it's a huge amount of money?'

'I knew you would ask that. There are apparently some elements of danger in the camp, in terms of the chemicals you will be handling. There are several that are extremely carcinogenic.'

Dougie thought for a moment, weighing up all the factors.

Carruthers continued, 'There is one more thing to consider before you decide anything; I am not going to be with you; I may not even be here for my last lectures.'

Dougie raised his eyebrows in surprise.

'I have blood cancer. Unfortunately, it has already spread to some of the soft organs. I personally believe that it may well have been caused by the chemicals I just mentioned.'

Carruthers paused, waiting for his words to sink in. Dougie was silent, lost for words.

'I therefore have a big favour to ask you. I have a son at college in London, also studying Chemistry. He is reaching the end of his second year and is looking for a final year project under the guidance of a PhD student. I know you are taking the PhD there also. He will take some convincing, but I want you to take him on. He will be devastated by my death, but I am sure that you will be at your most persuasive; his name is Paul.'

Dougie nodded and felt a tear come to his eye. He had only really known Carruthers for a few months and only met him properly twice but felt he had known him for a long time.

'I will accept your offer, Sir; that includes the summer camp in Canada.'

Carruthers proffered his hand which Dougie accepted and shook vigorously.

'I am off now, Dougie, but remember when my lectures start you know nothing of this conversation.'

Dougie raised his hand to stop him going, 'George, what about the research documents in the bank security box?'

Carruthers stared at Dougie as though he was mad and then relaxed.

'Of course, that information is absolutely key to everything, make sure you retrieve that information as soon as possible.'

With that parting remark, Carruthers wheeled round and left Dougie standing alone in the café.

CHAPTER – 10

THE FINAL LECTURE

During the final term, Dougie received an email from Carruthers confirming that he would receive the offer of the PhD. In a separate document were the details of the Canada assignment; they were very precise, and attached were details of the £100,000 payment. Carruthers also shared further information on how to access the security box as soon as possible.

It all sounded very real, and Dougie was now convinced that there was some truth in the rare metal catalysts theory. He was determined to research it thoroughly before the start of his PhD and the project trip to Canada.

That afternoon prior to going to the library, Dougie went to the bank and got access to the security box. Inside there were a lot of papers with detailed research and a couple of invaluable leads. At the library Dougie knew exactly what he was looking for, thanks to the information in the security box. The main one was a book by an eminent scientist from the 19th century, it was by Claude Devoir and the title of the book was Chemical Reactions.

For an hour, Dougie checked the book index on the Library PC until he found its location. Rather excitedly with his heart pumping Dougie walked past the huge, cavernous corridors of books that led to the Chemistry section. There was the book, a green volume, a little moth-eaten and tattered at the edges.

He took the book down and turned over the first few pages to locate the index. He wasn't exactly sure what he was trying to find, but his eye caught the title of a chapter on the breaking of the hydrogen–oxygen bond. Quickly, he turned to the right page and started to read. The first few pages were not very intriguing highlighting the bonds as the strongest known in nature, but then it started to discuss the role of the catalyst in breaking the bond. Catalysts made of a combination of well-known metals such as Copper could be combined with some of the rare earth metals to form unstable compounds. When the strongest H-O bonds, such as those found in water, were passed over the catalyst, the H-O bonds, Claude had observed, were broken to form other compounds, such as ethyl alcohol. The main problem was the instability of the compound, which meant it could only be used once or twice, and this led to incredibly high costs due to the rarity of the components. Claude had concluded his experiments but had added a footnote at the bottom of the page that, although it was an interesting area that probably merited further research, until the catalysts were more stable, it would not be worth extensive investment.

Dougie closed the book with a sigh. He strolled back to his room, glancing skyward at the increasingly dark clouds. It looked like the predicted storms were rapidly approaching.

Lying down on his bed, he contemplated the next steps and listened to the pellets of rainwater splattering against the window. It was strangely mesmeric, and soon Dougie drifted off into a deep sleep.

It was nearly 2 am when Dougie was woken up by a bleep on his smartphone.

It was a message from Carruthers.

'Sorry to bother you so late, but I am not going to cover the rare metal catalysts in tomorrow's lecture as I believe that the information may get to the wrong people at the university. Can

I meet you on the bridge by The Barge, as I have some important information to give you? Please confirm. If you can meet it will be at about 12.30 just before what I now believe will be my last lecture. I will fill you in when we meet.'

Dougie replied immediately, 'Yes, that is no problem.' He could not get to sleep after that; he tossed and turned all night. The bleeping alarm at 8 am came all too soon.

He stretched out and glanced across at Dave, who was still sleeping soundly.

Dougie wondered what to do for the next few hours and decided to have a wander around town. At around 11:45, the sun was just filtering through the clouds and the coldness of the previous few days had disappeared to be replaced by a warm, southerly breeze. Dougie leaned over the bridge and suddenly the deep gloom of the previous days started to evaporate. The punts were lined up, ready to be taken out by mostly students and a few tourists. On the opposite bank, a heron sat completely still, scanning the water's surface for its first meal of the day. Dougie quickly surveyed his surroundings and noticed Carruthers slowly making his way towards him, shuffling in his usual awkward manner. He was taken aback by the sudden change in Carruthers' appearance. His cheeks had turned a sickly grey and appeared to be stretched tightly over his bones, giving them an eerie sheen. Even his piercing blue eyes seemed dull and unfocused. Dougie was about to speak but Carruthers just raised his hand to silence him.

'Yes, I know I look awful, and I need to be quick,' Carruthers whispered quietly.

Carruthers slid his hand into his coat's inside pocket and withdrew a small brown envelope.

'This,' he said, 'is all you need to get to Canada and you do not need to worry about the security box.'

Dougie took the envelope and felt a lump in the bottom of it.

He looked at Carruthers quizzically.

'That's just a small disk describing all my fruitless research so far, but it also will give you some pointers on what do when you return.' Carruthers paused, coughed into a pocket handkerchief, and continued. 'I think that is all you need?'

Dougie raised his eyebrows. 'Why so quick?'

Carruthers nodded, 'Yes, there is a reason for that. I have just been told that I probably only have two weeks left now.'

Dougie gasped, 'My God, that's so sudden, I have so many questions.'

Carruthers nodded, 'Yes I know, I will try and answer as many as possible.'

Dougie took a big breath, 'I suppose there are two main questions: why did they target your family, and what does the research in Canada entail exactly?'

Carruthers, clearly struggling for breath leaned closer to Dougie and whispered quietly into Dougie's ear. 'Well, it's the same answers that I briefed you on all those months ago.'

He continued, 'We have already discussed the catalysts that could break the hydrogen-oxygen bond; that is really the easy part, the huge challenge is the breaking of the carbon-oxygen bond, which so far has proved totally insurmountable.

He leaned closer, 'However that didn't stop me being targeted by a person or persons unknown who believed that I had discovered the holy grail of the chemical world.'

Carruthers coughed violently, scaring the flock of gulls that had settled on the boat slipway just beneath them.

'Somehow, they thought that I had carried the knowledge with me to Canada; unfortunately, they were very wrong. They weren't targeting my family; they were after me.'

Carruthers paused for breath, 'So this brings me to your second question. While I was in Canada, I was approached by a consortium that offered me huge sums to carry on the research. My role was to be one of three team leaders and recruit a number of volunteers.

'On top of that you will also be funded by Rhys Williams; he is the Executive Chairman of Shetland Petroleum.' He paused. 'He is a hard taskmaster, but very fair, he is genuinely interested in green energy alternatives. He has funded me for the last three years and I have already mentioned you. Again, you will need to meet him in the next few weeks.'

He held on to Dougie's shoulder and said, 'Going back to the consortium though, one of those volunteers was going to be you, but now you are going to have to take a more senior role.' Dougie nodded. 'OK, so what do I do?'

'Well, Dougie, you need to read the instructions, but basically, you have just a few weeks; firstly, you need to accept the PhD. You should also get acquainted with my son Paul, who will be invaluable when you return from Canada,' Carruthers coughed again, then a smile crossed his lips. 'He will need some persuading, though, and most importantly, it has to come from you; he cannot know it's my idea.'

Carruthers drew away. 'I must go now, I must make final arrangements, enjoy Canada and look after my legacy. Everything you need to know is in the envelope and contained on the USB stick.' With that remark, Carruthers turned and walked away. It was the last time that Dougie saw him alive.

Dougie wrapped his coat tightly around himself as he made his way back to his digs. His hand clenched the envelope firmly, and a whirlwind of thoughts engulfed him. How to tell Dave; what would Canada be like; what would his role be?

Back at the digs, Dave was still asleep, so, not wishing to disturb him Dougie opened the envelope and retrieved the USB stick. Inserting it into the side of his laptop, he opened the first file with all the instructions on how to get to Canada and what to do when he got there; it looked fairly straightforward. The second and third files were the E-ticket and access to the bank account for the funds. The rest seemed to be a summary of all of Carruthers' research, all pretty comprehensive information.

A few weeks later, Dougie settled into a seat on an Air Canada flight wondering what was going to happen over the coming weeks. It was surprisingly simple to tie up all the loose ends in Cambridge. Dave had been incredibly understanding and encouraged Dougie to accept the offer as it will be worth the effort. Though it meant Dave might not see Dougie ever again.

After Carruthers' death, Dougie had a meeting with Paul and offered him a PhD. He also had a difficult meeting with Rhys Williams but managed to handle it well overall, and was all set to see what Canada would bring.

PART-2

MEET THE TEAM

CHAPTER – 11

ECHOES OF THE PAST

Dougie had been daydreaming and awoke with a jolt. He remembered this all so clearly and really wished he had never taken the decision to go to Canada. He even regretted the chance meeting with Carruthers in Paris. He looked around one final time, recalling the bizarre occurrences of the past few months as he flipped through the pages of a file. He was searching for answers for what happened in Canada.

He remembered all the people he had met in Canada, their faces still etched in his memory, their voices faint echoes in his mind. He wondered what had happened to them—Jock O'Neill with his quick wit and rugged charm, James White with his quiet intensity, Sean O'Paul who always had a story to tell, Abdul Rehmann with his sharp intellect, and Graham Southwell, the stoic yet dependable rock of the group. And of course, George Carruthers, who transitioned from his university professor to a trusted friend.

His mind drifted back to that day, a day he often relived in the quiet moments when memories resurfaced. He could see himself in his office, the large windows letting in the cold, crisp Canadian air. He had been the lead researcher then, a title that came with both prestige and pressure. The morning had started like any other—coffee in hand, a stack of papers waiting for him on the desk, the usual hum of activity in the background.

He remembered the moment when he opened file, the plain manila folder that seemed so unassuming, yet it held within it the details of the project and people involved in it. It contained names—O'Neill, White, O'Paul, Rehman, Tom, Carruthers—and more. These were the people who had been chosen, appointed to work on the ambitious project that had brought them from all over the world.

As he flipped through the pages of the same file, each name brought a face to mind, each face brought a memory, and their story how they became involved in the project. Was it all meticulously planned, or was it just a series of coincidences that had drawn them together? The way they had each come to join the project was, in hindsight, almost unbelievable.

CHAPTER – 12

JOCK O' NEILL

Jock was a typical ginger haired Scotsman, if there ever was such a thing. He was an only child and had had a rough upbringing. There was continual bullying at school, and he had learned to take care of himself, often turning up back at home with bloodied features and dishevelled clothing. His father was a kindly man who ran a small grocer's shop in the heart of Aberdeen old town, away from the harbour. He had health problems. Jock had always suspected that his father's ailment had come from the smog from the oil fires and coal burners on the quayside. His father died at the age of 57, from heart and lung problems, when Jock was just 13, leaving him to look after his mother who was also in very poor health. This meant that he had to leave school at 15 with practically no qualifications. When Jock's mother passed away just before his 16th birthday, he was left homeless, until his uncle kindly took him in.

Jock hated it, and always yearned to go to sea, particularly on the big oil tankers that were always docking in Aberdeen, bringing ashore the liquid gold from the North Sea.

One day in late summer, Jock was sitting at the dock watching the oil come ashore via a pipeline direct into the major oil refinery just up the coast.

He felt a tap on the shoulder, 'Are you looking for work, young man?'

Jock looked up to a grey bearded grizzled face. He immediately felt a tinge of excitement and a huge adrenaline rush.

'Yes, I am,' Jock stammered.

'I'm George,' he said thrusting a huge, blackened paw towards Jock.

A quizzical look appeared on George's face. 'How old are you?' asked George.

'My name is Jock, and I am 18 years old,' he lied.

George continued, 'Well, we sail in 6 hours; can you be here at this spot by 9 pm tonight?'

'Yes, yes of course!'

The thrill of it all took over Jock, and he didn't hesitate before turning around and sprinting back to his uncle's apartment by the dock who was away on business for a few days.

Jock's thoughts raced as he glanced around the small but exceptionally tidy apartment packed with Uncle Gordon's memorabilia everywhere: trophies of his sailing triumphs, consecutive Player of the Year awards at the local golf course and, of course, the Angler of the Year in 1992. Jock opened the kitchen drawer looking for a pad of paper and a pen. After scrabbling around, he found both and hastily scrawled a note.

Dear Uncle Gordon
Thank you so much for looking after me for the last few months. But I have decided to go and find my own fortune and go to sea.
Love Jock

Jock squinted at his note and thought that it was a little too short so added an afterthought.

P.S. I won't forget you.

He carefully placed the note under the Angler of the Year trophy, grabbed his bag and rushed to the docks. Inside the bag, he carefully gathered all of his beloved belongings making sure to include his favourite teddy bear. He felt a twinge of emotion as he remembered how his mother had given it to him after a rough day at school. He also put as many clothes as he could fit in and all the cash he had saved (a magnificent £32.55). He took a deep breath and gently closed the front door of the apartment, possibly for the last time.

George was already waiting for him and gestured urgently to him. 'Great, I am glad you are here so quickly, we need to move away from shore now.'

'Why?' said Jock.

George shrugged. 'I made a mistake; the high tide is going to be a much greater surge than normal.'

Jock looked puzzled.

'Doesn't mean we cannot get out of the harbour safely,' George said with some exasperation creeping into his voice.

'Get on board Jock, tapping on his shoulder; we leave port in 20 minutes.' And that was a new beginning for Jock. Little did he know he would never see his beloved Aberdeen again. The first thing he had to understand about ship life was that the youngest person on board would be given all the dirty jobs, and that was certainly the case with Jock. They had barely left port when he was asked to check all the on-board toilets, and there were nearly 30 of them. It was a repellent task, and, on several occasions, Jock retched and had to steady himself before moving onto the next toilet. The tanker was bound for Jeddah to get refilled before departing for Calais and then back to Aberdeen. After that, the entire crew were to be transferred to a tanker bound for the Far East and then onto Australia. Despite the demanding schedule, Jock felt alive for the first time since the death of his mother.

The crew loved him, and, despite their initial unfriendliness, they soon introduced him to the life of a sailor, The weeks turned into months and then into years as Jock moved from tanker to tanker. By the time he had turned 19 Jock had circumnavigated the globe at least 30 times.

In those days, the Cold War was well and truly over and Western vessels were permitted into Russian waters. Jock's vessel, the SS Carmarthen had been one of the first to enter the Black Sea. The Carmarthen was an old vessel nearly 20 years old, with black sides streaked with brown channels of rust. It was one of the older breeds of tanker and not in the super tanker class, but still capable of carrying 250,000 tonnes of crude oil.

Jock was already used to the famous sailor phrase of the 'run ashore' and was really looking forward to setting foot on Russian soil for the first time. The landing horn gave three blasts as the huge tanker turned ever so slowly to come alongside the massive oil terminal.

Jock glanced across at George and asked what the name of the port was.

'We're in Novorossiysk,' he said, 'It's a bustling city located in Krasnodar Krai, Russia.'

As the country's primary port on the Black Sea, it played a crucial role in exporting grain. In recent years, after opening its borders to the West, Novorossiysk had also become a major hub for crude oil exports. The city had even been given the esteemed title of 'Hero City' for its contributions and sacrifices during times of war.

Jock stepped ashore and waited for his usual supportive gang to join him on the quayside.

'Where to,' Jock shouted, so he could be heard above the noise of the huge, throbbing diesel engines.

Jimmy, who was always the tour leader spoke first, 'Don't worry Ginge.' (Jock's ship nickname, for obvious reasons). 'I have spoken to the Port Manager who has given me a whole list of likely establishments.' Jimmy paused, 'The best places are in the maze of small streets branching off the main square, unsurprisingly named Lenin Square.'

Jimmy sounded much more informed than normal until Jock realised that he was reading over a whole sheaf of handwritten notes that he had hastily scrawled following his conversation with Gergio, the Port manager, a couple of hours earlier.

The Carmarthen crew stumbled down the ramp leading to the quayside, and Jock felt a pump of excitement, wondering what this new adventure would hold for him.

The crew headed to the town. The first bar, they visited, was actually boring with lots of grey-haired Russians with beards smoking dark-coloured cheroots.

Jimmy looked around and gestured towards Jock.

'Ginge,' he whispered into Ginge's ear. 'I hope this is not typical of everywhere,' Jimmy grimaced. 'Here are the roubles we collected on the ship earlier, see what you can do.'

Jock pushed his way through the crowded bar, dodging and weaving between drunken Russians who had clearly consumed more vodka than they could handle. His goal was to reach the bar, where he hoped to get the attention of a red-faced, burly Cossack sitting at the end. However, when Jock looked over, the Cossack was engaged in a heated conversation with another intense customer. After waiting impatiently for a few minutes, Jock finally caught the bartender's eye. He quickly pointed at the various bottles of vodka on display behind him. 'Any of those will do,' he stuttered.

The Cossack wheeled away and grabbed one of the open bottles with one hand and six grimy glasses with the other. He held out his hand and Jimmy thrust a handful of roubles into his still-open hand. He calculated roughly that it was less than a fiver for the entire bottle. A couple of other clearly inebriated Russians lurched towards them, supporting each other to keep from crashing down. Jimmy leaned over to Jock and cupped his hand onto Jock's ear. 'We will be out of here in a few minutes, Ginge,' he whispered loudly. 'There is a decent club down the road.'

Jock scanned the bar with a smile, hoping that the next place would be an improvement from this one. As he looked around, his eyes landed on a short, round man dressed in a crisp business suit. The man was sitting at a small table in the corner of the grimy bar.

He wore horn-rimmed spectacles; below his rather pointed nose was a neat black moustache. That was not what caught Jock's interest. Sitting next to him was a gorgeous girl, no more than 20. She had a perfect complexion, long black hair, beautiful eyes, and an instantly engaging smile. She nodded towards Jock and patted the empty chair next to her.

Jock glanced at Jimmy and the rest of the crew, who were engaged in animated conversation with a crowd of Russians and decided to see what this intriguing couple were all about. With animated steps, he lurched over towards the couple and sat next to the girl.

Looking at her close, he found her even more gorgeous. Her hazel-coloured eyes twinkled with amused pleasure and, as Jock sat down, she thrust out a slender hand with nails coloured deep purple.

'I am Natalia,' she said staring straight into Jock's face.

Jock felt uncomfortable for a moment before stammering. 'My name is Jock, but most people call me Ginge, for obvious reasons,' pointing to his hair. Natalia looked puzzled for a moment before getting the joke and then threw her head back and laughed loudly.

Natalia then turned to her companion. 'This is Abdul; I am his personal assistant.'

'Well, I am, how do you say it in English, Scottish.' I have just come from the big tanker on the harbour,' Jock interjected.

'You are Scottish, OK.'

Abdul looked uncomfortable for a moment before he, too, thrust out a hand in Jock's direction. 'Abdul, Abdul Rehmann.'

As he walked away, Jock cast a quick glance over his shoulder at the group of sailors he had just left. Abdul noticed his gaze and turned to look at Natalia.

'Your friends?'

Jock nodded. 'Where are they going?' Abdul enquired.

Jock tried to remember the name, 'Something like the Vodka-Tease bar.' It was Abdul's turn to laugh.

'That is a very expensive bar,' he paused 'Do you have £1,000 spare?'

Jock looked uncomfortable again.

'I guessed not. I have a proposition for you,' Abdul smiled slyly and continued.

'I manage a number of oilfields both here and in the Middle East.'

'This is good for now, but I need a right-hand man to manage all my sub-managers in these fields,' Abdul said.

Jock looked puzzled. 'Is this something you want me to do?' He paused. 'But you don't even know me?'

'Ah! but we do,' he looked at Natalia, who nodded vigorously.

'Natalia has been very diligent and thorough in looking at all your background.'

Abdul continued as a brawl developed behind Jock, 'We know you have no dependents and that you have ambition; you cannot be bribed and would find anyone who accepted or offered them totally untrustworthy,' Abdul nodded at Natalia who opened a battered brown leather attaché case. Dipping her hand inside, she came out with a sheaf of closely typewritten papers.

She handed them to Jock, who took them somewhat gingerly. 'What's all this?' he enquired.

Abdul just smiled and gave Natalia a knowing look.

There were a few moments of silence as the brawl continued behind them with a cacophony of shattering glasses, raised voices, and the booming sound of the burly doormen as they tried to intervene.

Jock glanced around, saw he was in no immediate threat, and then turned to the papers and tried to make sense of all the various clauses and legalese.

Being dyslexic, none of it made any sense. He turned to the

back two pages which showed an array of calculations. Jock pointed at the last figure. 'What is this?'

Abdul turned the paper round and looked where Jock's finger had rested.

'That's your monthly salary.'

Jock's mouth fell open wide, and he just stared in astonishment.

'Is there something wrong? It doesn't include performance bonuses if that is a concern.' Abdul continued, 'And of course, there is a generous travel allowance.'

Jock still could not speak; the monthly salary alone was more than he had earned in total from all his time at sea.

Finally, he spoke 'Where would I be based?'

Abdul nodded. 'Initially here, and then you would be based all over the Middle East.'

Jock queried, 'When you say here, what do you mean?'

'You will have a flat here and spend a couple of years learning the ropes.' 'You won't be totally alone; Natalia here will look after you,' Abdul stated. 'Do we have a deal?'

'Yes!' Jock said and felt the same adrenaline rush he had felt years back at the dock.

'Meet us back here at 6 pm tomorrow, by then we will have all the papers sorted.'

'Do you have your passport?'

'Yup, do you need it?' Jock asked quizzically and retrieved it from his back pocket.

Abdul reached for it among the glasses. 'I will give it back to you fully authorised tomorrow.'

Thrusting out a hand towards Jock, he said, 'Until tomorrow then!'

Natalia smiled as they arose and headed towards the door. She let her hand linger on Jock's thigh for a little longer than necessary, 'da svidahnia,' Natalia whispered,

Jock gave Natalia a quizzical look.

'Goodbye Jock, until tomorrow.'

Jock glanced around the bar, which was rapidly emptying, with just a few stragglers clinging to their last glass of vodka draped on the bar.

He grinned and lifted himself to his feet. The vodka was starting to take effect and he lurched somewhat awkwardly to the open door. The doormen were still there and looked somewhat knowingly at Jock.

Jock wasn't sure how he got back to the ship, but he found himself lying face down on his bunk in his tiny cabin, just as the first glimmers of sunlight came through the porthole from a Russian dawn.

Morning came with a hangover and confusion. Had last night really happened or had it been a rather lovely dream? He wondered as he glanced across the cabin at his roommate. Shaun was still dressed, snoring loudly, with a small dribble crawling from the corner of his mouth. He had obviously had a good time, there was a smell of perfume and vodka mingled together in a heady concoction in the room.

Yup, Shaun had definitely had a good time.

He glanced around the cabin and thought this might be the last time he would ever see this cabin... Again.

Jock clambered up the stairs onto the fore deck, making his way past the upturned lifebelts and underneath the life rafts and lifeboats. He took in a lungful of the crisp cold air, holding it in for a few seconds before exhaling deeply.

With every passing moment, he became more and more convinced about accepting the proposition. The rest was relatively easy, no one tried to persuade him to stay, even Jimmy. They all gave him a hug as they lined up one by one to say their farewells. Jimmy was last, and Jock was sure there was a tear in his eye. 'Damn wind,' Jimmy said gruffly, wiping the tear away and then whispering in Jock's ear: 'Good luck Ginge, I'll miss you.'

With a gentle push, Jock felt himself propelled towards the gangway.

Clutching two large knapsacks, with all his possessions, he found himself back at the bar from last night.

It was already busy as he burrowed his way into the bar.

There, sitting in the same table as the previous night was Natalia looking even more demure and beautiful than the previous night.

Jock looked round, 'Where's Abdul?'

Natalia smiled enigmatically, 'He is just concluding the last few items in the office; we are to meet him back at your apartment later.'

'We can cover a few essentials now.'

Natalia reached into the briefcase and removed a whole sheaf of papers.

'What's all this?'

'Most of it is just house stuff.' 'House stuff?'

Once again Natalia smiled in that most beautiful way.

'Abdul is going to be at your apartment a little later.'

'Where is it?' Jock felt his voice raise a pitch or two as he could hardly control his excitement.

Natalia thumbed through the papers, looking slightly puzzled and then relieved as she found exactly what she was trying to locate.

She placed a photo in front of Jock.

Jock squinted at the photo; it looked like a boat bobbing in a small, secluded harbour.

'Am I going to be living on the water?' asked Jock incredulously.

Natalia tilted her head back and a joyous laugh escaped her lips, one that Jock would soon become accustomed to and cherish.

'No, Jock, look behind the boat at the apartment block,'

Jock squinted again at the small photo and could see, though rather indistinctly, a modern six- or seven-storey building set in gardens which bordered the tiny harbour.

'Where is this?' Jock was stammering now as he truly could not believe his fortune.

Natalia laughed again. 'It's barely 15 minutes from here.' She pointed in the vague direction of the main harbour.

Jock was speechless for a moment and struggled to find the right words. After a moment of silence, he finally blurted out, "Can I get you a drink?".

Natalia reached forward and gently caressed Jock's forearm. 'That would be really lovely.'

It turned out to be much longer than a few minutes, as it was nearly midnight before Natalia and Jock emerged from the bar. Jock stumbled forward as he missed the step and found himself being supported by two arms from behind. They were surprisingly strong.

'Don't worry, Jock,' Natalia whispered. 'I will look after you.'

Look after him she certainly did; the first few years were like a whirlwind.

It was clear that Natalia had set her sights on Jock; within three months she announced she was pregnant, and Jock did the honourable thing, immediately asking her to marry him. It was a very quiet affair witnessed by two dockers in a small Russian Orthodox church on the outskirts of the city.

Over time, Jock had become one of the most trustworthy employees who worked for Abdul. Abdul was very seldom to be seen. He was always overseeing all his overseas interests, which were mainly in the Middle East but interspersed with visits to Venezuela and North America, increasingly so.

Natalia was determined to provide their son, Ivan, with the best education possible. With the help of Abdul, she found an excellent preparatory school for him. As he got older, Natalia sent Ivan to a boarding school called Stowe in Buckinghamshire, a rural county in the South of England that she had never heard of before. The education at Stowe was exceptional and Ivan excelled there, earning a spot at the prestigious Cambridge University. Following in his father's footsteps, Ivan chose Fuel Technology as his main subject of study.

Jock was also increasingly away until he announced to Natalia that they were going to be leaving their beloved home country and moving permanently to Saudi Arabia on the Red Sea coast. Natalia didn't protest too much; she had found it increasingly boring, being home alone for long periods of time with only herself for company.

The move took place quickly and within a month, they were living in an ultra-modern block on the outskirts of the new oilfield. They had only barely been there a month before Abdul turned up at their flat one evening looking flustered. He had barely slumped in the large armchair in the corner of the apartment before blurting out.

'I am involved in a complicated project in Canada that I need some help with.' Abdul looked shifty, but leaned forward so Jock and Natalia could hear him more clearly.

'We will go for a month or two, but the pay will be extremely financially rewarding.'

Natalia and Jock exchanged glances. Natalia's was one of resignation. She had heard it all many times before.

'You go, Jock. I am not moving anywhere.'

'Well, why not!' Jock said casually, feeling the familiar excitement in his blood.

'And so it begins,' Jock said as he packed his suitcase.

The plane journey was long, but uneventful. Abdul had become more relaxed as time passed. The first part of the journey to Dubai was dry, which Jock did not enjoy. But once they arrived in London and then continued on to Montreal, alcohol was easily available. Jock indulged in a variety of Scotch whiskies and washed them down with Scottish lager. He eventually fell into a deep slumber, punctuated by occasional snores.

It felt like no time before a hand gently touched his shoulder and a dark brunette stewardess whispered in his ear. 'Sir, can you please fasten your seatbelt and put your chair into the upright position. We are about to land in Montreal.'

Jock jolted himself upright in his seat and peered out of the cabin window of the brand-new Airbus. In the fading late afternoon light, he could see the myriad of lakes that littered the landscape in Northern Canada.

The pilot's voice boomed out, 'Ten minutes to landing, fasten your seatbelts.' After landing in Montreal, customs was a surprisingly quick affair. The customs officer just gave a cursory glance at Jock's much-used passport and handed it back to him. Abdul also had little trouble. They both strode out into the crisp cold air. Abdul glanced towards the parked cars just behind the taxi rank and saw what he needed.

He nodded at Jock 'This way.'

Dragging their large suitcases, they headed across the parking lot towards a Land Rover.

Jock raised his eyebrows.

'There is a lot of off-road travel involved,' Abdul said bluntly.

Jock nodded, thrusting his suitcase into the large luggage compartment and jumping into the back seat. For some reason, Jock felt excited, but he also had a sense of foreboding.

It was late in the evening before they arrived at their final destination.

The Land Rover was well suited to the journey as over half of it involved bumping along a series of dirt tracks. After what felt like an eternity, they finally reached a large clearing in the midst of a desolate landscape. It looked like some sort of military barracks, with a white stone building at the north end that seemed to be specifically constructed for its purpose. Thin wisps of white smoke billowed from the chimney atop the structure, giving off a faintly eerie vibe.

Abdul turned to Jock and smiled: 'We are here,' and pointed towards the house. 'Let's go.'

The inside was deceptively large; the far wall was covered in a number of prints, mostly large oil tankers but there were a few old cargo-bearing sailing ships. There were a couple of old rugs stretched out in front of a log fire, which was burning fiercely. In the corner was a large pine table underneath the window, where two tanned men sat hunched over some papers, in deep discussion. They barely looked up as Abdul and Jock entered the room. Abdul cleared his throat, 'Hmm, James and Graham, this is Jock.' The shorter of them thrust out a heavily ringed hand.

'James White, good to meet you, Jock, I have heard a lot about you.' Jock hoped it had been positive.

He turned to the taller man and was immediately struck by the intensity of his eyes, which were the deepest blue Jock had ever seen.

'I'm Graham, Graham Southwell.' Graham smiled, and Jock instantly felt he would get along with him.

Abdul smiled and nodded towards the back room. 'Let's eat; it's late.'

The back room was just as spacious. A massive range cooker, fuelled by logs, dominated one side of the room, while a gleaming silver fridge stood in the far corner. A round table sat in the centre of the room, still cluttered with plates from breakfast.

One of the men hastily grabbed the plates and clattered them into the large sink in the corner. Graham then gestured Jock to sit down, while James put out a selection of cold meats on the table. Abdul waved them away, but Jock was ravenous and piled food onto the various dishes with gusto. There was little talking at the table, but once he finished eating Jock felt completely exhausted.

He was dying to ask numerous questions, as he had done on the flight over, but Abdul had been completely evasive, promising answers only when they were in Canada.

'Jock, your room is the first on the left on the first landing, I need to discuss a few things with James and Graham.'

Jock wanted to ask but was cut off immediately. 'Don't worry; all will be revealed in the morning.'

Jet lag and racing thoughts kept Jock up all night, his mind spinning with the true reason for his presence here. Eventually, he drifted off into a deep slumber, only to be stirred awake by the dawn's light creeping through the window.

Washed and showered, Jock hurriedly put on some clothes and stumbled down the stairs. The kitchen was spotless and empty, with not a single person in sight. In the main sitting room, the three men were huddled in deep discussion.

Abdul looked up; 'Ah, come and join us; we need to fill you in about a few things.'

Jock slumped into the fourth armchair and looked quizzically at the three of them.

Abdul cleared his throat and began, 'Jock, we have known each other for 20 years. I have always trusted you for your honesty, straightforwardness and, most of all, for your discretion. And I know your contribution to this project, too, will help us achieve our objective.'

Abdul paused then continued. 'This is 15 miles from the nearest town or significant inhabitation. The work we have started here is extremely discreet and we cannot afford any leaks.' He said with a serious tone and then smiled.

'Let me tell you a story. The most precious commodity on earth is still oil; yes, I know alternative sources of energy are in vogue, but oil is still by a long way the number one. Many of the wars in the last few years would not have happened if it had not been for the Americans' love of the product. However, even I realise that, sometime within the next 20 years, oil will start to run out with no serious replacement in place. That's where this place comes in. I have been in touch with some research students and a couple of university professors who believe that there is an alternative to both oil and gas resources.'

Jock raised his eyebrows: 'What would that be?'

Abdul paused once again, 'Ethanol and its gas ethane. There is a belief that ethanol can be manufactured from natural resources such as air and spring water.'

Jock was no chemist, but this sounded impossible.

Abdul laughed when he saw Jock's expression: 'No Jock, it's not just a case of bubbling air through water, and hey presto, magic, we have ethanol.'

Jock kept silent, but his jaw dropped open in surprise.

'There is a catalytic process involving rare metals which completes the transformation.' Abdul could see Jock's eyes glazing over. 'You don't really need to know how it all works; I will explain your part in a minute.'

Abdul waved his arm out towards the trees outside the building.

'That is why we are here; this area is the richest source of rare metals in the world. We have several small excavation sites close by and a small distillation plant just beyond the clearing where we can extract all the metal we need.'

Abdul looked at Jock and continued, 'I want you to manage the catalyst manufacturing process; this means arranging delivery of all the raw materials; managing the teams when they arrive here and supervising the manufacturing process. Are you up for it?'

Jock nodded.

'The most important thing to remember is that the raw materials involved are extremely toxic and need very careful handling.'

Jock nodded again, this time more fiercely.

'Well, that's settled then; let me show you around the site. You will see that there is a lot of preparatory work that has already been done.'

Jock looked at Graham and James, and asked, 'What are your roles, if you don't mind me asking?' Graham was about to answer but was stopped by Abdul.

'It's not crucial, but just know that they possess a vast amount of knowledge regarding the catalytic process we're implementing here. They have spent the past two years overseeing the construction and choosing local workers for the project.' He continued, 'To create the holy grail of the energy world has long been thought impossible, but if we can do it, we will create an everlasting fuel which is carbon neutral and at best carbon negative, so it could reverse the global warming process. However, we are at the beginning of a very difficult journey, and no one knows where it will end. I do, however, have financial support from two other parties across the border in the USA and back in England. Also, we believe that, together, we have assembled the right team for the job. It won't happen overnight; we are all hoping for the best results.'

Abdul turned towards the door; everyone dutifully followed behind him.

He glanced behind as they approached the first of two huts. Inside were ten bunk beds, a small seating area with three leather couches and a kitchen area in the corner.

'This is just the living accommodation for some of our guests. Some of the teams will sleep here. The others will sleep in the other two accommodation huts,' he said.

Jock interposed, 'When are they due?'

'You have a couple of weeks to get things sorted properly. Let me show you the laboratory huts.'

They all strolled across the clearing to the two huts on the other side.

'This is where the hard work will be done.' Abdul pointed 'The slightly smaller hut will be where results will be correlated and recorded.'

Outside the door of the main experimental hut was a box filled with what looked like sophisticated gas masks.

'Take one, Jock, you will need to wear it inside.' Jock raised an eyebrow inquisitively.

James answered before Abdul could speak.

'Abdul mentioned that the chemicals used in the process are toxic. This is particularly the case in here. We use beryllium, sodium and also francium. Francium is highly unstable, with a radioactive half-life of just over 20 minutes when exposed to air.'

'They all give off fumes, with beryllium being particularly nasty. It causes a lung disease called berylliosis.'

Jock glanced around the hut as he stepped inside; it was full of packages, and hundreds of specimen bottles; several of them had curls of smoke drifting towards the ceiling where they hung menacingly.

Abdul thrust a few papers into Jock's hands. 'These will give you a clear idea of what will be coming in over the next few weeks, what is already in place, and where and how they must be stored.'

Jock studied them in detail and immediately started making plans.

Outside, Graham and James wandered back to the rather superior lodgings on the campus's border. They lay in their separate rooms, both wondering when anything would eventually get going; it had been months since either of them had seen their families. Graham fell asleep after a few minutes, but James just tossed and turned, and his mind drifted back to beautiful beaches in Australia, where he had spent most of his life.

CHAPTER – 13

JAMES WHITE

James White, born James Charles White, grew up on the Sunshine Coast of Australia, just north of Brisbane. It was, without doubt, the most idyllic place on earth. Noosa was a great place where the beaches were white sand and not choked with tourists. He was the youngest of four siblings and, although by far the brightest, he was also the laziest. Although he had a first-class degree in chemical engineering, rather than pursue that path, James spent most of his days doing part-time jobs on the white sands of Noosa. He spent virtually every day perfecting his surfing techniques and soon became a qualified instructor. It was a great life, but James always thought there was something missing.

He had a deep passion for the environment, and one day while glancing at the local paper, he noticed a course that caught his interest. It was titled simply, "Oil and the Environment," and the lecturer was a renowned chemist, George Carruthers. The course was scheduled for three months later and was also in Brisbane, so James didn't think much of it at the time and stuffed the paper into his shorts pocket for future reference.

A couple of weeks later, while he was necking cocktails at one of his favourite beach bars with Sylvie, one of his many girlfriends, he mentioned the course.

Sylvie looked at him intently, 'Wouldn't you want to stop this?'

'Stop what exactly?' slurred James.

'This!' Sylvie waved her hand towards the increasingly large crowd that had gathered on the terrace just in front of them.

'They have all come down here in big gas-guzzling cars looking to outdo each other with the biggest engine.'

James nodded, 'I suppose you are right Sylvie, but then you nearly always are!'

Sylvie laughed out loud, and James joined her.

'I tell you what, James, if you sign up for this course, so will I and we can at least have some directions on how we can save the planet. Let's sleep on it and we can decide next week.'

They clinked glasses, slipped off their stools and wandered outside to the now empty beach.

With long, sun-bleached locks flowing down to his shoulders, a permanent tan, and piercing green eyes, James embodied the quintessential Australian. As they strolled along the beach, carefully avoiding any jellyfish in their path, Sylvie caressed his hair and whispered in his ear.

'What are you thinking about?' she asked.

'Oh, nothing really,' James paused, 'well, I wonder what my parents would have thought of all this, it's a real shame that they are no longer with us.'

'I know, but they would have been so proud of what you are trying to achieve, don't you think.'

'Yes, I guess in a way, I want to enrol in this course because of them,' James continued. 'My dad's sickness was likely caused by years working in the mines, and my mom died too young from a broken heart.'

Sylvie squeezed James' hand tightly as a comforting gesture.

'Let's get a drink at the bar,' she said.

Sitting at the makeshift bar James retrieved the crumpled form from his shorts and smoothed it out on the bar top; it gave clear instructions on how to apply online. Opening the site, they both filled in their details.

Sylvie furrowed her brow and asked, 'How are we supposed to get down there?'

'Well, it's only a month-long, so maybe we can get the train and stay in one of the Airbnbs on the outskirts of the city?' James shrugged his shoulders, 'I am not sure what else we can do.'

'Yes, that will work,' she smiled.

Finishing their drinks in the increasingly noisy bar, they wandered rather haphazardly back to James' place, a spacious large two-bedroomed ground floor apartment only five minutes' walk from Noosa beach centre.

Lying in bed together, listening to crickets chirping, they knew it was really a fantastic life, with no worries and a great future.

James mumbled, 'Oh well, we have enrolled in the course now, no turning back,' and drifted off into a deep sleep.

CHAPTER – 14

GRAHAM SOUTHWELL

In just three short months, the time had flown by, and they were already on their way to Brisbane. They were filled with enthusiasm as they prepared to start the course. Getting there was trickier than expected as the day they were due to set off also coincided with the start of the typhoon season, and their train was delayed by over two hours because of all the debris on the line. Finally, however, they alighted just outside Brisbane and made their way to what would be home for the next few weeks.

It had been a long time since either of them had been to the city, so they decided to take a boat trip down the Brisbane River to see the sights before their course started the next day. The boat was very much like an old paddle steamer modified with a diesel engine (Sylvie and James simultaneously thought that this was not very environmentally friendly).

Both had forgotten how Brisbane was both cosmopolitan and very tropical. The banks of the Brisbane River were lined with Eucalyptus trees, from where came sounds of the cockatoos, parrots, and a whole variety of other wonderfully colourful species. As the boat drew close, the flocks of birds rose in unison, creating a wonderful natural rainbow. James felt sombre for a moment. He had read somewhere that, because of climate change, 10% of the native bird species would become extinct. He nudged Sylvie and whispered this into her ear, and she nodded in silent agreement.

The boat stopped outside one of the many streetside cafés. A booming voice came over the boat speaker system.

This is the final stop on the tour. You can either return on the return trip, which leaves in about two hours, or take the trolley bus, which leaves regularly from just across the road.

Sylvie looked at James and said, 'Let's just hang around here for a while.'

'OK,' he smiled.

They grabbed a halloumi burger from one of the many street stalls and meandered along the riverbank so they could veer off to one of the many parks.

To their right, just before they entered the park, was the famous Gabba cricket stadium, where many overseas cricket sides had perished. Sylvie grabbed James' arm and they strolled through the park admiring the many monuments, which were reminders of Australian history. The afternoon soon turned into dusk when they reached the centre of Brisbane after a leisurely trip on the Brisbane trolley bus service. Next to their location was a brightly lit bar with many tables spread outside rather haphazardly. It was a suffocatingly warm evening, and as they settled down to a few iced beers, they couldn't help overhearing the next table.

'Graham!' A very loud voice, obviously English, drowned out everybody else's.

'Of course, I care about the environment, I wouldn't pay a fortune to do this course otherwise.'

'Oh, just shut up Graham, get off your high horse for a moment,' retorted an equally loud shrill female voice.

'OK, I will,' said Graham, 'but only if you get me another cold beer.' The whole table laughed.

They quietened down as the evening went on, and the flow of beers eventually dulled the conversation.

Towards the end of the evening, James couldn't resist wandering over and introducing himself.

'Are you all English?' he said rather obviously. 'All except Janet, she's our tour guide,' said Graham.

'I couldn't help overhearing but are you all going to be on the course tomorrow?' James asked almost apologetically.

'No, just me and Janet,' he smiled at her. 'We are really looking forward to it, despite my complaints you probably overheard earlier.'

James gestured Sylvie to join them. She hesitated and then pulled up a chair and joined in the conversation.

'Well, what do you reckon, James? Is it going to be worth hearing what Professor Carruthers has to say or not?' asked Graham.

'Well, as you said, it better be worth it for the cost of the course.' Everyone nodded.

The next day, they took the bus, which conveniently stopped right outside their residence, and made their way to the city centre. The course was being held in the Hilton, right in the middle of the business district. A good-sized crowd had gathered in front of the checking-in desks as James and Sylvie made their way to the front and found their new English friends.

Soon they found themselves in a large lecture theatre situated towards the back of the hotel, overlooking the swimming pool and the tennis courts. There must have been over 40 other registrations. James made sure that the four of them were all sitting together.

They were all getting a little restless when Carruthers appeared from the side entrance walked in front of the lectern at the front, paused, and casually looked around at the audience.

'Well does everyone know why you are here, and do you really want to be here? Because what you are going to find out over the next few weeks is what a mess the world is in and what you might be able to do about it.' He paused again, 'Do I need to say anything else?'

Everyone murmured in what seemed like agreement.

'Well, I will begin,' he said firmly.

Carruthers started by scrawling two chemical formulae on the whiteboard familiar to everyone. 'H_2O and CO_2. Water and carbon dioxide. Two of the most common chemical compounds on earth.'

There were a few nods.

James thought to himself, I hope it's not all going to be this basic as that would be a real waste of cash.

The next few hours actually proved fascinating. There were plenty of videos and lots of interactive equations. The first day was all about the damage that the burning of oil and hydrocarbons was doing to the atmosphere, in particular the impact of global warming on the unique Australian wildlife and habitat. It ended with a dramatic picture of the damage to the *Great Barrier Reef*, as a reminder of how bad it really was. The rest of the course continued in the same fashion.

At the end of the second to last week, the four of them decamped to a bar just outside the main campus. It was an idyllic spot, completely outside with white tables and chairs that tumbled down to the riverbank. They had found a lovely shady spot just under the bridge where the various wildfowl nibbled at crumbs of food the tourists had left during the day.

It was turning into a relatively cool evening with a slight breeze from the south removing some of the suffocating heat of the day.

They had settled down and were just through their second round of drinks when Janet looked up and shook Graham's shoulder gently.

'Don't look round anyone' (and of course everyone did.) 'Isn't that Carruthers over there?'

James turned slightly and immediately recognised the familiar features. 'Yes, shall we invite him over?'

'I don't know James; he looks pretty engrossed in his papers.'

At that moment Carruthers lifted his head and saw the foursome; he raised his hand in acknowledgement and beckoned them towards him.

All four somewhat sheepishly wandered over to him.

James spoke first, 'Sorry, Professor, we didn't mean to disturb your drink.' Carruthers waved his hand at the four empty seats.

He smiled and they all felt immediately at ease.

After a silent moment, Carruthers said, 'Well, the obvious question... have I gripped everyone's attention over the past few weeks?'

They all nodded vigorously.

Carruthers smiled again. 'Well, the final week should really open your eyes to the possibilities.'

Everyone leaned forward expectantly.

'I will also have an offer to anyone willing to listen,' he continued after taking a sip from his cold beer. 'You have heard me talk a lot about alternatives to fossil fuels. Well, in a few months' time, I will have access to some funding to build a camp where this can be explored in more detail. The initial funding will come from Saudi Arabia but after that from a more multinational consortium. He continued. 'Indeed, after the end of this course, I head to Paris to drum up more support.'

He paused.

James was the first one to speak again. 'Where is this camp going to be, and what would you be looking for from us.' He waved his hand over the rest of them.

'Well, the answer to the first question is most likely in Canada, which I will definitely know by the end of the course. In answer to your second question, I believe I will need a couple of willing volunteers to supervise the building of the camp, with the willingness to spend a couple of years away from home to find a solution that can reverse global warming and save the environment.'

Graham raised his eyebrows. 'Why Canada?'

'Well, it's a bit like here in Australia: lots of remote areas and plentiful raw materials. The big difference is that key raw materials will be right there on site.' Carruthers said.

Graham and James looked at each other and nodded.

In almost unison, 'Well, some of us could be interested; what do we need to do?'

Carruthers grinned. 'Let's catch up next week when everything is confirmed in terms of location and, more importantly, funding.' He looked at his watch, 'Well I must head back now to my hotel, I have several calls to make. All of you enjoy your drinks and think clearly about what I said and the commitment you would need to make.'

With that, he pushed his chair back, stood up, and, with another wave, he was gone.

There was a stunned silence around the group before they all tried to talk at once.

'Two years is an awfully long time, but on the other hand, perhaps we really can make a difference.'

'I don't know, James,' Sylvie shook her head. 'Let's just wait and see what he comes up with next week.' She continued, 'It will have to be really financially worth it to commit to so long.'

'Alright!' said Janet, 'Let's drink to it and see what next week brings.'

The next morning, they all jumped on the trolley bus, just about in time for the start of the course (as per usual). Settling in the normal positions all together in a tight group at the end of the bench nearest the exit. Carruthers strolled in his normal laconic fashion and fixed his eyes on them, fleetingly, before scanning the rest of the group. He paused.

'Well, this is the last week, everyone, and it is going to be a bit different.'

'Up to now, we have looked at all the devastation that hydrocarbons have caused to the environment. This week I am going to examine the possible solutions, and I also want to make it totally interactive.'

He stopped to make sure everyone was engaged.

'Well, let's start by asking a question, what does anyone think would solve the current climate crisis?'

Several hands were raised.

Carruthers looked around. 'James, what do you think?'

James glanced around before answering. 'There are so many alternatives now: electric vehicles, hydrogen-powered vehicles, wind power, solar power. Surely a combination of those would work.'

'You are right, but none of those is going to satisfy the growing energy requirements of countries such as India and, of course, China. On top of that, we in the West can scarcely complain of countries such as Brazil and Mexico also want to grow their economies by using natural resources. After all, that's what we have done over the last 150 years. On top of that it was their natural resources that we exploited.' he paused and gave everyone a moment to ponder.

'The answer is more complicated than that. We must find a solution that somehow takes carbon out of the atmosphere and at the same time gives a workable energy solution.' He paused again and looked around.

'Any thoughts?' There was silence. 'I didn't think so.' He waited a few moments and spoke further.

'Well, this week we will look at all those energy alternatives that James mentioned and a few others. Believe me there are many of those. Today we will look at the greatest hope of the 21st century, electric vehicles.'

Through the next four days, he went through all the solutions that were currently in vogue, and explained the virtues of them, but also their serious limitations. By the Thursday evening, the foursome was in a sombre mood as they sat round their usual table by the riverside.

Graham started the inevitable conversation. 'Well, what will tomorrow bring, do you think?'

James immediately replied, 'Well, I'm hoping that tomorrow he'll explain the purpose of the camp in Canada. Maybe that really will be the best and only solution. I know we're not all sure about going there. However, I still believe if the reward is great then we should all go for it.'

He thumped his fist on the table and raised his glass as did everyone else.

'To Canada.'

Everyone fell silent before raising their glasses again. This time they just clinked.

However, on the way back to the lodgings, Janet and Sylvie held back from Graham and James, who were talking excitedly a few yards in front of them.

Sylvie spoke first, 'I am not sure about this, Janet; two years is an awfully long time to be away. Those long Canadian winters don't appeal to me much either.'

Janet smiled and, in a hushed tone, said, 'I am not going Sylvie; I know Graham is super keen, but I don't think I could face it for all that time. We have already had the discussion and I think he has already accepted that. I can always come out for a few weeks in the summer until it gets too cold.' She shrugged her shoulders.

Sylvie went silent, and as they climbed the stairs to the lodgings, her mind was made up, too.

James was already lying on the bed when she entered the room, his eyes only half open. He raised a finger to his lips as Sylvie came alongside him.

'I know what you are going to say Sylvie, you're not coming with me, are you?'

Sylvie protested, 'Why do you think that? I might not have made my mind up yet.'

'Well, I saw you talking with Janet, and I just had a gut feeling.'

Sylvie nodded, 'I'm sorry, but I just don't think I can do it.'

'I understand,' he held her hand gently.

Soon after that, they snuggled into each other and fell into a deep but often fitful sleep.

The following morning, they were on the trolley bus to the hotel for the last day of the course.

After they sat down, Carruthers strolled into the theatre followed by an impeccably dressed Arab gentleman. He waited until the hubbub died down and then raised his right hand.

'Okay ladies and gentlemen, let me introduce you to Abdul Rehmann, Abdul will tell you a little about himself and then we will move into our final lecture.'

Abdul spoke for several minutes about his position as CEO of Arabian Gulf Oil Corporation and how, unlike for someone from that region, he was keen on finding urgent alternatives to oil. He was passionate and convincing.

The next part of the lecture was extremely technical but outlined some of the potential for, as he put it, 'a real financially viable alternative to hydrocarbons.'

The lecture finished around lunchtime, which was the scheduled end of the course, and he placed the folder with all of his notes in front of him.

He finished the course by saying, 'It's been a real pleasure knowing all of you and I wish you every success in the future. Could I just ask those who have shown an interest in the other project to wait behind so I can fill them in on the logistics and other details?'

With that, he sat down at the front of the group, who filed out of the various exits.

It was a great surprise that, in the end, only James, Graham, and Carruthers remained in the room.

James asked, 'Is it only us two then?' Carruthers nodded and said, 'It is. It's a shame your girlfriends don't want to accompany you, but from my research you were the best qualified ones in the group anyhow.' He retrieved two folders and handed them to both.

'Inside you will find everything you need. All the details of the required work, how it will be financed, and, most importantly, how you will be rewarded.' He smiled at them. 'I think you will find it most rewarding. I am leaving tonight for Europe, so your main point of contact is going to be Abdul. His contact details are here as well.'

With that, Carruthers proffered his hand and shook hands with them both warmly. He turned his back on them and strolled out of the room in his normal easy stride.

That night was both gloriously happy and, at the same time very sad. Despite all their good intentions, James and Graham realised that they would be seeing very little of their respective partners over the next two years. After a brief drink, they decided that, rather than head back to their homes it would be a good idea to stay a further night.

They had already checked out of their Airbnb, so they decided to splash the cash and see if any rooms were available in the Hilton.

They were lucky enough to find a two-bedroom suite available at a discounted price, and they eagerly accepted the offer. They strolled down to the bar by the river one last time, reminiscing about their first night together. As emotions ran high, they all knew that their wonderful time was coming to an end. James and Graham had carefully studied the package and it seemed too good to be true: $C 500,000 upfront and potential for even more money upon project completion. It was almost unbelievable.

It was a couple of weeks later that Graham and James met again at Brisbane airport, each clutching a first-class ticket in one hand and pulling a huge suitcase with the other. They both grinned upon seeing each other and headed toward check-in.

They finally landed in Montreal almost two days after leaving Australia.

It was mid-afternoon. Breezing through customs they both scanned the waiting greeters.

It was Graham who spotted him first. Towards the back of the waiting crowd was a tall, burly man in his early fifties with long grey streaked hair hidden by a baseball cap. He held aloft a placard with both their names in bold red ink. They strode towards him with hands outstretched; he ignored this and simply said, 'James White? Graham Southwell?'

They both nodded.

'I am Don Fordly, and I will be your pilot today. Have you got warm clothes?' Without waiting for an answer, he continued. 'No worries, I have some warm jackets on the plane.'

'Plane?' asked Graham politely.

'Weren't you told? Where we are going is inaccessible by road at the moment and the only way in is by way of a private airstrip.

Don't worry; it's perfectly safe and only a couple of hours away.' Don looked at his watch. 'Anyway, we must hurry; we only have an hour before our take-off slot.'

Don led them through the gradually clearing arrivals hall and down a few corridors until they reached a small two-engine plane on the grey tarmac.

As the sun began to set, shades of green and purple illuminated the plane in an eerie manner. 'Come on,' said Don 'There is a possibility of some bad weather coming in.'

The flight was smooth, and they landed in the middle of a small basin covered with trees except for the cleared airstrip. They drew to a close, and Don stepped out, letting the two visitors follow.

It was a bitterly cold evening for late October; they were relieved when Don indicated a cabin nestled among the pine trees with white smoke billowing from the small chimneys.

Don said, 'This will be your home for a while. There is electricity from a small hydro plant from the lake just a few hundred metres away and plenty of food and rations. Heating and cooking are from the wood chip boilers; all very environmentally friendly.' Don grinned and then continued, 'Anyway, I will give you a couple of days to enjoy the surroundings before I bring the crew up here to start work.'

With that, he left and headed back to his plane, it taxied around and then took off heading back in the direction they had just arrived from.

James and Graham looked around the cabin.

Don was right; it was well equipped, there was a huge freezer at the back of the cabin, a grey stove covered with all the necessary utensils, and a comforting log fire well-lit by Don or by one of his crew though in need of replenishment from the pile of logs next to it.

James looked at Graham and nodded, 'I think we are going to be alright here. Graham. I am really knackered though; I need some sleep. I don't think I have had more than four hours in the last three days. Graham agreed and they both headed towards the back of the cabin where there were two inviting bedrooms.

They must have slept for nearly 12 hours because the next thing they saw was the sun filtering through the windows of the cabin. Their meal was satisfying and exactly what they needed - Canadian bacon with an abundance of eggs, cooked by one of the locals who had been hired to assist during this initial phase.

It was time to explore, so, pulling on the warm jackets that Don had left them, they opened the cabin door to be greeted by an icy cold arctic wind. The sun, however, was still strong, and in the rarefied air of Northern Quebec, it felt especially pleasant. They looked around and then studied the maps and diagrams that Carruthers and Abdul had given them. It looked very ambitious.

Firstly, there was the access road that needed to be built to the nearest intersection by the lake, some 3 km away. Then there was the construction of sleeping quarters, all to be made from logs forested locally. Finally, and most important was the transportation of the very specialist laboratory equipment that was coming in from overseas and the raw materials only found locally.

Two years was an ambitious target.

James looked at Graham, 'First things first, let's take a look around.'

Walking through the dense foliage of the Canadian forest, with the canopy towering above them, it was like a picture-perfect scene. As they neared the lake where the access road began, there were multiple open areas, including a large section that seemed to be a popular spot for local wildlife. According to reports, there was a family of bears living in the vicinity, but fortunately, they didn't happen to run into them on their stroll.

The first couple of days passed quickly and soon there was a host of local workmen ready to get started. Graham had a construction background, whereas James was a chemist, so Graham took charge of the initial proceedings.

Fall turned into winter, which led to a rapid slowdown, nevertheless, after three months, over 60% of the road had been constructed.

It was time for a two-week break, and both headed down to Florida to meet their respective partners.

Prior to their departure, they had a lengthy conversation with Abdul. They expressed concern about not hearing from George Carruthers and asked how he was doing. Abdul was evasive, simply mentioning a family emergency that had taken him out of the picture for the moment. He also acknowledged some health issues he was dealing with. They gave him an update on the progress of their project as well.

To adhere to the timeline, Abdul increased his workforce starting in late February. The call ended with a thorough discussion of the experiment huts, necessary equipment, and a lengthy list of chemical raw materials needed.

Graham looked at James after the call and asked, 'James, you're the chemist. What are all those raw materials about?'

'I think it's pretty obvious mate, he is trying to create some sort of new fuel source. It's sort of following the lines of Carruthers' last lecture,' James replied.

Graham nodded, not really understanding what James was going on about.

'Anyway, Graham it looks like we should be back on track for the end of next summer. I do wonder about Carruthers though; what do you think was going on with him?'

'I know, it sounds really sad, especially after all the help he gave us to get here.'

That winter was particularly cold and lonely as Sylvie and Janet had decided not to come across. Janet had got herself a part-time job at Brisbane Cricket Ground for the forthcoming test series, and Sylvie didn't want to come all that way on her own.

James and Graham took a flight to California and spent two weeks on the beaches there where James painstakingly showed Graham how to surf. It was all over too quickly, and after a two-month break, it seemed like a dream when they returned to Canada.

The permafrost was just easing, and spring was just about to start, but there was a bitterly cold Arctic wind and still a foot of snow on the access road. The whole site looked particularly desolate. Things were better the next morning. They had managed to get the generators and both log fires going.

Don had been there a couple of days before and had stocked up the freezer with enough food to last them until summer. It was around 11am when they heard the sound of a diesel engine and looking west along the access road, they both saw the welcome sight of the snow plough.

The area was now officially open for business.

In the following weeks, there was a flurry of activity. As promised, reinforcements had arrived and quickly completed all of the living quarters. Next were the experiment huts, which required extensive attention. Due to the hazardous chemicals used, multiple filters were necessary along with top-of-the-line air ventilation and conditioning systems.

When the workers finally finished set up of labs , they were dressed in clothing more suitable for surviving radioactive fallout. They wore full face masks, covering their entire bodies from head to toe with clothing that extended down to their ankles and up to their necklines. Additionally, they all wore heavy-duty gloves that reached up to their elbows. No skin was visible at all.

Graham turned around to ask James questions. 'What's this all about, James?'

'These chemical and raw materials are extremely toxic not only to the skin, but especially if inhaled. When we have all the guinea pigs, (sorry laboratory workers) turn up, we have to make sure that they can work under the absolute safest conditions.'

Graham nodded 'I see; will you actually need me after this is all in place?'

'Of course, it will be vital that every day we make sure that the ventilation and air conditioning areas are performing to the highest standards. On top of that, I expect that you will be the site safety officer when we get everyone here,' James replied.

Abdul's team spent about two weeks bringing in the chemicals and testing all the sophisticated array of equipment.

When they were finally satisfied, they left as smoothly and as quickly as they had arrived.

'What next, James?'

'Well, firstly we are expecting Abdul here in the next few days, he is bringing an oil expert, Jock O'Neill, and then it will be all the chemistry experts.'

A few days later, James found himself lying on the bed, reflecting on his meeting with Jock, who seemed like a nice enough guy with his thick Scottish accent.

CHAPTER – 15

SEAN O'PAUL

As Dougie flipped the pages, he looked at the list of experts, Dougie Fields, Sean O'Paul and Tom Dingwall were marked the most prominent.

At the very moment when Dougie was reading about Sean, he recalled how Sean was full of enthusiasm when he joined the projects and headed to the Canadian site. The story that he had shared about it still brought a smile to Dougie's face.

Sean was back in school in South Dublin when Father Benedict softly whispered into his ear. 'You'll never make a businessman like your father.' It had been a tough few years for Sean, his mother had been in an institution since he was 10 years old, and he had been bought up by his strict maiden aunt, who had never let him associate with other children.

His father was an oil magnate living in Texas and he was lucky if he got to see him more than twice annually.

When he was on the cusp of manhood; his father had somehow managed to secure a place at an exclusive private school near his residence in Austin; it was not quite Yale, but it was just as expensive.

Nevertheless, he barely knew his father, he was looking forward to this new chapter in his life.

The Mansion House was an imposing building built out of the finest Texan sandstone. It was situated in beautiful surroundings of some 25 acres of virgin Texas land. On the grounds were all manner of native trees, Redwoods, Cedars, Lolobolly Pine, and other exotic varieties. Two small streams pierced the grounds to the north of the grounds merging into a single stream to the southwest. In the triangle that was created by the streams, the building was an edifice of great beauty, a triumph to the great Nicholas J. Clayton. Built in 1895 as a Catholic mission bringing religion to the Native Americans, it now survived as one of the most prestigious schools in the North American mainland.

It was here that Sean found himself staring in awe at the cavernous main hall roof as each of the new boys was introduced to the Dean of the University and to his home group tutor.

The Dean, James Manley, looked Sean in the eye and shook his hand vigorously, 'Good morning Mr. O'Paul.'

Sean took in his stare and replied, 'Good morning, Sir.'

He turned to his tutor and exchanged similar pleasantries.

David Smith Jr smiled and said, rather menacingly, 'We have heard a lot about you, Mr. O'Paul, and not all of it particularly good.'

As the two men walked on, Sean wondered what that had been about.

As he walked up the wide stone spiral staircase led by one of the older students for a tour, he was still thinking about it. The tour leader stopped at each area of interest pointing out the various study areas, the Gymnasium, the late 19th-century library, and the recently added annexe containing an indoor swimming pool.

Sean was impressed.

Finally, the tour leader turned to the influx of 20-odd students and said, 'That's all for indoors; now if you could return to David, your Home group tutor, he can take you outside to the apartment blocks where you will spending the next four years.

This time, down in the huge Atrium, David did not address Sean, but rather brusquely said, 'OK, all of you follow me.'

Dutifully, the students trooped out after the huge 280-pound frame of David Smith.

Sean had done a little investigating on David prior to his arrival at the university. He hadn't discovered too much of his background apart from his age (just 40) and professional sporting career as a footballer playing as a line-backer for Dallas before his career was cruelly cut short by a ruptured spleen.

His academic career had been based on his love of Chemistry, specialising in inorganic chemistry. This was obviously of interest to Sean as this was to be his major subject during his time at the college.

Finally, after what seemed like a 10-mile route march, Sean arrived at the apartment blocks. His apartment was particularly secluded under the shade of a giant Redwood tree with only 12 students in the block. Sean looked around the room; it was fairly sparse but adequate, with an oak chest of drawers and a wardrobe and desk to match. In the far corner was a curtain that covered a shower suite. Sean saw his trunk already had been delivered; with a sigh he opened the trunk and quietly shut the door behind him.

It had been a hot, steamy, and sticky day with temperatures well into the mid-nineties, far too hot to do the unpacking.

Sean carefully lifted the heavy trunk from the bed and lowered it to the floor, where it landed with a satisfying thud. He closed his eyes and allowed himself to relax for a few blissful minutes before drifting off to sleep. When he woke up, the room was nearly pitch black. Peering at his watch, he realised he had been asleep for a few hours.

There was plenty of movement from the wildlife that had gathered outside; ground hogs, deer, and birds who hovered above the trees shrilling out their tunes and waiting for dusk to arrive.

There was plenty of action in the apartment blocks as new students started to arrive from the other year groups. Thirty courses could be studied at The Mansion House with a heavy emphasis on the pure sciences of Biology, Physics, and Chemistry. The thirty courses had approximately fifteen students in each area meaning nearly 2,000 students in total. Sean couldn't help but think about the reason for all the additional buildings scattered around the campus. They had been built in the 60s to meet the rising demand for higher education.

From his window, he could see a frenzy of students scurrying between the main Student Hall and bar, as well as the central building on campus. Sean realised that he should also start moving, as he had a meeting with David at 6 pm to discuss the first semester's syllabus. Hurriedly slipping into a pair of jeans and throwing on a loose t-shirt, he made his way through the crowds. As he walked, he couldn't help but wonder what the next four years would hold for him.

It was easy to find David, he had his back to the bar surrounded by a clan of eager followers, including most of his fellow new students.

They all clutched a bottle of local beer or, in some cases, water or cranberry juice. David, himself had his large hand nailed to a large glass of draft ale. David gesticulated enthusiastically at him to join the group.

A cold beer was thrust into his left hand; he took a long gulp and let the ice-cold liquid swill down his parched throat. The conversation that afternoon and evening meandered around the course curriculum and future plans everyone in the group had over the next few years. Sean looked around at the other members of the home group and wondered whether their aspirations were really possible or just pipe dreams. He decided on the latter.

After peering at the name badge pinned to her, Sean spoke to a rather timid student he had met earlier in the day.

'What are your plans, Emily?'

'Nothing really, Sean,' she said, rather defensively.

'What're your reasons for coming to the Mansion House?'

In the recent past, Mansion House has been a very male domain; it has only recently admitted female students. Emily was only the fifth such annual entry.

Emily paused, sipped her warm glass of orange juice, and said coyly, 'My father felt I was too introverted and needed to enjoy a more expansive existence. Anyway,' she continued, 'I have always been totally fascinated by the pure nature of chemistry.'

Sean nodded his head vigorously in agreement. 'Me too!' he exclaimed, 'My father kept me isolated in a Franciscan monastery until I was 17 and I have only just come to Texas to join him.'

'Maybe we can link up later,' he said cautiously.

'Maybe, we'll see.'

She turned away and immediately engaged in another conversation with another one of the fresh-faced students. Sean returned the little huddle of male students by the open bay window and re-joined their conversation on the greatest chemists ever born. He glanced at his watch and noticed it was past midnight. Time to retire, he thought to himself. Placing the empty beer bottle on the table and feeling a little giddy, he wheeled around and headed back to the apartment block. He tripped over his own feet a few times, but he was in good spirits. The evening air was warm and pleasant, with the chorus of crickets playing in the background and fireflies guiding him back to his room.

The first year at Mansion House passed rapidly. It reinforced all his previous educational knowledge from Ireland.

Sean found that degree education in the USA was essentially no better than the final year of sixth form in Ireland and it was not until the beginning/middle of the second that parity started to be achieved. On top of that, most US degrees lasted four years as opposed to those in the UK and Ireland, which were mainly three years.

Social life consisted mainly of drinking in the bar most evenings and then retiring around midnight. Every Friday, they would make a trip down to the nearby town. However, the residents were not very welcoming towards them since the average age of the town's population was over 70 years old. The local bar, known as 'The Punchbowl,' was a cosy gathering spot for the neighbourhood. It was the only place that offered home-cooked meals, and on weekends it was popular among younger locals. The floor of the bar was cluttered with a mix of old wooden chairs and worn white tables, with chipped paint flaking off the legs. The perimeter was lined with cubicles big enough to fit eight men each. This was where Sean and his friends typically spent their nights. Beer was served in well-used chipped glasses or by the bottle, and food consisted mainly of one-pound steaks that were grilled on an open fire. Served with home fries, they made a welcome change from the Spartan food served back at the house.

The owner, John MacPherson (Mac to his regulars), had red hair flecked with white streaks and bristling red eyebrows. He had a short fuse and did not take kindly to the Friday night student pilgrimage to his pub, even though it probably doubled the weeks' taking. Occasionally, he brought in a local band, who crooned through a country and western set, interlaced with some modern classics.

It was the last Friday after the first-year exams, Mac was also in a surprisingly good mood. Sean had found forming relationships with his fellow students quite tough, except for his relationship with Emily, which had started to blossom in the last few weeks. She had begged him to stay quiet over it, as she was positive that she (and they) would be teased mercilessly. Sean sat upright as he realised Chuck Williams was speaking directly to him. 'What did you think of the inorganic exam, Sean?' Chuck asked.

In the moment, Sean was confident that his answers were enough to earn the highest score. However, after a few hours had passed, doubts began to arise. While the first three portions of the test seemed straightforward, the final question was rather unclear and open to interpretation.

Chuck nodded vigorously. 'Yes, yes I agree,' he said apprehensively, 'but still think I did enough.'

Sean nodded and then, distracted by the band's preparation, he turned away to gaze in their direction.

Sean's mind wandered again, and he stole a glance at Emily. She was deeply engrossed in conversation with a fellow second-year student, making it impossible for Sean to catch her attention. They had already discussed their plans for the upcoming summer, wondering if they would be able to see each other at all. It seemed unlikely; Sean was set to return to Ireland for a few weeks while Emily was flying up to Canada the next day to spend the summer at her family's cabin by one of the many lakes near Toronto.

Both Sean and Emily had excelled in their first year and were on track for top honours. The second year flew by quickly, and the final exams posed no major challenges. Emily and Sean grew closer over the period of two years.

They both headed to The Punchbowl to celebrate the end of another successful year as they always did.

This summer, Emily was going to a villa near Nice in France. Sean could not decide what he wanted to do in the summer. It had been two years at Mansion House, and he had just one year to go to the final exams.

It took him a week to get over Emily's absence, but then he finally got his act together. Realising that he would have to head back to Dallas despite the suffocating heat of mid-summer, he caught the bus at the end of the second week of his separation from Emily. It took nearly five hours to reach the ranch and, as he passed through the gates, he felt a sinking feeling in his stomach.

He glanced around the spacious room in the vast ranch. It was blisteringly hot in Dallas that day, with a hot savannah breeze snaking up from the Gulf coast. Sean could feel his cotton shirt sticking to his back. He took another sip of ice-cold water and thought about options.

A couple of hours later Sean was propping up a bar downtown with the delightful name of *'Sheri's Pleasure'*. He felt the alcohol bring a warm glow to his cheeks as he surveyed the scene. In the far corner, a group of lads were raucously egging each other on to higher and higher stakes at the pool table.

In the quieter area next to the restrooms stood several couples most of them nursing a bottle of beer or the local whiskey. It looked like most of them were waiting for a table.

'What would you like to drink sir?' asked the barman.

'I'll have another Bud,' Sean said.

While he was waiting for it to come, Sean looked at the group of lads. They were very animated with a lot of arm waving and fist thumping. Grabbing the bottle in his right fist, Sean sidled over towards the group to eavesdrop on the conversation. They were earnestly discussing the merits of an alternative for oil.

'For sure, it will run out in the next 50 years and then everyone will be stuck,' the tall, lanky, acne-scarred lad furthest away said.

Everyone nodded in solemn agreement.

Sean could not resist making a comment.

'Surely, that deficit could be covered by fusion or hydrogen-based fuels,' he interjected.

'That may be so,' a lad with a footballer's physique said, 'but it won't really be a viable alternative for gasoline.'

He thrust out a huge paw towards Sean, who grabbed it and then it was shaken violently up and down.

'Tom, Tom Dingwall.'

'Sean O'Paul.'

'Join us,' said Tom. Sean did not need asking twice, and immediately joined the discussion.

The discussion ebbed and flowed until, as the end of the evening approached, Tom took Sean to one side and asked immediately, 'You seem really interested in all this stuff. What are you doing the rest of the summer?'

'Well, I don't really have any plans and then I have my final year in Mansion House, Austin'.

'Well, why don't you join us?' Tom said, 'I am sure we can find plenty to talk about.'

'Where are you off to then?' Sean asked inquisitively.

Tom touched his nose, 'It's one of the beach resorts on the Gulf coast. First, it's a great way to earn plenty of greenbacks; it's hard work, lots of bar work and running around, but boy do you deserve the beer at the end of the day.'

Sean thought to himself, why not, better than being stuck here doing nothing.

'When do you leave, Tom?'

'Well, actually, it's tomorrow'.

'Oh OK, let me call you tonight when I have had a chance to think about it. I didn't realise it would be so soon.'

Sean groaned; his head was going to feel sore tomorrow. He weaved towards the door, narrowly avoiding several stragglers still lingering over their last drink. Outside, Sean took in a deep breath in the still warm air and headed towards the flashing lights of the taxi rank across the road.

By night, Sean's mind was made up, he did not know why, it was crazy, but he was going to join them on this adventure.

At home, Tom looked at the door closing behind him and thought back to his own rather turbulent past.

CHAPTER – 16

TOM DINGWALL

It had been an unusually warm day in Texas, Tom looked at his family huddled around the black ebony wood table in the palatial front room of the ranch. The ranch was typical of the area: ten bedrooms upstairs, and six reception rooms, of which the largest was a 2,000 square foot breakfast room, where the family spent most of their time. The grounds were enormous, with some 10,000 acres of prime grazing, with 500 head of top-quality cattle.

Texas was still the second-largest oil producer in the World. Tom's father, John Dingwall, owned many of the oil fields in Texas and the new offshore exploration fields in the Gulf of Mexico. He was also very ambitious, and he had just formed a company to manage his investments, Houston Oil. He was determined that Houston Oil would one day be the largest oil company in the world.

Tom's world shattered when he learned that his brother Jeff was dying of leukaemia. That same afternoon, in a cruel twist of fate, he also received the news that he had been accepted into Yale. His father, with a mix of sorrow and pride, had delivered both pieces of news in a single breath. For the first time, Tom saw genuine happiness in his father's eyes for him, even as they both stood on the edge of despair.

Tom struggled to find his voice. "How long?" he finally asked. His father, still avoiding his gaze, replied, "You leave in October."

"No, no," Tom stammered, his voice trembling. "How long does Jeff have?"

John looked up; his face was ashen white. He had aged at least ten years within the last two-three weeks.

'Oh my God, no!' Tom cried.

He looked at his father again, something was wrong, very wrong. He was breathing only very short breaths and gasping for air.

'Father, are you OK?' Tom asked nervously.

'Get your mother!' John whispered under his breath. He gestured with the back of his hand toward the open study door. Tom, in haste, stumbled over the edge of the carpet as he hurried through the ranch, heading toward the decking where he hoped to find his mother. His voice rose in panic as he ran, "Mum, come quick! It's Dad!" He repeated it again and again.

His mother appeared at the open doors leading to the decking; her face reflected fear and anxiety. "What is it?" she asked, her voice barely audible.

"It's Father," Tom said urgently. "He's struggling to breathe."

Without delay, Sally rushed past Tom and sprinted toward the study.

John was lying almost lifeless on the desk clutching a bundle of papers, still breathing but with shortened rasping breaths.

Sally looked into his husband's terrified eyes, 'Tom please go back to the main courtyard and see if Dave is still rounding up the cattle; if he is, I need him to come back here as quickly as he can. In the meantime, I will phone 911 and get some medics out here immediately.'

Despite choking back her emotions, Sally spoke with clarity and direction.

Tom whirled round and, slamming the study door, dived through the nearest open full-length window.

He screamed, 'DAVE, come quickly.'

Dave came immediately and not long after, the medics arrived too. They glanced at John and realised that, although serious, he was not in a life-threatening condition. They placed the clear plastic mouthpiece over John's mouth and released gentle bursts of oxygen through his open mouth until his breathing became steadier. The senior medic glanced at Sally and gave a quick thumbs up.

Tom grasped his mother's forearm and hugged her 'He will be fine, Mother.' He sobbed in short breaths.

Later that year, after Tom's brother's demise, his father's condition worsened. His father now struggled to get out of bed, barely able to make it to the en-suite bathroom, let alone manage the cattle and oversee the ranch hands. Tom also knew that he could never embrace his father's way of life. He needed to break free before it was too late.

As he glanced around his spacious bedroom, his eyes locked on the slats of the blinds shielding the room from the relentless midday sun. His decision was clear—he would pursue the path of black gold and earn his Chemistry degree at Yale. *Forget the cattle and the oil; young Dingwall was destined for a different future.* He said to himself firmly.

Tom did not really enjoy college life. Sure, the end-of-week parties were fun, and the end-of-semester parties were even better. But after a while, Tom was even tired of these socials and yearned for something different. Every day at college felt the same. The same lectures and the same familiar faces became a monotonous routine until he attended one lecture. The inorganic chemistry class near the end of his second year where a guest speaker sparked curiosity. The speaker was George Carruthers, a well-spoken English professor from Cambridge University who grabbed everyone's attention. Carruthers spoke at length about the end of oil production and the future beyond it.

It was strange to hear the idea of a world without oil. After the lecture Tom met Carruthers, determined to find out more information about his newly introduced idea.

Carruthers explained that he was on a world tour, with Australia as his next stop. He even explained about the research site in Canada and how he was very close to securing US funding for the 'magic' catalyst that would solve the world's energy crisis and reverse the effects of climate change forever. Tom mentioned his interest in the oil industry and his father's oil business in Texas. They exchanged mobile numbers and agreed to stay in touch.

After the third year ended, Tom went to see his father. John was in a miserable state, confined to a wheelchair to move around. His once sharp piercing gaze had been dulled by drugs and constant pain. He had passed on the power of attorney to Tom's mother, Sally, who now oversaw all decisions, both on the ranch and in the thriving oil business.

Later that evening, as Tom retured from an evening at the bar and sat with his mother, Sally looked up from behind her gold-rimmed spectacles. A sharp, quizzical expression crossed her face, her brow deeply furrowed with concern.

'What do you make of this, Tom?' she asked directly.

She passed a letter to Tom across the wide table. Tom flipped it over and glanced quickly through the contents. It really was puzzling; the letter was from Abdul Rehmann with reference to the conversations Tom had with George Carruthers almost 18 months ago.

The letter was an invitation to Tom to work away in Canada on a research project on alternative energy sources.

It was a bit vague. However, the money was really enticing. Three months work and 100,000 dollars upfront with an option to extend it for a further nine months.

'It seems too good to be true, Ma. But I am intrigued.'

He paused for thought. 'I think I will give them a call,' he said.

The phone on the other end was picked up after the first ring.

As the conversation progressed, Tom turned towards his mother again with a huge grin.

'Well, it's not for a year, Ma, but they are offering a great package. They will put the money into my account at least three months in advance. It is still puzzling though; they talked about research into new fuel sources, but I have no idea why I have been selected, and there was no mention of what would be expected of me once I get there. The person on the phone also mentioned some other first-class chemists, joining me on this project. I actually met someone earlier this evening who would be a great fit and also would be keen to go. I don't know what his commitments are though.'

'Well, you know I don't want you to go, Tom,' Sally said sadly. 'But it looks like you have made up your mind, I am not ready to lose my other son,'

'It's not for a year Ma, I know that it's a cliché, but it could all be just pie in the sky.'

Sally shrugged her shoulders and wheeled away into the kitchen behind her. As she retreated, the phone rang again.

This time it was Sean on the phone.

'I have been thinking about you,' said Tom. He mentioned the communication from Abdul Rehmann.

It was just past 7 am when Tom stirred in his bed; the early morning sun had just started to filter through the slats on his window. Stretching his arms, he sat up and made his way towards the window. Sliding open the blinds, he stood on his veranda, surveying the extent of the rolling fields that seemed to go on for miles. Luckily, he had packed his trunk the night before, so now it was time to get moving.

There were now six in total going to Galveston for the summer, including Sean. After a quick breakfast and curt goodbyes to Sally, he was on his way to pick up Sean.

They only stopped once prior to arriving in Galveston, which would be home for the next eight weeks.

Lunch was a rushed affair at one of the many roadside restaurants en route. It was early evening before they reached Galveston, just as the sun was setting over the shimmering clear blue waters of the Gulf. Sean gazed over the ocean and immediately thought that it was going to be an enjoyable summer, no matter how hard he had to work. As with the previous summer, it was hard work but very rewarding. Tom introduced Sean to everyone in their group.

It was, at times, very busy but also quite monotonous; it was not until nearly the end of the fourth week that Tom got a chance to see Sean alone. They found themselves at the back of the group on the familiar walk along the boardwalk one evening.

Tom grabbed his moment.

'Sean, you know when we first met, we were discussing alternative fuels.'

Sean paused for a moment and looked fixedly at the ground and then turned towards Tom.

'Well sort of, but it was all very hypothetical, wasn't it?' Tom smiled.

'Well, I have an interesting proposition,' he said. 'After I met you on the first night, I got home to find a letter waiting for me. Its contents were quite strange but the gist of it was that there is an opportunity to work in Canada in about a year's time. It will be to look at alternative energy sources. That is interesting, considering my background.' Tom chuckled and then continued.

'Anyway, the financial rewards are quite staggering; $100,000 upfront and weekly payments of at least $5,000. All lodgings are paid for along with food and any expenses.'

Tom paused before Sean interjected: 'Why are you telling me all this?'

'Well, it's simple; they, (whoever they are) have asked me to find one other person. They are quite specific that they must be a chemist, with no ties, preferably just graduated. I thought of you as an ideal match.'

Sean thought for a moment. 'You kind of caught me off guard. I have lots of questions, The most obvious being, who is funding all of this?'

Tom replied, 'To be honest. I don't have the complete picture. All I know is that it appears to be funded from three areas: England, Saudi Arabia, and the USA. I know all about the Saudi Arabia funding because this came directly from my lecture courses.'

Tom went on to explain the events of the previous year and the discussions he'd had with Abdul Rehman.

Sean nodded in approval and said, 'Well, it's certainly interesting, but, as you know, I have not graduated as yet. I know you say it is in a year, but a lot could happen in that period, and I might not even graduate!' He paused for a minute. 'So, what are the next steps, in any case?'

They had reached the end of the boardwalk as it curved gently into Galveston Harbour, where the rest of the group had stopped, waiting for them both.

'Let me get a few more details, I am sure we will have more time to discuss this,' Tom said.

It wasn't until the last night that they were able to chat once more and then only briefly. The next day Sean was going directly to Austin by plane.

All Sean was able to say over the last of many cocktails in their favourite bar overlooking the harbour was a few words. 'Tom,' he shouted over loud hubbub. 'I am definitely in, let's keep in contact over the year.'

Tom raised a thumb in acknowledgement.

On the flight back to Austin, Sean had a lot of time to think and wondered if he was really doing the right thing. *Ah well,* he thought to himself, *nothing ventured*!

When college started, it was much easier than he thought it was going to be. Emily had decided to take a gap year and travel around Europe, which meant he literally had no ties.

He knuckled down to the final year project, which coincidentally was on the role of catalysts in chemical reactions. The last year drifted past quite slowly, and although there was time to drift down to 'The Punchbowl' for the usual Friday night event, it did not seem quite the same without Emily there with him.

He had fallen behind a bit on his work, so he decided to stay over Christmas to catch up. It was quite a surprise when he received an invite from Tom to spend a couple of days with him at the ranch. He headed down on Christmas Eve and met Tom at the Dallas bus station.

He smiled, looking at the Christmas decorations as they travelled along the main highway out towards the ranch.

'I have news from Canada,' Tom finally blurted out.

'All the funding has been approved for me and you will be getting a call in the next few days. The difference is that you will be receiving a call from the US side of the bargain. They cannot approach me because of the conflict of interest. My funding is coming from Saudi.'

'Conflict of interest?' Sean said with a puzzled look on his face.

'It's because of my connections to the oil industry, I cannot be seen to be working against them, so it is all very secretive,' Tom added.

'Oh, I see; so, when will I be getting the call?' asked Sean.

'From what I understand, it will be in the first week or so in January, so for now and the next few days, Christmas and our hospitality.' replied Tom enthusiastically.

Tom was a very welcoming host, as well as his mother. They had even bought Sean an expensive Christmas present. Sean was very apologetic that he had nothing to give in return.

The festivities helped take Sean's mind off things. There seemed to be an endless stream of relations and friends coming to see the strangely spoken young man from Ireland.

It was almost exactly a week later that Sean received a phone call. An officious voice asked him his name, and when Sean gave his details, he was put through.

'Hi Sean,' a gruff but friendly voice announced, 'I am Grant Lyons, I am the financial director of Gulf of Mexico Oil.'

Sean waited for him to continue, 'Do you know why I am calling?'

'I think so, is it about the Canada project?' replied Sean.

'Yes, that's right, you come highly recommended not only by Tom Dingwall, who I know you know very well, but also, we have been in touch with your college to check on your credentials.

'I am most impressed, and I am willing to fund you providing your results at college are as predicted. What do you think about that?'

'That's great to hear, Grant, but getting a little more detail would be great.'

'Do you mean around the project? If so, that is easy. Our consortium is trying to assemble the top young brains in the chemistry world to examine alternative fuel sources to hydrocarbons. Several oil companies like mine are trying to follow the same route. However, this project is taking a different tack. We are trying to think outside the box and not looking at hydrogen fuel, nuclear, solar or wind power.

'So, the Canada project is hopefully going to take steps to solve the problem by other means; and that is where you come in.'

'OK, Grant, what will be the next steps? I am definitely in.' Sean said, sounding confident but feeling apprehensive.

'That's great, I will be in touch.' Grant said bluntly. The line disconnected.

The next few months went quickly. Sean and Tom kept in touch on a regular basis.

If anything, Tom was more on edge than Sean. He too had very little communication with the consortium apart from a couple of calls from Abdul confirming arrangements and a potential starting date

CHAPTER – 17

THE FINAL PREPARATIONS

'I have booked a great restaurant in Fort Worth tonight so we can really catch up properly. It's a great place, most famous for its steaks and a trapeze artist swinging above you as you enjoy your dinner. The steaks aren't small either, as you will see. And I felt before we leave for Canada, we must treat ourselves,' Tom said.

Sean smiled, 'That sounds absolutely perfect, Tom, I cannot wait.'

As expected, it was brilliant. The menu itself was quite astonishing. The average size steak was 24 oz, but for those who were not faint-hearted, there were steaks of 48 oz: enough for a family of four, let alone a single diner. Sean watched in amazement as the trapeze artist swung over the heads of diners as he tried to make his order. It was all quite spectacular.

Tom was clearly in his element. Having been there several times, he was familiar with the waiting staff, as he addressed them all by their first names. He also did not even bother to look at the menu, which he had left closed in front of him.

'I'll have the 20-oz rib-eye, with peppercorn sauce, the creamed spinach and French fries,' he said to one of the waiting staff in a voice loud enough to be heard over the clamour all around them.

It was what Sean had been waiting for, 'I will have the same as him please.'

Without a doubt, it was one of the best steaks Sean had ever tasted. It wasn't until they finished the meal that the conversation turned to Canada in detail. Tom leaned over so he could speak more quietly.

'I think it is going to be great; they are talking about the money transfer at the end of the month. It looks like you and I will be team leaders, though I am not exactly sure why?'

'I must admit, I am getting a little anxious about it all.'

'You will be fine, Sean, I am absolutely sure, anyway, let's get out of this place before it gets too exciting. I think they usually have fire eaters and acrobatics later on!'

They made their way back to Tom's new Miata convertible parked just in front of the restaurant. Both just about squeezed into the small bucket seats. It was a pleasant drive back to the ranch through the peach tree-lined avenues, where the fragrant smell of their blossom still lingered in the night air.

Soon they entered the open highway and quickly picked up speed.

'I love your new car, Tom.'

'Yes, it is sort of a present from my mother to try and persuade me not to go away.' Tom gave a sideways glance to Sean in the passenger seat. 'Don't worry Sean, it hasn't worked.'

They both laughed heartily.

It was somewhat of a relief when Sean and Tom received a call at the ranch, barely two weeks before their departure.

Grant, his funder, immediately got to the point.

'Sean, as we discussed, we have chosen you specifically to lead one of the teams once you are in Quebec.' Grant paused. 'Apart from yourself, you obviously know Tom, and the other key individuals on the chemistry side are James White and Dougie

Fields. Also, there are some more individuals who will look after the construction side of the plant; you will meet them when you arrive. Well, that's all for now, Sean; good luck, and I will be in touch again soon.' With that, the phone line went silent.

Tom looked at him. Sean just raised his thumb before remarking, 'I think it's all sorted, but I still don't know why I was picked above anyone else; it's all very peculiar.'

'Don't ask the questions, Sean, just take the reward. Let's go down to Sheri's and celebrate.'

Tom wanted to say farewell to all his local friends, most of whom were somewhat jealous of his change of fortune. Tom whistled in the back of the cab as it hurtled along the dusty roads towards downtown Dallas.

When they opened the door and sucked in the icy cold air-conditioned climate, ten or so friends gathered to say farewell. Having consumed few Buds, they were in boisterous spirits. Tom soon took up the threads of conversation; evidently, they were all equally confused over the exact purpose of his and Sean's mission.

As the conversation revolved around topics such as oil conservation and more importantly what would happen when it ran out, Tom noticed another guy about their age inching closer to their group.

'Hey buddy,' Tom called out excitedly. 'Come join us,' he gestured with his index finger towards their group. Sean was also drawn into the conversation. Sean had to leave soon as he wanted to visit Dallas before their departure to Canada. It was therefore quite an early end to the evening, and Sean took a cab back to the ranch alone, leaving Tom with his friends and the protracted farewells.

Sean felt bleary-eyed as he groped for the loud buzzing emanating from the annoying alarm clock perched on his small bedside cabinet. He groaned inwardly as the time showed 5 am, just an hour before he was due to leave.

He decided to leave a note on the kitchen table explaining his early departure, and then he set out to meet his airport ride at the ranch gates, which were a mile away.

Back at the ranch, Tom had not stirred. He had got in around about an hour before Sean had left, with considerably more beers inside him. After Sheri's had closed, they had moved on to a late-night pool club before ending up in an all-night burger bar. Tom remembered very little beyond getting in a cab and arriving back home.

When he awoke, he had vague memories of the night before and hoped he had done nothing foolish. He strolled down a wide pine staircase to the entrance hall, with his head still throbbing. There was no one in the breakfast room, but it had obviously been occupied, as the two enormous veranda doors were open to the patio.

On the patio table was an unfinished glass of orange juice and the remnants of a croissant. Tom wondered where his mother was for a moment, then remembered that every morning, she went out to the far reaches of the ranch to check on the livestock and give instructions to the head of the ranch.

Opening the fridge, he found it stacked with various juices, breads and meats. Helping himself to a large glass of cranberry juice and a couple of croissants, he settled down for a morning's relaxation before contemplating what Sean was up to at the moment.

Sean had just landed in Austin and was on his way back to his college digs. On arrival, he opened the door to an immaculately cleaned room. The first thing he noticed were two envelopes, both from the college and both marked private and confidential. In all the excitement, he had forgotten about the results, so he opened the first one somewhat nervously. The first words were, "Congratulations, Sean. You have been awarded a first in Chemistry." After that, there were lots of details on how to collect the necessary paperwork and attend the award ceremony.

The second letter was more interesting, it detailed a couple of potential options for later in the year, one of which was a junior position in the UK branch of Gulf of Mexico Oil. It was not due to start until later in the year, but the rewards looked great. Again, his immediate thought was this must have come via Grant Lyons. The other two offers were related to postgraduate work at the university, but Sean immediately felt that he had had enough of college, at least for the time being. There was no need to rush into doing anything at the moment.

Feeling tired, he stretched out on his bed, falling asleep almost instantly. He did not wake up until nearly 10 pm that evening; realising he was feeling completely starving, he wondered if he had time to get to the late-night restaurant but settled upon the 7-11 just outside the campus instead.

Walking back to his room, he dug into the nachos and had practically finished them before getting back. Looking around the room, he knew that there was a lot of packing to be done over the next few days. Luckily, Tom had agreed to let him store most of it at his place.

The week sped by, and soon, it was time to say goodbye to his room for the last time. He had lots of happy memories mingled with some sad ones. He also had a few regrets, in particular the end of his relationship with Emily, his first and only love.

The shrill sound of his phone ringing startled Sean. It was Tom calling. 'Hey, Sean, everything alright?' Tom asked without waiting for a response. 'I'll meet you at the same spot as last time, by the information desk.'

'Yes, that's perfect,' replied Sean.

Back at the ranch, Tom had had a quiet week, trying to avoid his mother's icy stare whenever they saw each other. On the day of Sean's departure from the ranch, they finally made a peace agreement. Tom promised to call her at least once a week without fail, and he would come back and take over her responsibilities when this period of foolishness was over. Tom agreed, just to keep the peace, but secretly thought that it was unlikely.

Sean duly arrived back and met him as agreed. This time there was no trip to the 'Circus Restaurant'. The drive back to the ranch was in silence and it was not until they entered the final track leading up to the ranch entrance that Tom spoke.

'I got a First, Sean.'

'That's great, Tom, so did I!'

They excitedly went over their expectations for the next few months.

Sally had very reluctantly agreed to give Tom and Sean a lift to the agreed pick-up point.

When they reached it, Sally looked at her son. He looked both excited and somewhat anxious at the same time.

'Tom, are you OK?' She asked cautiously, sharing his apprehension.

'Of course, Mum,' he said dismissively. 'Why wouldn't I be?"

'I know you don't want me to leave, but I will be back,' he hesitated, 'I promise,' said in a much quieter tone.

As he got out of the car and retrieved his luggage, she gave him a quick peck on the cheek and then Tom disappeared into the swirling mists of heavy morning dew that already swathed the downtown bus station.

Tom turned to Sean, eager to get started. They both climbed onto the bus, tripping over each other's feet in their haste. As more passengers filled up the space around them, they knew they were finally on the long and exhausting journey to Canada.

After two days of travelling by bus, they decided to stay at a sprawling motor hotel on the outskirts of Washington, DC. In the sweltering heat of summer, staying in a poorly air-conditioned motel was far from enjoyable.

The next day, they continued their journey on the bus and arrived at their destination in the dead of night, the old bus screeching to a stop. "We're here, get off," the driver announced. Sean and Tom yawned and stretched as they peered outside. The darkness was heavy and disorienting, making it difficult to distinguish any objects besides the other vehicles that looked similar to the one they had just disembarked from.

Tom and Sean jumped onto the pebbled ground. Their feet felt a crunch as they landed back on terra firma. Tom scanned the horizon as fireflies flittered in the suffocating night air. The humidity was stifling. Both grabbed their heavy bags and stumbled towards what appeared to be a row of army barracks.

A torchlight waved from side to side in the distance.

'This way,' bellowed a deep disembodied voice from beyond the flashlight. 'This way.'

Clutching their bags, Sean and Tom were shepherded into the furthermost cabin. Sean looked around at the stark surroundings and thought inwardly about the last time he had been in Canada with Emily just a couple of years earlier. It was certainly a very different and almost surreal feel.

As they entered the cabin, they saw several others lying on beds all fast asleep. With a cursory nod to each other, Tom and Sean found the only two remaining uncomfortable narrow beds. Within seconds only, steady, rhythmic, shallow breathing could be heard from all the bed's occupants. Tom winked, and Sean tried to wink back. Soon they drifted to deep sleep, oblivious of the fact that this would be the last time that both of them would be truly happy and content.

PART- 3

CANADA

CHAPTER – 18

IN CANADA, WEEK ONE

The next morning, there was a loud rap on the door and all the occupants stirred.

'Wake up,' boomed a voice from outside the cabin. 'It's time for breakfast!" the disembodied voice softened a little.

Sean looked at his watch and blinked; it was only 6 am. Sleepily, he pulled on a pair of track pants and a sweatshirt and gingerly made his way to the open door. All the rest followed in disorderly fashion, most of them pulling clothes as they walked to a central barbecue area where they could see glowing coals.

Wafts of smoke carrying appetising smells of maple syrup and smoked bacon drifted towards the group of half-dressed, rather dishevelled men. Sean also noticed a couple of women at the end of the group, who looked like they were part of a management team. Breakfast was taken in silence as most people were still in shock at the early start or still exhausted from the journey the day before. Polite small talk started to erupt as the plates were cleared away. They were then disturbed by the booming voice again; it appeared to emanate from a bearded giant standing behind the now extinguished barbecue.

'Back here in 20 minutes,' he said brusquely. He spun round and headed towards the large cabin set aside from all the smaller army barracks.

Sean looked around; the dawn sunlight was just filtering through the leafy canopy of giant maple trees. Even at this time of day, the humidity was starting to rise, and he could see steam starting to curl upwards from the dark emerald green mossy carpet at the edge of the forest. Tom, who was usually so confident in any situation, was starting to feel very apprehensive and beginning to wonder what he had got himself into.

The group stood, waiting expectantly in front of the management hut. Sean did a quick count up and made it 22 individuals, all men, and mainly in the twenties or early thirties, as far as he could ascertain. Jock, standing at the back of the group, was, of course, older.

The bearded giant exited from the management hut, closely followed by two men who appeared to be of Middle Eastern descent.

There was a deathly hush and then the shortest man of the group spoke. 'My name is Abdul Rehmann, and I guess you are all wondering what you are doing here?' Abdul peered over the top of his rimless gold glasses expecting an answer from his small audience.

There was no response.

Abdul continued, 'These huts,' he pointed at the huts just beyond the barracks. This is the place where you will be working for the next few months.'

He continued, 'The work will be hazardous and at times dangerous.'

Tom thrust his hand up. 'Why dangerous?' he asked.

'The chemicals you will use to extract the rare metals are both toxic and highly flammable.'

This time Sean raised his hand. 'Yes, what is it?' Abdul asked impatiently.

'I thought we were looking for alternative sources of energy; so why are we extracting rare metals?'

Abdul continued. 'Some of you, possibly not you young man, will be aware that we are investigating catalysts that can be used in chemical reactions to create these new sources. Anyway, these chemicals are highly toxic and, in building this establishment,' he waved his hand around indicating the whole campus, 'we suffered one or two fatalities from a lack of care.'

Abdul paused, taking stock of all the ashen faces now looking at him. 'This will not happen now we are in full production mode, so there is no need to worry excessively. There are numerous forms to fill in, including a disclaimer and a whole set of safety forms.'

Abdul paused again before asking, 'Are there any questions, please?'

There was no response.

'OK, great! Hugo will divide you up into groups of five or six for induction and a small tour into camp life.'

Sean was in the first group to be picked and he was delighted to see that it was the same group as Tom.

He stepped forward and thrust out a hand to the other three men.

'I'm Sean O'Paul and this is Tom Dingwall who arrived on the same bus as me, and you are...?'

Sean faced a man in his 40s with a shock of red hair; 'I am James O Neill, but everyone calls me Jock.'

'Nice to meet you, Jock,' Sean said pleasantly. 'And you?'

'I am James White,' stammered a tall, tanned individual.

'That's not an American accent, James; where are you from?' asked Sean.

'I am from Queensland, Australia.' James spoke in hushed tones as though he was somewhat ashamed of his background. 'Great to meet you too.'

Sean smiled and turned to the last of the group, a bespectacled young man, thrusting his hand into his.

'I am Dougie Fields. I'm a chemistry undergraduate from London, England.'

Then they all huddled together, waiting for Hugo, the bearded giant to direct them to their laboratory hut.

Once inside James and Jock got together and compared notes. James nodded a couple of times and then approached the three men in his group.

'Okay, just to give you a bit of background, I have been here on and off for a couple of years. Don't mind Abdul; he's not the best at being tactful. When he mentioned the fatality, it wasn't related to the chemicals. It was an accident caused by carelessness during the construction of one of the huts.

'However, the gases and chemicals that you will be exposed to over the next few months are toxic. It is therefore really important that you wear protective clothing, including full face masks.

'Also, I would be interested in knowing how you got invited, so perhaps we can have a chat towards the end of the week. What I do know is that the consortium has singled you three out as key individuals, as we try and make progress.' James paused for a moment before continuing.

'Anyway, the main purpose of the first week is to familiarise yourself with the set-up here and give you an understanding of what we are trying to achieve through this research project.'

James waved his hand in the direction of a small room at the side of the hut, gesturing at the collection of protective gear inside.

'If you get into something that fits you, I can show you around and explain a little bit more.' James shouted above the noise of the whirring machinery.

The clothing had a futuristic feel, almost like they were plucked from the set of a sci-fi film.

Not an inch of skin was visible, and they could only speak to each other through helmet microphones.

'This hut,' James explained, 'is one of the two main experimental huts. This is where we extract the purest forms of the rare metals and try to combine them to create catalysts. These catalysts, as I am sure you must have heard, are called metallates; they have almost magical powers. They can break chemical bonds that have never previously been broken, at least not effectively.'

Tom, Dougie, and Sean looked around. At least 15 other people were dressed in similar clothing.

Tom asked the obvious question, 'Who are all these people?'

After a short pause, James answered, 'They are all local people with a little chemical knowledge; basically, you three will supervise them.'

They meandered through the long tunnel of a hut before stopping in front of three workstations.

'This,' James explained, 'is where we will look at different combinations of rare metals to try and achieve optimum results. We will measure the success of each before it passes into more vigorous testing in the second hut. The second hut has a whole host of environmental devices. This equipment will test the ageing process of each catalyst by accelerating one year's wear and tear into just a month. The defence industry uses such machinery to look at the viability of paint on military aircraft.

'The second set of machinery will attempt to measure how many times a catalyst can be reused before disposal. This is critical. These catalysts are extremely expensive and need to be used hundreds of times before becoming economically viable. Unfortunately, they are quite unstable, and many will only last three or four times prior to disintegration.'

James paused, 'Any questions?'

Tom spoke first 'Well, loads actually, but I guess they can wait until we actually learn the ropes.'

Dougie and Sean just nodded in agreement. 'OK,' said James. 'Let's get started.'

Dougie was excited to work on the rare metals he had studied. The other two seemed less enthusiastic but were captivated by the whole concept.

'So, James, are we looking at every rare earth element or just a few select ones?' Dougie asked.

'Well, we are going to try all of them or as many as possible. Familiarise yourselves with this hut, which will be your home during the day. One last thing: I must introduce you to Graham Southwell. He is not a chemist but knows how all this machinery works and is also in charge of safety on site. I will bring him around shortly, as you must meet him today.'

James paused and then brought out a sheaf of papers from his inside pocket.

They were marked:

- Week One Team 1
- Week One Team 2
- Week One Team 3

Each section contained a series of chemical experiments, complete with a list of necessary substances and step-by-step instructions for mixing them.

'For the first three weeks, Sean, you will be in charge of Team 1, Tom in charge of Team 2, and, Dougie in charge of Team 3.' James said before handing out the sheets.

'It is up to you how you handle these experiments; you can either do one a day or vary the quantities to create a slightly different compound. Or you may prefer to do all five experiments simultaneously every day and then vary the quantities on a daily basis.'

James sighed. 'Personally, I would go for the first option, mainly because you will need to document the results so carefully. A metallate, in the broadest meaning of the term, is a compound created between two metals. A simple example would be nickel ferrate, which is a compound of iron and nickel.

'Metallates have been found to be excellent catalysts for all sorts of chemical reactions. It was found only by accident a few years ago that metallates made from rare earth elements could be used to break chemical bonds like the carbon-oxygen bond and the hydrogen-oxygen bond. Therefore, the purpose of these experiments is to try to discover the most stable metallate, and the one that is the most effective in creating an alternative fuel. This would be something like ethanol which is already used to enrich gasoline to lower carbon emissions.' James paused, 'Does all that make sense?'

All three nodded, hiding their uncertainty.

'OK then, let's get started... Oh! Just one more thing. After you have prepared the metallate it has to be weathered in the hut opposite.' James raised his thumb and pointed behind him. 'I think Graham will give you a tour of that hut bit later today. Anyway, I have got to brief the other teams, so I will see you later!.'

James turned his back on the trio and made for the door. All three looked around; in front of them were the three groups of willing workers ready to take their instructions. Behind them were three neatly laid-out benches stacked with carefully labelled chemicals. Above each bench, each team number was clearly labelled. There was plenty of space between each bench for team members to move around and circulate. Over in the distant corner, three laptops were already connected and ready for them to analyse all of the data and draw correlations.

'Okay; let's get started.' Tom said into his helmet microphone.

Sean and Dougie gave a thumbs-up, and they went to their respective parts of the hut, where their teams were waiting expectantly.

It was well into the afternoon before any experiment could begin. As with any experiment, they had to make sure they had the right chemicals in sufficient quantities. Then, the finished results were elaborately tested before being analysed and recorded.

Inevitably, the first two days would involve much trial and error. The chemical reactions needed constant supervision, meaning only one-third of the team could take lunch and afternoon breaks at any one time.

Once the initial excitement wore off, the work became monotonous and dull. The constant trips to the stores to fetch more chemicals were tiring. However, it was the process of putting on and taking off protective gear that proved to be the most exhausting. Each time took over 20 minutes, adding to the already draining nature of the work. Luckily, they had a fantastic team of workers from nearby towns, comprised of both men and women. The workers had been handsomely rewarded in an area where employment was mostly seasonal or confined to fishing on nearby lakes.

As the sun set each day, they gathered around the campfire to discuss who had the best team, while enjoying barbequed steaks and locally brewed ale. Over the course of the first weeks, all five of them became close friends, with even Graham and James joining in the evening festivities. Despite the lack of success in creating a metallate and the absence of any investors, there was an easy-going atmosphere among the group.

Over time, synergy shifted within the group. Dougie and Tom really got along, whereas Sean felt a little bit out of it and tended to stick to his own devices. Of course, James and Graham had been together for over two years, but they, too, mixed in at every opportunity. At the end of the week, James and Graham visited the local township to sample the local nightlife, particularly the small micro-breweries on the township outskirts. They took it upon themselves to introduce the new threesome to the delights of extremely strong local ales.

It is still a mystery how they managed to return to camp on Friday. Thankfully, they all got back safely.

The next morning, the group ate breakfast in silence until Tom finally spoke up. "Last week was tough, but it's only going to get harder from here on out," he said. "What do you guys do for fun on weekends? Just staying at the camp can drive us crazy."

James nodded, 'Well, we visit the lakes, rent a boat indefinitely. I 've booked an extra one for the period all of you are out here; it's free to use whenever you want. We tend to spend our time cruising on the lake at weekends. The fishing is absolutely great, and we often frequent a couple of beach bars on the other side of the shore.'

James smiled knowingly and tapped the side of his nose. 'Don't worry Sean, they don't have beer from micro-breweries.'

Everyone laughed out loud at Sean's obvious discomfort.

The following weekend, the five of them visited the lake and a beach bar.

James and Graham explained their favourite hangout over the previous couple of years has been 'The Shellfish Backwater'.

From the exterior, it didn't look special. The door hung open, revealing peeling blue paint and bare window frames. On the landing stage, a few planks were missing, creating a dangerous gap. Outside the bar, tables were haphazardly scattered along the beach, with faded umbrellas providing minimal shade. Despite its run-down appearance, this place was renowned for serving the freshest shellfish on the lakes - their scallops were especially delicious. And to wash it all down, they offered a selection of Ontario's finest wines from the Niagara region.

As the cormorants and seagulls dived for their scraps in the early evening sunshine, the dappled shadows cast eerie shapes on the crystal blue water. It was perfect.

Everyone swapped stories of how they had arrived in Canada.

James and Graham told of their meeting with Carruthers in Brisbane and how Abdul had persuaded them to join the expedition.

Dougie nodded at this point. 'I will have to tell you all the stories about Carruthers when you have a few hours,' Dougie said with sadness in his voice.

'You know he passed away a couple of months ago and also the tragedy surrounding his family?' Dougie paused. 'Actually, I don't think it was very far from here where the tragic incident happened. There was some sort of boating accident. It was all very mysterious, and I never really got to the bottom of that mystery. What was nice, though, was that Carruthers introduced me to his son, who is assisting me in my PhD back in England. He seems really nice, and very passionate about this project.'

Graham interjected. 'I just wondered Dougie, where did you get your funding? You know most of us had a Saudi connection, except Sean.' Sean nodded in agreement.

'Mine is coming from the UK part of this triangle. The investor is Rhys Williams, CEO of Shetland Oil. I am not sure how he fits in with the Saudi arrangement and Sean's connection here in the USA.'

Sean shrugged his shoulders, then spoke. 'I have been thinking about this for a long time, the whole thing seems very random, but on the other hand, very selective. It seems to me that the Saudi part of this trinity seems to be pulling the strings.'

Tom nodded again and said, 'I think it would be a good idea to try and get Jock to join us one evening. He seems like a reasonable sort of guy; he might give us some insight into what is intended in the ultimate plan.'

Tom looked at Graham and James and continued.

'How well do you know him? Has he been here as long as you guys?'

Graham rubbed his chin. 'He's mostly kept himself to himself out here. But yes, we should see what he knows.'

As the sun began to dip below the horizon, the radiant hues of a Canadian sunset danced across the serene surface of the lake, creating a breathtaking sight.

'We best get back to the other side of the shore, I am sure there will be plenty of time to continue this discussion on another occasion,' James said.

All five wandered down to the end of the landing stage, where the boat was still tethered.

It already seemed a long time since they had all first arrived at the camp.

CHAPTER – 19

CANADA-WEEK TWO

The alarm shrilled loudly, drowning out the sweeter sound of the morning birdsong.

Tom blearily opened one eye, then the other and stretched out his arms and legs.

'Time to wake up, guys; another week awaits.'

Sean and Dougie weren't in the mood to be disturbed, so they ignored Tom's pestering until it became unbearable.

'OK, OK, Tom; we heard you. Just give us a few minutes more, please,' Sean implored.

'We haven't got that long; look around you; everyone else is already having breakfast.'

Dougie now fully awake, 'OK I guess we better get going.'

The second week didn't go well. Everything that could have possibly gone wrong did. Tom frantically searched for his protective goggles but couldn't find them. Sean accidentally dropped a vial of dangerous beryllium, and to top it off, Dougie's helmet microphone wasn't functioning properly. All three were relieved when Jock arrived, hidden behind layers of thick protective gear, and joined them for lunch. He also looked tired of dealing with endless paperwork, daily arrangements, and investor calls.

Shaking hands with the trio, he asked them how they were finding life at the camp. There was silence for a moment.

Tom was the first to speak. 'Well Jock, to be honest, it's all a little strange. We were given sheets by James at the beginning of last week which gave us the tasks expected in the first week. By the way, none of these were achieved last week. Then yesterday when we were at the bar across the lake; we realised that none of us really know why we are here and, more importantly, why we were chosen.'

Dougie and Sean nodded in agreement before Sean added. 'We thought perhaps you might be able to give us some answers.'

Jock was quiet for a moment with his chin resting in his gloved hand. 'Well, I can try, but I have only been here for as long as you. However, I think I can provide some background. Perhaps we can head over to this bar one evening. No promises, but I may be able to fill in some gaps.'

The trio nodded, somewhat satisfied.

'OK, that's settled then, let's try to meet on Friday, probably best without James and Graham though as they don't really know much.'

With that, Jock turned his attention to the other groups waiting to start on the week's work.

The rest of that week went much the same way.

It was not until Wednesday morning that the first minor breakthrough came when Dougie discovered that he was able to create a semi-stable metallate using beryllium and cerium.

He was so excited that he nearly forgot to enter the test results on the laptop. Clutching the test tube with both hands, he went to the weathering hut. Graham was already there, he showed him how to operate the various machinery. He clarified that the goal of this step was to speed up the process of weathering by subjecting the end result to different atmospheric elements. This entailed subjecting the product to intense UV rays and then switching to freezing temperatures. This exposure would be done on the product in sealed test tubes, with air and moisture removed.

Dougie nodded his understanding, it all seemed completely rational. He looked around the hut and pointed to a sealed area at the back of the hut. It looked like a completely sealed chamber with an interim pocket between the weathering room and the room beyond.

'What's in there, Graham?'

Graham paused, took a deep breath and explained. 'This room has been sealed hermetically to prevent any moisture or contaminants, leaving only an oxygen and nitrogen atmosphere. It took James and me a year to create this environment. In this room, we have set up equipment to test the products you are creating to see if they will work as intended. After that, we plan to expose the product to pure CO_2 and water multiple times in order to break down the carbon-oxygen and hydrogen-oxygen bonds. The goal is for all of us to work together and hopefully discover the catalyst we are searching for.'

Dougie nodded excitedly.

'I guessed it would be something like that.'

'I am not sure what the investors had in mind when they started on this project. I have only really been involved in the construction of all the huts and this area. You should speak to Jock.'

Graham continued, 'I am mainly anxious to get home to Australia now this initial phase has been completed, but they want me to stay to supervise this area, as I am really the only one who knows how it's put together. James is great on the chemistry side and can analyse everything you produce, but apparently, they need me until this is finished, whenever that may be.' Graham shrugged his shoulders in resignation.

'Anyway, Dougie, let's see if this first sample is going to work. The sooner we get a finished product, the sooner we can all get home!'

As Dougie exited the weathering hut, a thought crossed his mind for the first time: maybe what they were searching for was beyond even their wildest dreams. Also, how would it fit in with everything he was doing with his team back in England? So many questions and not nearly enough answers.

When the weekend arrived, they accompanied Jock to the Shellfish Backwater.

On that particular day, they had received news that the lone metallate created by Dougie on Wednesday was deemed unstable and marked as unsuitable for further examination in the main database.

Over the first drink or two, Jock told them various anecdotes from his colourful past and tried to provide as much information as possible about what the investors were trying to achieve.

It was quite apparent that Jock was in the dark about many of the objectives of the camp.

His limited knowledge of chemistry did not make matters any easier. However, he did mention that Abdul was a fiercely determined person whom he had known for over two decades. Once he set his goal and timeline, he became relentless in achieving it. After a few rounds of beer, the conversation became more open, and the three men voiced their concerns about the overall objectives and the tight deadlines they were given.

Jock then leaned in and spoke honestly. 'I don't believe the investors truly care about the end result. It's mostly just a show for the environmentalists, to demonstrate that they are genuinely trying to find alternative energy sources.

'There is also definitely more to the three investors than meets the eye. Take Abdul, for instance, I am sure has other significant backers. As I said, I have known him for 20 years and have never known him to be so furtive and evasive. He even told me to be careful about socialising with you all, so he wouldn't be that happy I am here tonight.' Jock paused and gulped the local ale.

'This is really good though. So, I guess I am sorry not to be able to help you a bit further, only to say that if you can produce something in the next few weeks and keep your heads down, you should all be out of here in no time. Also, I am guessing a lot wealthier.'

Tom piped up. 'Thanks, Jock, I guess you cannot really give us too much detail. However, there is definitely a connection to George Carruthers' death, and it seems to be a link between Abdul's three investors and his backers. I think we all believe in this theory,' Dougie and Sean nodded their heads in agreement.

'It would be great to get some more answers.'

Jock sighed, 'I wish I could be more helpful, but I am kept in the dark on a lot of things and especially this project. Anyway, guys, enjoy your beers, I guess it's going to be hard few weeks ahead.'

CHAPTER – 20

CANADA -WEEK THREE

The third week started well, with successes registered with the trio, and five or six metallates were being evaluated simultaneously.

Sean, however, was becoming more and more depressed. He was missing home comforts and could not stop thinking about Emily. He was also getting annoyed with the friendship that was developing between Tom and Dougie, who clearly had a lot in common. They had also managed to bond more closely with James, and were often in huddles in the early evening, excluding him.

As the week drew to a close, things finally reached a breaking point. Sean had spent the entire day working tirelessly, successfully creating two more metallates. Despite his accomplishment, he was completely drained and collapsed onto his bed in their hut, falling asleep almost immediately. Instead of waking him, the rest of the group decided to leave him sleeping while they went off to The Shellfish Backwater without him.

Sean woke with a start, just as the last rays of sunshine filtered through the weathered green slats of the blinds covering the nearby window overlooking his bunk bed. His immediate thought was to wonder where everyone was. It did not take him long to realise that they had left without him. Although he was annoyed, he felt strangely calm and instead decided to take an early evening stroll in the forest that stretched down to the lake shore.

It really was a beautiful evening. The birds chattered urgently as they settled into their nests for the night, and the owls hooted as they began their evening routines of hunting for food or searching for a mate. As Sean approached the lake, he saw that both boats were gone. *Bastards* he muttered to himself in frustration.

But as he gazed out at the peaceful scene before him, with the vibrant colours of the sunset reflecting off the water and cormorants diving for their last meal of the day, his anger dissipated. He was about to turn back when he caught a faint sound coming from behind some maple trees about 50 yards away. Despite the wind rustling through the leaves, he strained to hear what was being said and cautiously moved closer in an attempt to eavesdrop without being noticed.

It was clear that one of them was Abdul, but he did not immediately recognise the other voice. It was only when Abdul addressed him in quite an anxious tone that he realised it was Grant Lyons, his benefactor.

'I know you have concerns, Grant, but it has only been three weeks so far on really concerted efforts.' Abdul stammered towards the end of his sentence.

'Well, we will give it to the end of six weeks and see where we are up to then,' Grant affirmed.

Then they started talking more quietly and Sean struggled to catch anything more than the occasional word. He didn't like the snatches he heard, like 'withhold funds', 'let someone go', and 'pay-off', it was all most disturbing. He even forgot about his own annoyance at being left stranded at camp.

In some confusion, Sean meandered back to the lodgings. He sat down on one of the rattan armchairs and waited for the others to arrive back.

Meanwhile, at the bar, Dougie, James, Graham, Tom, and Jock were well into their third drink and any initial pangs of guilt about leaving Sean behind were well forgotten. Dougie was deep into his story of how he had become involved with George Carruthers and all the shenanigans he had encountered in Europe.

'I am, of course, really sad he has now passed on, but, as I said, I am now looking after his son Paul, and we are researching alternative fuels. Nothing like this, though; it is and always will be on a much smaller scale.'

Everyone nodded in agreement.

No one doubted that if it hadn't been for George and some of his remarkable work, this would never have happened. They all shared more details of their own tale.

Finally, after all their stories, they all agreed that this had been the most successful week so far, with some real progress being made as they swallowed the last bottle of Ontario Sauvignon. It was quite late when they reluctantly stumbled down the rocky path to the quayside where both boats were moored.

CHAPTER – 21

WEEK FOUR

Sean woke early on Monday. He didn't speak to Dougie or Tom about the strange conversation he had overheard and spent most of the weekend meandering around the camp's locality. While they were having breakfast on the veranda, there was a flurry of activity around the manager's lodgings. Just before nine, the door opened, and Abdul stepped out, closely followed by Grant Lyons. Jock and Graham dutifully followed a few paces behind them. James gestured towards them and the group of all the other local workers to gathered around them. Grant waited until everyone was there and then started. 'First of all, I want to thank you all for all the progress so far.' He paused and then looked directly at Tom, Dougie, and Sean who were just at the side of the main group.

'A special thanks to our team leaders who have been instrumental in those efforts. I initially planned to close down the project after this week, but I have decided to keep going for another three weeks; then we can review things as I am sure it will all be much clearer then. Moreover, I am going to stay here this week, so if any of you have any concerns, please see me. Either now or any evening, I will be available any time.'

He paused again. 'Well, I won't keep you any longer, so let's get back down to work.'

With that, he simply turned around and made his way back to the managers' hut leaving the group in a stunned silence.

Tom looked at Dougie and shrugged his shoulders. Sean smiled inwardly and then made his way over to the experiment hut. He started quite slowly, with many thoughts swirling through his head. Finally, he decided to speak with Grant privately as he was funding his participation in this experiment. He wanted to concentrate his time this week on beryllium, where there had been most of the success the previous week. He worked in silence, glancing occasionally at Tom and Dougie, who were busy giving instructions to their respective teams. They, too, had decided to concentrate on beryllium as it seemed the most likely avenue for success. There were indeed several successes in the first two or three days with a total of six separate metallates created.

Graham came over on Wednesday afternoon and was clearly happy with the results. He took all the samples to the environmental hut, labelled them carefully, and placed them in the machine that accelerated the ageing process.

In a few days, these samples will be taken out and assessed to see how well they worked. The results from the last batch had been disappointing, but there were some hopeful indicators. He secured the door and headed back to their designated area in the management hut where James was waiting.

Sean was not the only one feeling a bit homesick. Jock also was missing his family; even though it had been only four weeks it seemed a lifetime since he had last seen Natalia. On top of that, Ivan, his only son, was due back from college for his final term, and he didn't want to miss his homecoming.

Above all, Jock was getting a little suspicious of Abdul's motives. Why would the magnate of a major oil conglomerate want to look at alternative energy resources? He glanced at his watch and made a mental note to get hold of Abdul or Grant and preferably both before the end of the week, before Grant leaves.

It was an incredibly hot and sultry day and sweat trickled down his shirt, staining both back and front. He strolled over to the fridge, grabbed an iced tea, gulped it down in one and settled down for what he hoped would be another quiet day.

Meanwhile, in the experimental hut, Sean debated whether he should share the conversation he overheard with Dougie and Tom. Ultimately, he decided against it.

Suddenly, his thoughts were interrupted as Graham burst into the hut, clearly agitated. He spoke quickly into his helmet microphone, tripping over his words in excitement.

'Who has samples 3245 and 3267 for weathering treatment?'

Sean and Dougie looked at their iPads and shook their heads.

Tom raised his hand and replied, 'I think they are both mine Graham.'

Graham raised his hand indicating for Tom to follow him outside.

'What's this all about Graham, is there a problem?' Tom asked.

Graham just smiled and shook his head, 'Far from it, Tom, far from it. Follow me.'

They both took their suits off and strolled over to the weathering hut and stepped inside.

'No need for full protective clothing here Tom; if you just wear these aluminium gloves, I need to show you something.'

He carefully removed the two samples from the rack behind the weathering machine. Graham carried them over to the digital spectrometer in the corner. Pouring a small drop of the liquid into the two test tubes, he inserted the first tube into the slot on the top of the device. He looked at Tom.

'You know what this does; this basic technology hasn't changed for 50 years; it's just got more efficient. So, this is sample 3245.'

Tom nodded silently.

After 20 seconds the results appeared on a compact laptop plugged into the back of the machine. A graph appeared on the screen. Sean could not make it out that clearly, but it seemed to show peaks at carbon, oxygen, hydrogen, and a couple of much smaller peaks.

Tom looked at Graham and shrugged his shoulders.

'What does that show then Graham,' he asked.

'Let me show you,' said Graham excitedly.

He found the red button at the bottom of the screen and clicked. The analysis came up immediately.

85% ethanol

14% water

1% other

Again, Tom shrugged his shoulders.

'Well, that's just diluted alcohol, not of much use.'

'It's pretty fantastic Tom, as this has come from just water and carbon dioxide in the air. Anyway, that brings me to the whole point of bringing you over here.'

Graham reached for the bottle labelled 3267 and went through exactly the same process as before. This time, similar peaks were seen on the graph, though more evenly spread.

Graham grinned. 'Shall I click the red button, or will you do it this time, Tom?'

Tom waved his hand for Graham to do the necessary. This time the results were extraordinary.

99.999 % ethanol

0.001% others

Tom stood for a moment, his mouth agape at the astonishing result. Graham looked at the result, too, as he still could not believe it.

'So, to make it clear, we have pumped over 1000 litres of water mixed with air over your catalyst. From this, we have produced pure ethanol, fuel grade ethanol. In other words, it looks like you have cracked the final great mystery in the chemical world; turning water into alcohol. It's almost biblical. We have also, at the same time, weathered your catalyst for the equivalent of 8 years,' Graham laughed out loud.

Tom leaned forward: 'What now, Graham?'

Graham looked at him and squinted, his eyes narrowing in concern.

'I am not sure we should do anything now. Let me log this result along with the exact chemical breakdown of the catalyst.' He added, 'Don't say anything at the moment until I have verified the results which should be later today or tomorrow morning,'

Tom nodded sagely and made his way back to the experiment hut, with his hands shaking with excitement.

As he stepped into the room, both Sean and Dougie glanced at him out of the corner of their eyes. Tom simply nodded in response and returned to his workbench. Later in the early evening, Tom revealed the results of his experiments had been fairly positive, but he wouldn't know anything further until all the tests had been completed.

Both Sean and Dougie stared intently at Tom, hoping to extract more information from him.

'Oh, all right if you won't tell us let's just go across the bay and have a couple of beers; maybe that will loosen your tongue a bit,' said Sean with some exasperation.'

'OK,' said Tom, 'that will be just fine, but I can't promise anything.'

'Shall we ask James and Graham?' Sean asked.

'I don't think so, I think they have a meeting,' said Tom, knowing it to be a blatant lie!

As they relaxed in the quiet Shellfish Backwater, Dougie and Sean pushed Tom's strange actions to the back of their minds. They sipped on wine as the sun set beautifully before them, reminiscing about all that had happened over the past few weeks. For Tom, this was the first moment in a while where he felt truly content, and he enthusiastically joined in on the conversation.

It was well after dark when they finally made their way back to camp. It was very quiet, with all the lights out.

Earlier in the evening, Graham had spent a couple of hours studying the results which he still couldn't quite believe. He had taken copies of the formula and loaded them onto two flash drives. Then he decided to take the short walk down through the forest to the water's edge to admire the sunset in its full-blown technicolour. Whistling an old song, he did not notice the footsteps behind him, and neither did he feel anything as an unknown assailant struck the back of his head with a rock. He was instantly unconscious and was dragged to a small rowing boat and unceremoniously dumped in the bottom of it.

It took only ten minutes to row out to the deepest part of the bay in the now pitch-black darkness. With the weight of two hefty rocks, he was dumped off the boat's edge and swiftly plunged to the bottom of the bay. After waiting a couple of minutes, the assailant rowed back to shore, moored the boat in the same place, and made tracks for the huts.

That night Sean felt restless. Tossing and turning, he had all sorts of weird dreams, and it was somewhat of a relief when he was dragged out of his broken sleep by Tom vigorously shaking his left shoulder.

'Wake up Sean,' Tom whispered into Sean's ear.

'We have a pre-breakfast conference announced, I am not sure what it is all about!'

Sean, Dougie, and Tom quickly dressed up as they noticed workers from the other huts making their way towards the central area.

In the middle-stood Abdul and Grant, accompanied by James and Jock, with a line of people forming behind them. Abdul coughed politely to clear his throat.

'You may wonder why I have got you all here this early in the morning,' he stated calmly.

'Well, you may notice that Graham left us unexpectedly yesterday evening; he left a note that he had been called away on a family emergency and will not be back for some time.'

Abdul paused and glanced around to see if there was any reaction. Seeing there was none, he continued, 'Because of this sudden departure, I will now be taking control of the weathering hut and James here will take a more active role in the experimental hut. Jock will still be doing the administration. Is that clear or does anyone have any questions?'

Tom was about to raise his hand but resisted; it all seemed very odd. He made a mental note to look into the weathering hut to see what had happened to his samples.

Seeing no reaction from his audience, Abdul simply said, 'OK, back to work then, you all know your roles.'

He wheeled away, followed by his entourage back to the huts on the far side of the camp.

There was a hushed murmur among the rest of the crowd as they gradually dispersed to finish off their breakfasts at their lodging huts. Sean also felt uneasy. He was wondering if it had anything to do with the conversation he had overheard, but then quickly dismissed it as a conspiracy theory. Anyway, his mind was made up, he was planning to leave the camp as soon as possible, maybe as soon as the end of the week.

It was a cheerless morning in the experiment hut, with none of the usual encouragement from Graham. This also translated into their work efforts. That day, they were unable to produce anything of note. Around lunchtime, Tom decided to take a walk over to the weathering hut. It was late summer, and the sun was gradually imparting less heat as it filtered through the leafy canopies. As he approached the hut, there was a rustling among the leaves, and a startled small deer darted back into the forest. It was quiet as Tom climbed up the couple of steps to the hut entrance. Glancing around, he tried to open the door, and to his surprise, it was open. Looking inside, nothing much had changed from the previous week. There were stacks of tested samples in racks above the main weathering machine which was still whirring around. Tom glanced inside and saw a few samples in the final stages of testing. He approached the spectrometer but could not find either of his samples. However, next to the spectrometer was a memory stick, which had been partially hidden by a sheath of papers. Cautiously, Tom inserted the drive into the side of the nearby laptop and checked the files. It was clearly Graham's memory stick, as listed on the files were a few personal items. After searching the file, he found one named result. Tom carefully downloaded this onto the laptop and then copied it onto a spare memory stick. Replacing everything where it had been, Tom retraced his steps back to the experiment hut and resumed his work again, making it appear as if nothing had happened.

Dougie mouthed at him through his face mask, 'Where have you been?'

Tom raised a finger to his lips and indicated that they would speak later.

CHAPTER – 22

SEAN'S DEPARTURE

In the meantime, Sean decided to head over to the management block to tell them he wanted to leave. His conversation with James was quite friendly and surprisingly easy. James shrugged his shoulders and nodded as Sean went through all his reasons.

'OK, Sean, if that is what you want to do, I can make arrangements tonight and you will be able to leave by tomorrow lunchtime.'

'Oh, thank you, James. That is such a relief.' Sean thrust his hand towards James, who grabbed it and shook it warmly.

Sean wheeled around and then, without another word, headed back to the experiment hut. A grin slowly spread across his face as he envisioned Tom and Dougie's expressions when he would share his exciting news with them. He decided to share it during his farewell drinks that evening.

At 6 pm when Sean and his friends were at The Shellfish Backwater. At around 8:00 pm, he finally blurted out the news to Jock, Dougie, and Tom. It was astonishing how unsurprised they all were. Dougie was the first to break the silence with his words.

'I knew you weren't happy Sean, but surely you can wait until the end of the programme in two weeks or so?'

Sean just shook his head, 'I had no idea it would be so intense. No, I need to go now for my own sanity, I am lonely here.'

'Also, I have been offered a position in a major oil company based in London, which is too good of an offer to refuse right now.' Sean paused to see if there was any reaction, but there was just a general nodding of heads.

Tom stood up and, clutching Sean firmly, he whispered gently in his ear so the other two could not catch his words.

'Before you go, I need to tell you something. I will speak to you later tonight.'

With that, he pushed Sean away, exclaiming, 'I will miss you, mate, and all your funny quirks.'

Before they headed back to camp, they consumed a lot more alcohol, but rather than getting morose, the evening became more boisterous, and it was well after midnight when they reached their lodgings.

Sean could not sleep and sat outside the hut in the chilly night, staring at the constellations in the pitch-black sky. He was just nodding off when he felt his shoulder being grasped firmly and looked up to see Tom's reddened face barely six inches from his.

'I am glad you are still awake, Sean; I need to tell you something now, as you are leaving tomorrow, and I won't have time to pass this on.' Tom paused and gazed into Sean's face, looking for agreement; Sean nodded quickly.

Tom continued, 'Before Graham left so suddenly, he had tested a couple of my samples and there were some quite astonishing results.'

'What do you mean, Tom?'

'Well one of the samples was nearly perfect, I had somehow created pure fuel grade ethanol from water and air using one of the beryllium catalysts. I mean it was perfect in every way. Then, the very next day, Graham goes away. I mean why would he? It was what he and James had been waiting for since they arrived over two years ago. It does not make any sense.' Tom sighed, waiting for Sean to reply.

'I agree, Tom, no sense at all. I thought he just had family issues, I did not know all of this.'

Tom lowered his voice even more. 'Now if Graham was forced to leave, or maybe something more sinister, where does that leave us? This brings me to why I need to speak to you now. I can speak to Dougie later. I have a copy of the formula of the catalyst in this memory stick.'

He retrieved the stick from his back pocket.

Tom continued. 'If I really have created this catalyst, it could be the answer to the climate crisis.'

Sean nodded.

They went back into the hut. Sean glanced around and decided he would treat himself to a last drop of whisky from the stash hidden in his kit bag.

CHAPTER - 23

THE CANADA DISASTER

The first sign of problems appeared at about 4 a.m. Smoke started rising through the floor, rapidly filling the hut. It was deadly, choking fumes. Dougie was first to notice anything, waking up just in time, violently coughing.

'Wake up everyone, fire! Fire!' he screamed.

He glanced out the door and was taken aback by what he saw. Quickly, he went around the hut, rousing everyone from their slumber. Besides their small group of three, which included himself, Sean, and Tom, there were three other newcomers who had arrived earlier in the week. In the chaos, he couldn't recall their names, so he just shook their shoulders and yelled into their ears, 'Get up, wake up!'

Tom stretched his limbs wearily, 'What's all the fuss about Dougie?'

'Come outside quickly,' Dougie screeched.

Tom and then Sean pulled themselves towards the door and looked outside. It was a horrific sight; all the other huts were engulfed in flames, climbing into the night sky, casting flickering shadows all over the site. The most alarming sight was the flames engulfing their hut. The thick smoke was drifting into their lungs as they grabbed what they could from their belongings and tried to wake the others at the far end of the hut. They stayed back to wake up their colleagues, but they were all clearly unconscious due to smoke and fumes. Dougie even tried to drag one of them from their bed but as he did so one of the overhead rafters came crashing down on his shoulder causing him to drop in pain. Realising that he might not get out himself, he covered his mouth with his t-shirt and just made it outside before the roof collapsed.

Three of them stood there terrified. Gaping at the carnage, just thanking God that, somehow, they had survived.

Tom was first to speak.

'Do you think anyone survived this disaster, and do you think it was due to arson?'

Sean was struggling to get his words out. But he answered, 'Yes, and yes.'

The heat was now so intense that they all retreated to the edge of the forest leading down to the lake.

'What can we do, Tom?' Dougie's eyes were wide open in terror.

Tom shook his head, looking at Dougie, whose face was streaked with ash and blood; the falling beam had caused a nasty gash.

'I don't know Dougie, let's just wait until the fire has died down a bit. I honestly don't think anyone could have survived this. Certainly, none of them who were caught in the inferno.'

Sean shook his head violently, he muttered under his breath.

'I should have gone sooner.' He was shivering, although the heat was intense.

The management hut was the only hut not in flames, presumably because it was a bit further away. Tom indicated to the other two, and they approached the hut with caution in case there was a sudden explosion. As they approached the hut, they saw a huddle just at the back, in safety from the now ferocious flames. Though the smoke was thick, they could recognise the silhouettes of Abdul, Jock, James and, they guessed, Grant Lyons, though they could not be completely certain.

Tom approached them first; he gasped, 'What the hell happened here?'

Abdul was the first to answer. 'Well, the initial thoughts are obviously sabotage; it's inconceivable how several fires could start simultaneously.'

He continued. 'The Canadian authorities are on their way and all of us must get to safety by the lake shore as quickly as possible.'

Abdul looked through the haze. 'How many of you are here?'

'As far as we know just us three from our hut, all the others were unconscious. We tried to drag them out, but the ceiling beams collapsed before we could reach them.'

Jock came over, overhearing the conversation. 'I tried to get in some of the other huts, but the heat was so intense. I don't think anyone else could have survived. We should escape as soon as possible in case there are any more explosions.'

When they got to shore, there was a motor launch ready to take the management team away.

Abdul turned to Tom, Sean, and Dougie.

'We are meeting with the authorities on the opposite shore, I have another boat coming for you in the next few minutes. They will take you to the bus and then you will stay in Toronto for a few days while everything gets resolved.'

The trio just nodded glumly in silence.

As the management team boarded the vessel, Jock turned around, his face was still smeared in ash from his vain attempts to rescue any survivors. He smiled wanly and discreetly gave them a thumbs up sign as if to say they shouldn't worry.

The motor throbbed into life and the boat headed out to the other shore. There was silence and then it was Sean, who had been muttering under his breath.

'It was definitely arson, and our dream of creating wonder fuel has quite literally gone up in flames,' he said emphatically.

Tom smiled, 'Not quite Sean, not quite. I have this still,' He slid his hand around to his back pocket and retrieved a small flash drive.

'So, what is that, apart from the obvious?

'As I told you earlier, well not to you specifically, Dougie, as all this crap happened, this is the jewel in the crown, the nectar of the gods, the answer to climate change.'

He paused and then continued. 'Uploaded on this flash drive is the formula that gave me such astonishing results. Graham could have explained it more eloquently, but unfortunately, he is not here either. I am going back to Texas when all this has died down to look into it more deeply. It may be that Graham was fixing the results to make himself look good in front of the management team.'

Tom paused, waiting for a reaction.

Sean was still muttering to himself, but Dougie was plainly on the same wavelength, nodding his head furiously in agreement.

His phone bleeped and a message appeared from Jock.

It was to the point. 'Your boat will be there in about 20 minutes,'

Dougie sighed and showed the other two as they settled down on the water's edge waiting for rescue.

CHAPTER – 24

THE AFTERMATH

As the boat sped to the opposite shore, Jock glanced at the grim faces of James, Abdul, and Grant and didn't know what to say. Most of the workers had perished in the fire, and it was particularly sad as they had provided him with great company when Abdul had been away on his numerous trips. Jock was also certain that the fires were not accidental. One or two, maybe, but certainly not six or seven simultaneous ones. He was going to raise it with Abdul, but Abdul was deep in conversation with Grant. So, he just bowed his head and let a few thoughts race through his head. What if the team had somehow found something of interest and this was just a way of covering things up? What if he had not been supposed to survive either? No, Abdul could not do without him. Jock snapped out of his depressing train of thought as they approached the far shore.

The morning mist had now fully cleared and on the pier, there were several uniformed policemen waiting to be filled in with all the facts. It was going to be a long day. Indeed, the questioning was intense and centred around the nature of the blaze and details of all those who had perished.

Afterwards, Jock sat down with Grant and Abdul and discussed the events and future strategy. They all agreed to the story they were going to tell (well, Jock didn't agree but he wanted to just keep the peace). Multiple fires started due to the highly flammable materials on site, and it was triggered by the high winds.

Jock was the first to add a further comment.

'What do we do now?'

Abdul stared fixedly at him for a moment and then snapped a reply.

'Let's get back to Saudi and forget about all this; there is a lot to catch up on.'

Jock nodded glumly and stared at his feet as the conversation once more descended into silence.

It was several hours later, after numerous car journeys, they were safely ensconced in a hotel room at Toronto Pearson Airport. Jock had some time to reflect on the previous few weeks and wondered why he had ever got involved with Abdul in the first place. He thought about his wife, Natalia back in Saudi, as he drifted off into restless sleep. It was going to be an early start the following day.

Meanwhile, back at the campsite, it was now a completely desolate scene; the blackened timbers lay on the ground still smouldering, with curls of smoke threading their way through the singed tree canopy. The firefighters had left, so all that could be heard were the sound of crickets and the gentle cawing of the birds.

Sean, Tom, and Dougie had also departed and were en route to Toronto. None of them had visited Bracebridge in Toronto before, so they were pleasantly surprised by the stunning views as their car arrived at the Bracebridge Inn.

Bracebridge was famous for its waterfalls and its location next to the Muskoka. As they strolled through the picturesque town in the evening, the horrors and devastation of the previous day felt like a distant memory. But deep down, they were all aware that this was far from over.

Following their time in Toronto and the conclusion of the inquiry, the three of them said their goodbyes and returned to their respective homes.

PART-4

THE NEXT CHAPTER

CHAPTER – 25

SAUDI ARABIA

In Saudi Arabia, Jock looked at his son Ivan, now 20, and wished he was as carefree as him. Ivan was at Cambridge University and was back for a few weeks before finishing his studies in petrochemical engineering. He would be taking his end of year exams in just a few weeks' time.

Jock, Natalia, and Ivan were planning to go to Athens for a week-long cruise. Ivan was excited to meet up with some of his college friends during the trip. Jock shared a knowing look with his wife, Natalia, who was the real boss in their relationship. She managed everything effortlessly, from controlling the household to keeping a tight hold on their finances, while Jock was free to throw whatever he wanted her way. They were both looking forward to this much-needed getaway.

Natalia's dream was to have a big house with a beautiful English garden, and that dream was about to come true. Stacked in their account was close to a million dollars. Not bad for a Russian girl from such humble beginnings. She was just over 40 years old, but she looked more like 25, absolutely gorgeous, with black long hair flowing over a beautiful bone china complexion.

She smiled adoringly at Jock. 'Yes, you better be on time. I am sure Mr. Rehmann will be waiting for you,' she said politely.

Jock thrust the chair back and planted a kiss on the top of his wife's head and gave a gentle push on Ivan's shoulder. He walked out through the adjoining door to their garage and climbed into his car.

As he got ready to brave the 120+ temperatures outside, Jock went over a few things in his mind. *Today's production meeting was going to be a bit tricky. Production in one of the wells had stopped, due to a faulty drill bit, which was not being replaced until the following Wednesday, nine days away. Also, number 2 well (out of a total of 10) had come across some unexpected resistance at the second reserve. The drilling is likely to take another week. On top of this, Rehmann is insisting on going at full tilt on 3, 4, and 5 wells, beyond the safety levels.*

As he pulled up to the building, he slammed the jeep door closed and took a moment to gather his thoughts before heading to work. He couldn't help but wonder what challenges lay ahead for him today.

Abdul Rehmann looked at his watch pacing up and down. He was a short heighted dapper man, always immaculately dressed. His black moustache was just about covering a thin upper lip. He had not changed at all since meeting Jock all those years ago. Abdul stopped to look outside. Since his return from Canada, he focused entirely on the oilfields as they were now the only source of revenue. His office overlooked the oil field with the derricks as black and stark monuments against the steel blue sky. Heat haze shimmered from the oil-streaked sand.

Abdul looked down at the week's production levels. He knew it was going to be a difficult one, starting with the morning meeting. He had to persuade Jock to accelerate the production on all the remaining wells. His masters would not permit any more cuts; the levels had to be maintained.

The door rattled briefly before Kristin entered; Kristin handled all the finance and salary issues.

'How's it going Kristin?' Abdul raised his eyes and addressed his personal confidant in his usual polite but direct manner.

'OK,' she said almost dismissively, 'but I think this meeting will be very stormy.' She looked anxious.

'Why do you think that?' said Abdul curtly.

'Jock was resistant to upping the production on three wells, let alone all the remaining ones,' she said shrugging her petite shoulders.

'There is no other choice! Unless we meet this month's target, they are threatening to close down production on all the fields permanently,' Abdul said, with despair creeping into his voice.

'Well, it won't be easy with Jock.'

Abdul heard a knock on the glass door and looked up from his work, seeing Jock's scowling face on the other side. He motioned for Jock to enter and take a seat. Jock chose the chair closest to the door as if he were already planning an early exit.

'Well, we'd better get started,' said Abdul firmly. 'Kristin, can you go through the figures.'

Jock hated this pointless exercise. It always went on for hours and today looked likely to be no exception.

Kristin handed out three sets of rather complicated finance papers and then went through each one in minute detail for the next two hours.

Despite the air conditioning being on full blast, the relentless sun shining through the window was making Jock drowsy. Abdul flipped to the final page and asked Jock directly, 'Do you agree?' Jock snapped out of his half-sleep and responded, 'Agree to what?'

In a firm tone, Abdul stated, 'I need production levels at maximum for the remaining wells.'

'That is just not possible; we are already at 98% capacity, 10% above maximum permitted safety,' said Jock. He stood up and glared at them both.

'On top of that, we had one man seriously injured and one killed last week. They were trying to repair a valve on the fly while we were still pumping.' Jock was in his stride now.

'It's an order, Jock, I have no choice,' said Abdul. Jock looked down at his feet and the whole room went into a deathly silence.

It was two minutes before Jock spoke.

He addressed assertively, 'I have no choice either Abdul. I quit... In fact, I quit now. This is really the last straw, particularly after what happened in Canada.'

Abdul raised his forefinger to his lips to quieten him. Jock stormed out of the room.

Abdul looked at Kristin; she shrugged her shoulders, and said, 'He'll be back when he's calmed down. He built this field up from nothing; he doesn't want to go, you know that Abdul, 'she said, nodding her head emphatically.

'Yes, I am convinced Abdul that he'll be back, where else can he go?' she reaffirmed.

'I am not sure, he looked pretty damn determined to me,' stammered Abdul.

Jock was still breathing heavily when he reached the site office. He sat at his desk and then started thinking. *This was no different to Abdul's attitude from the very beginning; he was always ready to compromise safety for revenues. On top of that he wanted to brush all the horrific events from Canada under the carpet. Well, this time he had gone too far.*

It was only a matter of time before there were more fatalities. God, how much was a man's life worth, more than an extra barrel of oil, that's for sure.

The more he thought about the situation, the angrier he became. *The bastard, the absolute bastard. This was a pathetic joke.*

Jock wiped the tiny beads of sweat that had collected on his chin.

The black internal phone jolted him back to reality with a single ring. 'Jock here,' he said gruffly.

A voice spoke urgently at the other end of the line. 'We have a huge problem on well 4; it seems to be leaking from the top valve,' said the pleading voice.

'Jeez, that was only repaired last week; what's the problem?' Jock demanded.

'The primary pressure valve has become dislodged, causing oil to spew from the hose connected to the central storage terminal,' said the voice with growing concern.

'OK, OK, I am coming over,' Jock said dismissively.

Jock grabbed his kit and was just about to leave when the phone rang again. It was the main gate.

A resigned voice said, 'Your wife and your boy are here.'

'Dave, could you do us a favour and bring them round to my office in a few minutes,' he said in a wheedling voice, as this was strictly against company rules 'I have an urgent issue with one of the main wells.'

'No problem, Jock,' Dave said assuredly, 'I will bring them right over.'

For Jock, this was the problem, no time for his family and huge expectations from the company. He grabbed his tool pack, slammed his office door shut and jumped into the awaiting company jeep. It was nearly two miles to the oil field, and Jock was still steaming when the jeep skidded to a stop in front of the leaking well. Jock grimaced when he saw the problem...

CHAPTER – 26

TWO HOURS EARLIER

'This,' thought Natalia was the best time in her life. She was with the son she totally adored, and just about to go to Greece with a husband who, though grumpy at times, was absolutely wonderful to be with most of the time.

She looked around the sterile flat, 'Soon... very soon, we will all be back in England.'

The walls didn't answer!

Ivan looked at his mother, 'What's wrong, Mum? Who were you talking to?' he said sweetly.

Natalia smiled and said, 'It's nothing, Ivan; I am tired of this monotonous life and can't wait for our holiday.'

She dragged all the baggage and her son into the company car that had been waiting patiently for over an hour.

Even in those brief seconds, the heat was totally overwhelming, nearly 130F.

'God, let's get to the sea, the coolness, away from this god-awful place,' said Natalia.

Luckily, the company car driver showed no interest in engaging in pointless small talk today.

On the way, Natalia took a quick glance at the desolate surroundings, the towering cactus, and half-hearted attempts at creating a human touch. *This job may have good pay, but especially in moments like this, it hardly seems worth it!* She thought.

The driver having stopped at the main gate, spoke for the first time that morning.

'Jock is at the well, but Dave can take you to his office to wait for him,' he said.

They stepped out of the car. Dave was waiting just outside the door in the searing heat next to the company Land Rover.

Damn this oppressive heat, thought Natalia.

The only thing on her mind was the refreshing sea breeze in Marathon, a town just 25 miles from Athens. Suddenly, she was jolted out of her thoughts. She was pregnant once again! Given her medical history – with only one functioning fallopian tube and a limited egg supply every six months – this news was unfathomable. She couldn't wait to share it with Jock when they arrived in Greece.

'Well, it would not be very long now. 'She looked at Ivan.

Natalia felt an impulse. 'Dave don't take me to the office; let's go and surprise Jock at the well. It would give us both such a thrill.'

Ivan nodded his head in vigorous agreement.

'OK,' said Dave, unable to resist Natalia's pretty smile, 'But you have to take the blame; you know Jock hates seeing you there.' He wagged his finger in a pretend display of anger.

The car skidded and headed off the tracks to the oil field a three-mile journey.

At the well, Jock had just arrived. There were four derricks in various states of disrepair. Gas burned off in flares from the top of each one giving an eerie feeling in the hell hole of immense heat. Grey pipelines were linked to four huge, upturned bowls. Oil was pumped into these bowls 23 hours a day. This gave one hour a day for the essential maintenance and repairs. Not enough time spent considering human lives. He looked at the glum faces upturned to top of the derrick, they all showed signs of exhaustion.

No wonder there were technical issues, Jock thought to himself.

While most competitors shut down operations for three hours daily, he was confident that they didn't deal with the same issues. He made his way towards the shack, the only structure remaining after a powerful dust storm had swept through and destroyed the field office along with the makeshift café and facilities. Now, these services were provided from a green caravan powered by a diesel generator.

Inside the shack, Chris, the site manager, sat looking very miserably at the readings from all the wells. He was surrounded by empty coke cans, screwed up crisp packets and curled up pieces of dried bread. When Jock came in, Chris did not look up.

He mumbled rather pathetically, 'Sorry Jock, I know you want to get away, I just couldn't...' he tailed off without finishing the sentence.

'It's OK.' Jock interrupted.

'Well Chris,' Jock paused with an exasperated sigh. 'Let's see what's the problem.'

Chris shouted above the noise of pumping mechanisms.

'It's that damn well 4 again. It always seems to be that one. I have no idea why.'

They went outside and Jock gazed upwards, his eyes shielded by his floppy, rimmed, stained hat.

As an executive, he knew he shouldn't really be doing this sort of work but it had been forced upon him by Abdul and also due to lack of general skilled help at the site.

He sighed inwardly. He couldn't see anything immediately but then soon spotted the problem. Somehow the high-pressure valve they had only replaced the previous week had eased itself loose again and a micro jet, almost like a black needle was arrowing towards the ground.

'Chris, come here, I need the pulley lift for Well 4.' said Jock.

Chris manoeuvred the lift into position, a crude yet effective machine operated by a series of levers. It would bring Jock to the necessary height of 100 feet, aligning him with the troublesome valve. After securing the safety harness over his shoulders, Jock hopped onto the platform. With careful precision, Chris and one of the other workers lifted the trolley until it was level with the valve.

Jock heard a noise in the distance and could see the cloud of dust, it was the site Land Rover approaching, and that meant that Dave had disobeyed his orders and bought Natalia to the site of the field. 'Damn him, Damn him.'

The jeep would be there in just a few minutes. 'Let's get on with it,' he mused.

Jock reached down to grab the massive wrench amongst the tangled jumble of tools at his feet. He was determined to fix the stubborn nut once and for all. However, he had no idea that the bolt was not just stuck, but dangerously cracked. The pressure from the oil flow was slowly prying it apart.

As Jock tightened the wrench, the bolt suddenly split into three pieces. Two of them fell harmlessly to the ground, while the third piece shot out with a force of over a megaton. It tore through Jock's skull as if it were paper, instantly killing him. Blood and oil splattered everywhere as he fell off the trolley, still attached to his safety harness in what seemed like slow motion. There was no pain for Jock, only an abrupt end to his life.

'Jock, I'm here,' Natalia called. But the words choked at the back of her throat when she realised that something had gone wrong – very wrong.

It took a long few seconds before she screamed and then she could not stop.

Ivan looked at Dave. 'What happened Dave?' he shrieked with a heart-rending bellow.

Dave shouted as loud as he possibly could, 'Ivan, take your mother back into the caravan; I will deal with this.' Ivan grabbed his mother's hand and shepherded her into the caravan making sure she could not see what was happening any more clearly.

'Just get him down, for God's sake get him down.' Ivan screamed at Dave.

Jock was still suspended from his harness some 50 feet up, gently swaying from side to side, a quite grotesque sight, like a ragged loose-limbed doll.

There was a deathly silence; the wells were all shut down now. Slowly Jock was winched down to earth.

CHAPTER - 27

LONDON, ENGLAND TWO
WEEKS LATER

It was a wet and windy afternoon. Ivan stared out of the window in the newly refurbished Hilton Hotel, Park Lane. It was his first time attending a funeral, and he knew it was going to be a difficult experience. He wasn't worried about himself, but he knew his mother would struggle with the whole affair. He fixed his stare across the road into the depths of Hyde Park, where the huge elms were swaying in the gales. Brown dappled leaves swirled around the steely grey branches. Everything, all of this, was bleak, matching the mood of the day.

Ivan's mother was with Uncle Boris, Natalia's half-brother. They both were supposed to be taking care of his mother together, but Ivan knew that most of the responsibility would fall on him. Uncle Boris wasn't very reliable in these matters. Ivan had managed to hold back his emotions until now, but a tear finally escaped and rolled down his cheek. He quickly wiped it away and continued to stare out the window intently.

Memories flooded his mind from the past few weeks and all the troublesome arrangements he had to make. Natalia, his mum had given up on most of it, leaving Dave and Ivan to handle everything. The most difficult part was when they had to transport his father's body to the undertakers in London. Seeing him lying peacefully in the coffin after being "repaired" made Ivan reflect on their time together.

When they were at the funeral parlour, Natalia confided in him that she was pregnant with a baby boy. She told him that as the man of the family, he would have to take care of both of them.

Ivan shrugged his shoulders at the thought; he felt that he had enough on his mind with his final exams rapidly approaching.

Meanwhile, downstairs in the hotel, Natalia had arrived back from several errands and strode across the marble floor of the hotel lobby. Her metal-tipped heels sent out echoes around the cavernous roof. She placed her leather-clad hand on the brass knob of one of the many doors leading from the lobby. She twisted the knob slowly and pushed open the gold-inlaid door.

Natalia looked vacantly at the vast number of flowers that lay over the floor of huge reception room on the first floor of the Hilton. Idly she picked up the first two huge bunches. Inscribed on the first bunch was a handwritten card; it said, 'From Dave, your first friend.'

Natalia couldn't help herself. Salty tears started to trickle down her already-flushed cheeks. Then she flicked over the label of the second bunch. She stared in horror. She couldn't believe what she was reading; pinned to the cellophane was a neatly typed card, obviously telephoned from overseas. She stared and read it very slowly twice. 'From Abdul your friend and colleague.'

As she read the words out loud, they stuck in her throat. She could not stop the anger welling up inside her. She had blamed Abdul for Jock's death, and his refusal to let anyone else look after the functioning of the oil wells. She was also convinced his death was, at best, unavoidable and, at worst, not an accident at all. She threw the flowers down and then lashed out at them with both feet. Soon, all that was left were a few broken stalks and a scattering of petals over the oaken floor.

Her anger had dissipated, and she suddenly sensed someone else's presence in the room. She spun around to find a startled chambermaid standing just inside the doorway, her eyes wide with surprise. Natalia brushed down her dress.

'Clean this up, please.' she screamed.

She brushed past the maid, not giving her a chance to reply. The maid, still shocked, brushed the debris to one side and rearranged the remaining bunches into a neat pile.

CHAPTER – 28

THE FUNERAL

The funeral was a solemn event, attended by Jock's many friends and some of Natalia's family. Ivan greeted the guests as they were introduced, but his mind was elsewhere. Natalia's cousin Boris sat next to him in the church and was very attentive. As Ivan looked around, he couldn't help but admire the beautifully engraved statues lining the benches. The sun seeped through the stained-glass windows, creating an ethereal atmosphere. Eventually, it all came to an end. Friends and family gave heartfelt speeches, and then the pallbearers carried Jock's coffin out while the congregation followed behind, with Ivan among the first in the group.

On the way back to the hotel in one of the funeral cars, Boris glanced at Ivan and saw a small notebook in Ivan's hand. 'What is that?'

Ivan quickly thrust it back into his black suit jacket pocket. 'None of your business, Boris,' he said indignantly.

Ivan turned away from Boris and stared at the usual bright frontages of the window displays along Oxford Street. Ivan wondered why he had remained so emotionless during the funeral and thought of the little notes he had jotted down in his notebook since his father's death.

The first page was simply titled 'Why?' Why had it happened, and what could have been done to prevent it? He listed many items but nothing substantial. On the next page, he listed many items that need to be resolved now.

Boris did not probe him about the notebook any further, so as they neared Hyde Park, he averted his gaze towards the front car where his mother and grandmother were travelling.

The first car approached the hotel foyer entrance. The black-suited driver opened the door and stepped out into horizontal rain. He clutched his peaked cap as gusts of wind threatened to send it skyward. With his other hand he opened the passenger door. First, an elderly lady, (also called Natalia) very gingerly stepped out. It was very evident that she had been crying.

The second car drew up close to the first funeral car, and Ivan waited patiently as his driver opened the rear passenger door. Ivan thrust his notebook back into his inside jacket pocket, along with his black pencil, and walked quickly towards his mother as she stood by the hotel foyer door.

'Let's go downstairs,' said Natalia, with her voice shaking.

Ivan and Boris followed Natalia through the entrance hall and into the lift lobby area.

Boris, finally asked, 'How are you feeling, Natalia?'

Natalia stared into the space in front of her, with the lift wheels whirring above as she at last spoke, 'I am still thinking about the service, it was so beautiful almost serene, and then everyone just sobbed through the whole service except me. I just felt so empty, and now I am so angry,' She paused, 'Do you know what that bastard did? He sent flowers. I just tore them apart and trampled them,'

Ivan looked bewildered. 'Which bastard Mum, as if he didn't know what the answer was going to be?'

'Abdul of course, I blame him 100% for what happened.'

Ivan wrapped his right arm tightly around his mother, tugging her towards him.

He whispered gently in her left ear so no-one could hear.

'I know Mum, I blame him too,' choking back tears. 'I am just trying to decide what to do about it.' He paused, 'I've written a few notes.' He patted his inside jacket pocket.

The doors opened into the sumptuous lobby of the newly refurbished Hilton. Natalia and Ivan paused their conversation and looked around them at the sumptuous beauty. There were tall oaken pillars inlaid with gold, supporting a beautifully carved Italian ceiling. In the corner of the first floor was the venue for the wake, so Natalia, Ivan, Boris, and the rest of the straggling entourage traipsed across the lobby and climbed the stairs to the mezzanine. The doors were opened wide and over 100 people were milling around, all speaking in hushed whispers. Ivan looked around, and for a moment, blind panic set in. He spoke again into Natalia's' ear.

'Mum, I feel really awkward, and I don't think I can put up with any more questions,' he whispered, 'I am just going over to that long black table covered in snacks. I will just stand in the corner.' Ivan knew his mother expected him to be near her throughout proceedings.

'Yes, yes just go, but please be close if I need you.' Natalia whispered under her breath.

'Sure, Mum, just give me a signal if you need me to come over and support you.'

Ivan gently stroked away a tear falling down his mother's cheek and quietly moved towards the end of the table. He positioned himself discreetly in the corner of the room but near enough to the various conversations so he could hear everything going on. He opened his notebook, retrieving it from his inside pocket, and listened to all the hushed chatter around him.

Occasionally he strolled across to food table to collect a few more sausages, sandwiches and some crisps, but then immediately returned to the corner.

As the evening wore on, the hushed tones got louder, and Ivan heard a few words that he immediately wrote down.

It was past ten o'clock when he moved from the corner and was propping up the bar having had too many glasses of wine and several neat vodkas. Boris strolled over to him. He looked at Ivan and, in his broken English, asked what he had on his mind. Ivan looked directly back at him and just nodded.

'I don't know what to say, Boris, I have just written a few comments down. Everyone in the room seemed to be blaming Abdul, and I think I tend to agree with them.'

CHAPTER – 29

HAMPSTEAD HEATH

It had been weeks since the funeral and the weather in London had turned a lot warmer. Spring had passed in its usual wet way, with occasional warm spells and summer was just around the corner.

Natalia and Ivan had recently moved to an old Georgian home on the outskirts of Hampstead Heath, London. Natalia was a woman of great wealth, with over a million US dollars saved up. While Ivan loved the vibrant atmosphere of the city, he was also eager to return for his final weeks at university. Over time both she and Ivan began to heal from their loss.

On Ivan's last night before returning to university, Natalia prepared a hearty stew for dinner. As they ate together, enjoying every bite, Natalia opened up about happier times when Jock was still alive. Ivan had a beer while Natalia savoured a glass of French Bordeaux. Eventually, Ivan dozed off next to Natalia, dreaming about the future where he would follow in his father's footsteps to become successful– but this time, he would be the one in charge, and people like the Abduls would work for him.

Ivan had chosen to research oil pioneers for his final year project long before his father's untimely death. As he approached the end of his project and began to work on his dissertation, he reminded himself to stay focused and get an early start. But with only two weeks left, he was falling behind. He would occasionally open his laptop, not to study for finals but to search for any information that might provide answers about his father's passing. Instead of doing general research like in previous terms, he was now solely focused on finding connections to his father. And finally, after days of searching, a breakthrough appeared. Just the day before, as he pored over unsolved cases and endless pages on his laptop, he stumbled upon a tenuous link between Abdul and his father's death. It may have been by chance, but Ivan felt like he was getting closer to solving the mystery surrounding his father's murder.

As Ivan scrolled through the old photos on his laptop, a familiar face caught his attention: his father's. In the group photo, he was grinning while hanging out with his colleagues during their days in Canada. Ivan downloaded both pages and looked closely at the background. He noticed a small silhouette smoking a cigar and engaged in deep conversation with someone else. Curiosity sparked within him as he searched for more information using the laptop's search engine. Typing in his father's name led him to recent events in Canada. There was a mention of mysterious research into oil alternatives, followed by the unexplained disappearance of one of the main researchers and a devastating fire that destroyed most of the campsite and resulted in multiple fatalities. No wonder Ivan's father had been quiet upon his return from Canada.

Ivan then searched for information on Abdul's career, which was easier to find than details about his own father's life. Posts revealed AGO's rapid growth over the last twenty years, with Abdul now at the helm of the company. But Ivan couldn't shake off the feeling that there was more to uncover, some connection between these photos and his father's death.

Ivan was confident that Abdul must have invited his father to Canada at that time. He just had to find a link, maybe through some of the other individuals named in the description. At that time, nothing was clear to him. However, he took note of some of the names, although they were not all named: James White, Sean O'Paul, Tom Dingwall, Dougie Fields, Graham Southwell, Abdul, and a few others.

He had a gut feeling that these names held the key to the truth, whatever it may be. The problem was figuring out where they were now; once he found them, he could piece together the connection between the photo, the reports, and his father's death. He returned to the library and searched for any articles or newspapers about alternative energy research. The amount of information was overwhelming, and it would take hours to sift through it all.

"I guess I won't be eating lunch or dinner today," Ivan said to himself as he delved deeper into his research. It wasn't until late at night that he stumbled upon a possible lead by chance. But there was still more to uncover. As he continued his search, he discovered potential links between the other people in the photograph. For instance, Dougie Fields was a Ph.D. student at Clerkenwell University.

Tom Dingwall, a postgraduate student currently in California, had a different area of expertise than Dougie. His research was funded by Houston Oil, and there seemed to be some collaboration between him and Dougie as they attempted to form an Anglo-American alliance in their research. Although his focus was similar to Dougie's, it leaned more towards biofuels. James White, who had previously been in Canada but returned to Australia, had recently passed away in a boating accident. Ivan struggled to find any information on Sean O'Paul and needed to conduct further research on him. Additionally, Graham

Southwell, another former research student, was currently missing. A shiver ran down Ivan's spine as he realised that two of the six individuals featured in the picture were now dead and one was missing. The remaining subjects were all involved in alternative fuel research. Content with his findings from the library, Ivan saved the collected material onto his laptop and backed it up on a memory stick before leaving.

He stepped outside and blinked, realising it was already past ten in the evening. Weary from a day of research, he made his way to his living quarters in the main accommodation building. He settled into a chair and opened his laptop to continue his work. Glancing around the room, which he shared with his school friend George, he couldn't help but feel comforted by its familiarity. The walls were decorated with George's beloved Marvel comics and oil-related memorabilia, including photos of gulf flares and early strikes in Texas. There was even a picture of George's father working on an oil rig. It all reminded him too much of home, causing a tear to escape down his cheek before he drifted off into a deep sleep.

The next morning came abruptly, as beams of sunlight streamed through the browned net curtains and woke him up. Groaning, he rubbed his tired eyes and surveyed the room. He glanced at the bed across from his own, occupied only by scattered sheets and pillows that had clearly not been used the night before. This was no surprise; George always had multiple girls spending the night with him, sometimes up to four at a time.

George was not concerned with his degree achievement, and indeed, he would be lucky to get away with a 2:2. In contrast, Ivan already had a guaranteed place with Anglo-Dutch Oil as a management graduate.

After the previous day's discoveries, Ivan was determined to find the truth. He wandered down to the library again, this time heading for the newly built technology area with a faster Wi-Fi connection so he could probe further and get some more information. He leaned forward, opened his laptop, and typed in the search field—'Sean O'Paul. 'Again, he found nothing. He tried again, but this time, he left a space between the O and Paul. Immediately, he was gratified to see three references. He leaned back from the screen and gave out a low whistle. The very first reference told him all he needed to know.

Sean O'Paul was a recent graduate at MEO (Middle Eastern Oil) in the UK Headquarters in Hays Mews London, Mayfair, looking into alternative forms of energy. He clicked on the 'Contact Us' field and took note of the number. He wandered back to the halls of residence to make the call. His mobile phone was in the room, and he needed to grab the printouts he had taken the previous day.

Ivan dialled the number with his hand shaking vigorously. Would this finally uncover the truth?

'Can I speak to Sean O'Paul, please?'

Yes, who is it?'

'It's Ivan O Neill.'

'Mr. O'Paul is busy on another call.'

'He will take my call; tell him it's Jock's son,'

The phone line went silent for a brief moment. Ivan could faintly hear hushed voices in the background before there was a rustling sound.

This time, a softer voice responded, 'OK, I will let him know you're on the line.'

Then, a gruff and harsh voice came through the phone, 'Yes?'

'I'm Ivan,' said Ivan introducing himself. 'Jock's son.'

The tone in Sean's voice immediately softened. 'It's a pleasure to hear from you, Ivan. How can I assist you?'

'I'm interested in discussing my father's time with you in Canada, specifically the fire incident.'

There was a noticeable pause before Sean spoke again.

'Well, Ivan, first of all, I am so sorry to hear about your father's untimely death. I didn't really know him that well as he was part of the management team. However, I am more than happy to chat to you. I will be in the office until the end of next week before I fly out to Malaysia for six months as part of my training course.' Sean paused before continuing.

Can you possibly get down here, sometime next week?'

Ivan thought frantically, 'Next Friday?' he stuttered.

'Yes, see you then.'

Ivan ended the call but was sure he heard a sharp click before the phone went dead.

Could someone have been listening? *Surely not?* Ivan kicked himself, he was definitely getting paranoid. He lay down on his bed, thinking about the peculiar end to the call.

He also thought carefully through the two threads that were developing with his research.

Firstly, they were all associated with alternative fuel research, and also 40% of them were dead. Maybe Sean would have the answers for him.

There was a rap on his door, and in walked George fresh from his encounters the night before. Despite all the flaws, George was the only person Ivan truly trusted. They had grown up together at Hoxborough Grammar School, and now they were at the same university. They shared the same principles and the same ideals.

Ivan was absolutely sure if he owned an Oil company in future, George would be his right-hand man.

'What shall we do tonight?' George shrilled.

'Just the usual.' The usual meant getting into their best designer jeans and heading down to their favourite riverside pub for a burger or curry. This was essential before heading up to Brown's in the main street for some drinks followed by their regular St Catherine's college disco. It was a great Friday tradition.

'Before we go on our mission,' said George, 'I need to tell you about something very strange.'

'Go on,' prompted Ivan.

'Well, you know you went up to the library earlier,' 'Yes,'

'Well, while you were out, there was a rap on the door; I was half asleep and struggled to open the door. To my surprise, there was no one there, just this envelope.'

George retrieved the envelope from his back pocket, it was screwed up, but the letter inside was still legible. It was written in capital letters.

'DO NOT SEE SEAN O 'PAUL OR FACE THE CONSEQUENCES.'

George shivered. 'Who is he, Ivan?'

Ivan sat down and explained his research over the last few weeks and his attempts to trace his father's earlier associates. He also told George about his earlier conversation with Sean.

Later that evening, Ivan, and George, as usual, went to St Catherine's retro disco dressed in eighties garb. George took matters into his own hands before they could take their course. It wasn't difficult to track down Abdul's contact information; he was active on all the popular social media platforms. George carefully considered what message to send and ultimately decided to keep it brief. He composed a simple note, stating that he knew details about the events in Canada and that there was no way Abdul could prevent Ivan from seeing Sean O'Paul. After a moment of contemplation, George sent the private message to Abdul.

He smiled to himself and looked at Ivan, wondering if he would approve of what he had done.

The seventies glam rock over the speakers started to fade, and Guns and Roses boomed across the room. The music washed over him, and Ivan watched George as he staggered away with another young girl. George was strikingly handsome. Big pooled blue eyes, long blond hair, and a permanently fixed toothy grin on a nutty brown face.

Oh well let him go; Ivan was still thinking of his research and the call from earlier in the day and he really could not be bothered tonight.

In particular, the acid trips that George took were something Ivan really could not handle.

He turned towards the bar and ordered another drink. Ivan let the large Bacardi and coke fizz through his head, and he felt himself lurching from side to side as the intoxication took hold. Ivan staggered across the pools of spilt beer and upturned plastic glasses and just about made it to the chairs at the side of the now packed and noisy room. He peered across the swirls of distorted lights and glistening faces upturned to the silver spinning balls. He thought that he saw George across the room tugging at a girl's sleeve, but it was all too much, and he drifted into a disturbed sleep.

In his dreams, he imagined the entire dance floor suddenly rising up and crashing on top of him. He gradually came round, blinking his eyes. A huge face framed in black hair and a large, peaked cap was looking into his face.

It was the local police. Ivan was instantly awake. He was still in the disco, but there was no music, just the hum of the amplifiers and a siren outside. Most of the students seemed to have left, and those remaining were standing around with pale faces.

'What is it?'

'Do you know George Sheffield?' the policeman said.

'Uh huh.'

'You best come with us.'

Somewhat bewildered, Ivan followed the two police to the police van positioned just outside the gate.

'Could you please tell me what the problem is?' They remained quiet, not offering any explanation. The van stopped outside the station, but still there was no response. Ivan looked at their unemotional expressions before making his way up the steps.

'Where can I find him?' Ivan asked with a sense of urgency in his voice.

'Come this way.'

Ivan went through both sets of double doors and entered into a dark, white-washed room. In the centre of the room was a small table with a plastic chair against one of the sides. On the other side of the table sat George, with his head buried in his hands.

George had not noticed when Ivan quietly appeared by his side. The sergeant who had let him into the room stood stoically by the door as he watched Ivan walk purposefully towards George.

'George,' he croaked. But it came out more like a hoarse whisper.

When George looked up, Ivan could see that his eyes were swollen and red from crying. 'I didn't do it, Ivan. I swear, I've been set up.'

Ivan's voice was strained with panic as Ivan asked, 'What didn't you do?'

George took hold of Ivan's face in his hands and said in a straightforward manner, 'She's dead...Ivan, she's dead!' The news hit Ivan like a ton of bricks.

He was allowed to stay at the police station overnight and make a phone call to George's parents, Diane and David, who promised to come as soon as possible the next morning. Ivan joined two young police officers in the lunch area; they were not much older than him. A kind desk sergeant draped a large blanket around his shoulders and told him what he knew about the events of the previous night.

The police had been called to the college at 1:00 am due to a disturbance reported by residents. One witness claimed to have heard high-pitched screams coming from the river side of the college. Three policemen went down to investigate and found George looking dishevelled and covered in blood. He was slumped over a bench by the river with two glasses turned upside down next to him. In between the glasses was the lifeless body of a girl, her chest covered in blood.

Ivan couldn't help but remember the words George had muttered just minutes before.

'What could I have done?' he wondered, feeling overwhelmed with shock and confusion.

The sergeant returned to the room and gently shook George's shoulder. He spoke quietly. 'I am sorry son; I have got to put you in the cell now.'

Once in the police cell, George suddenly felt very tired. Indeed, he put his head down on the wooden bench and fell asleep.

It seemed like only a few seconds, but suddenly George was awake again. Lights were flashing and George was certainly feeling the effect of the acid tab he and Shirl had taken earlier. George gasped and sobbed, moments before she died, he startlingly remembered.

There was a knock at the door and a policeman walked in. George saw a striped red and yellow man with a huge tongue lolloping from a green face. God this was a bad trip...

George felt something cold being pressed into his hand. He opened it and there was shiny silver blade. He felt the policeman press it against his thigh.

What was this guy doing? George watched as his jeans were pierced, and then watched with fascination. George stared at the psychedelic fountain as it covered him and with the colours his life ebbed away. George dreamt of Ivan and tried to remember. He could not focus now.

He tried to scream but it was just a pitiful whisper. He fell down to the ground, surrounded by his own blood. The man felt for a pulse and satisfied, slipped out of the cell into the night.

Ivan was oblivious to all of these events and had fallen asleep on the hard wooden chair in the police reception area. When he stirred from his broken sleep, he could hear other movements. He could hear outside the whirr of an ambulance's siren.

He looked up and heard snatches of conversation. 'How did he get the glass?' 'How long was he left alone?' 'Oh God.'

'What's happened?' Ivan queried the nearest uniform.

The fresh-faced constable no older than a boy turned to Ivan. 'He's killed himself, your friend George, I don't know how he got the blade.'

'Noooooo! Noooo!' Ivan screamed.

The police held him as he tried to get to the body of his dearest friend.

Once again, Ivan remembered the words George had muttered just minutes before. "What could I have done?" he wondered, feeling overwhelmed with shock and confusion.

Ivan turned round to see the bleached white faces of George's parents. The rest of the night flashed past after endless interviews.

Finally, totally exhausted, he fell asleep once more.

After less than an hour, he awoke with a start. Turning his face towards the light he glimpsed the back of a familiar head. It was Diane Sheffield. He had often met George's mother during school holidays.

With a cold grip ripping into his stomach, it suddenly came back to him.

His best friend was dead.

He spoke gently to Diane; 'I will find out who did this,' he stammered.

'George would never contemplate suicide, even if he was in serious trouble.'

CHAPTER – 30

NATALIA

Ivan wanted to inform his mother too. Natalia had not been feeling well over the past few weeks, so it was quite a nice surprise to hear from her only son. However, the joy quickly faded when Ivan recounted the events of the previous evening. Natalia asked for more information and promised to visit him the next day.

After putting the phone down, she felt very unsteady; as she sat, she felt a trickle of warm liquid down her inner thigh. It felt comforting but was immediately followed by a sharp stab of pain in the abdomen. Natalia immediately knew something was very wrong. After some time the pain subsided a little, but she decided to go to the hospital immediately as she was bleeding profusely. She called the emergency services number and explained the issue. Within minutes, an ambulance arrived. The paramedics examined and gave her a dose of morphine to ease the pain before they took her into the ambulance.

As she drifted off into a light doze, memories of her life flashed before her. She remembered her childhood in a small Ukrainian village near Odessa and all the events that led up to meeting Abdul so many years ago. It felt like just yesterday when they had first crossed paths. She didn't regret anything. She had a beautiful son and a handsome husband until the memories of that dreadful day flooded her mind. In a rush, she jolted awake and reached for her phone in her pocket. Ivan needed to know that she wouldn't be able to support him the next day. So, Natalia dialled his number but couldn't get through, she left a voicemail with a calm tone, trying not to sound too concerned. With a heavy heart, she drifted off to sleep again, this time getting some much-needed rest.

Later the next day, Natalia awoke to find several sets of eyes peering down at her, all looking very concerned.

'What's wrong?' She spoke with a tremor in her voice.

The nurse grasped her hand and spoke in a hushed whisper.

'I am really sorry Natalia, but as you probably know the blood you felt was because your pregnancy is over... we have lost the child.'

Natalia had probably realised this but still let out a shrieking wail and sobbed into her arm almost uncontrollably. Her grief was so overwhelming that she couldn't process what the other doctors were saying. She only caught snatches, such as 'CT scan showed something else,' 'Unexplained growth....' 'White cells count very low.'

As she stopped sobbing, she turned to look at them and stuttered. 'What does all that mean?'

The senior doctor said, 'What it means, Natalia, is that we need to keep you in for a day or two so we can investigate further.'

Natalia just nodded her head and sank her head into the pillow wondering what else could possibly happen to her and her family.

As she slowly woke up, she couldn't remember where she was at first. The room was pitch black, and it filled her with a sense of fear. Then, she remembered what the doctors had told her, and her fear intensified. *How would Ivan react when she'd tell him? Should she wait until after his friend's funeral to break the news?*

These questions swirled in her mind. She reached out for her coat in the cabinet beside her bed and grabbed her mobile phone.

There were multiple messages and missed phone calls. *How long had she been in the hospital?* She looked at her phone again and was surprised to see that it was nearly 15 hours. She pressed the buzzer next to her bed to call the attendant, and a couple of minutes later, the duty nurse turned up next to her.

She whispered quietly, 'I am glad you are awake, Mrs. O'Neill. The doctors will be here shortly. They asked me to tell them when you were conscious.'

After settling back, Natalia couldn't help but worry about what else they had discovered. She closed her eyes for a brief moment, only to snap them open when she felt five pairs of eyes on her. They all had serious expressions on their faces. She sat up straight, suddenly on edge.

The doctor with the ginger moustache was the first to speak. 'I am really sorry Natalia, but we have really bad news. The growth we found next to the uterus was cancerous and it looks like we need to operate immediately. We also need to give you a full CT scan to see if it has spread anywhere else.' He paused. 'I am so sorry to be the bearer of such bad news.'

Shocked, Natalia stared at all of them and then burst into tears. She wondered what else could possibly go wrong as she thrust her head deep into her pillow.

The entourage drifted away after having confirmed her operation would be first thing the following morning. Natalia looked at her phone again. Nearly all the messages were from Ivan. So, trying to calm herself down, she called him. After a couple of rings, it went straight to voicemail. It gave her the chance to look around the room. She was in a private ward.

There were yellow curtains partially covering the bay window at the end of the ward. The rest of the walls were a stark creamy off white. On the wall opposite was a TV monitor screen, which was muted, but she could see 24-hour news channels. The dour background and the now near silent atmosphere only added to her sense of unease and impending doom. She phoned Ivan again, and this time she got through. Trying not to sound too anxious and failing quite miserably, she told him that she was in the hospital and expressed her apologies for Ivan having to handle his best friend's funeral alone. Ivan promised to come and see her immediately after the funeral, though he was mystified by why his mother could not be more forthcoming with her answers.

As he hung up the phone, he reminded himself that he could only focus on the present moment for now.

CHAPTER – 31

GEORGE'S FUNERAL

The funeral was very quiet. It was attended by just 10 people, including George's immediate family and Ivan. George was of Irish descent, so the funeral took place within four days of his tragic death. It was a very peculiar atmosphere at the wake; it was almost surreal.

Although George had been Ivan's best friend, yet George's parents wanted him out of their lives as quickly and as humanely possible. And oddly enough, Ivan felt the same way.

As the evening wake came to a close, people slowly dispersed with puzzled expressions. No one could offer a satisfactory explanation for what had happened. Ivan eventually left and shook his head as he walked down the road towards the train station in Hampstead. He and his mother lived in a modest home near the edge of the Heath. The neighbourhood shops were still open, their lights flickering as they prepared to close for the night and pull down their metal shutters. As Ivan rode the tube back home, one thought kept repeating in his mind: why were so many people dying.

He reached home with a throbbing headache; he felt he was going to be sick at any moment. Somehow, he staggered to the kitchen and fried a couple of eggs and toasted the remaining two slices of white bread. It didn't really make him feel much better, but at least he was not feeling sick anymore. He turned and made his way back to his bedroom. Looking at the pile of dirty clothes in the corner, he just about found a few wearable items.

The journey to University College Hospital was slow due to some line issues and an electrical failure. Some 45 minutes later he found himself at the main desk and asking directions to his mother's private ward. The hospital wing was one of the newer ones that had been built under a public finance initiative and gave a feeling of a rather superior hotel. Ivan made his way to the top floor and negotiated his way down a long corridor to the room where his mother was staying. There were no nurses that he could see, so he opened the door and stepped inside.

He was shocked to see his mother's plight. Natalia had various tubes attached to her right arm and her complexion looked a really unpleasant shade of yellow. Ivan couldn't control himself; he burst into tears and flung his arms around her neck in an embrace hugging her as close as he could without disturbing the variety of tubes attached to her now fragile body.

'Oh my God, Mum, why didn't you tell me?'

Natalia's eyes fluttered open briefly for a moment and she gave a small smile of recognition.

The door opened behind him and in strode a stern-faced nurse followed by a trio of doctors.

'Mr. O'Neill,' asked the smallest of the trio of doctors. Ivan nodded glumly.

'Will you please come outside for a minute?' Ivan dutifully followed them out of the room.

One of them nodded towards the vacant chair in the nurses' station just outside the room.

'I am Doctor Arnold and must tell you this is a very difficult conversation. Your mother is very ill, but it was only apparent after she lost the baby she was carrying.' Dr Arnold paused.

'You didn't know Ivan?'

Ivan shook his head.

'Anyway, after she had lost her baby, we gave her a CT scan and an MMR. This was to make sure there was nothing else left behind. It was only after this that we found a couple of things of grave concern.' Dr Arnold paused again. 'I am really sorry, but we found,' he coughed apologetically, 'at least three tumours, the most serious being the one on the pancreas.' He waited for a response.

Ivan did not know what to say, he just looked straight ahead, his eyes glazed over.

Finally, he was able to stutter, 'How long has she got Doctor Arnold.' 'Only a few weeks, or maybe months.'

Ivan stared at the ground in front of him, wishing it would open up and swallow him whole.

Thoughts raced through his head, first his father, then his best friend and now his mother.

Could it all somehow be Abdul? He knew his mother certainly blamed him for his father's death, but surely, he couldn't have had a hand in his mother's fate and certainly not his friend George.

Anyway, he needed answers and needed them quickly. Fighting back tears he strode towards the lifts at the end of the corridor. He had to keep occupied, to keep him away from all these dark thoughts.

CHAPTER – 32

THE NEXT DAY

Ivan got no sleep at all that night; He just couldn't get a whole lot of weird ideas out of his head. The alarm on his phone buzzed at 7 am and, for a moment, he thought it was all a bad dream. Then he remembered all the horror of the last couple of days and woke up with a start. It was a struggle to once more head down towards the tube station and then the onward journey to Green Park.

Ivan alighted from the tube at Green Park and wandered down Piccadilly turning right into the narrow streets leading to Shepherd Market. Turning right towards Berkeley Square, Ivan traipsed along the south side of the square and finally right into Hays Mews where the small UK headquarters of MEO were based.

With some trepidation he pressed the answer phone on the door entrance. 'Yes, can I help you?' a disembodied voice announced.

'I am here to see Sean O Paul,' Ivan answered.

The door buzzed; Ivan pushed gently and weaved his way up a short flight of stairs to the first-floor landing.

As he opened the door on the first floor, in front of him a large buxom, kindly faced blonde woman in her late forties beamed at him.

'Sean will be with you shortly.' She gestured towards a seat in the corner for him to sit down.

Within a few moments, Sean emerged, looking every bit like the typical researcher. His face was tanned and weathered, likely from the sun or perhaps alcohol. His eyes were piercing blue, and his long ginger hair seemed to sprout from various spots on his face.

He looked much older than his age.

'Come in, come in Ivan,' he said positively; he thrust out his hand and shook Ivan's hand vigorously.

Ivan followed Sean into one of the small conference rooms and sat down on one of the plush fake leather chairs that surrounded a small oak table.

Ivan got straight to the point.

'Sean,' Ivan gulped in the air, 'I am trying to get to the bottom of a strange mystery.'

Sean nodded for him to continue.

Ivan went through his life story up to seeing his father die, Sean nodded sadly at this point,

Ivan paused briefly and then continued right up to his uncovering of the group in Canada and his friend George's demise.

Sean was silent for a good minute and then slowly rose from his seated prone position and flicked on his laptop. An image appeared on the opposite wall against the screen. It was not what Ivan expected. Nothing about the company: just a rather complex equation and a picture of a complex molecule.

'We will look at this in a moment,' said Sean rather mysteriously, 'First I need to look at the photo from Canada. Is it on your phone?' Sean paused again 'Do you think you could find it for me please?'

Ivan stared at the complex molecules on the white screen and then looked at Sean.

'Sorry, what did you say?'

'I said, did you have a picture of the group in Canada on your smart phone?'

'I don't, but I am sure I can find it.'

Ivan arose from his chair, and walked over to Sean's laptop, 'Do you have guest Wi-Fi?' Ivan asked politely.

'Yes, yes of course.' Sean blustered.

Ivan deftly searched through the archive files and after a few moments was able to bring up the pictures of Canada.

In the background were some log cabins, 'Ah yes,' Sean said after a few moments. He turned to face Ivan, 'Yes that is only a few months ago, and gosh I do look a lot younger,' he stated.

Ivan became excited, 'Do you know all these people?'

'Yes.' Sean said bluntly. 'Except him,' Sean pointed towards the man with his face half hidden in deep conversation with Abdul.

Ivan shook his head to acknowledge that he too had been unable to identify the man. Ivan explained all the extensive research he had conducted, including how he had sought out Sean. It was a strange coincidence that all the individuals involved in alternative fuel research were either deceased or ...

Sean nodded sagely and then flicked on the switch again to show the picture of the complex molecule.

'This is what it is all about!' Sean said.

A sudden thought came across Ivan, 'Do you think that Abdul and this other man were involved in this alternative fuel research?'

Sean nodded vigorously.

'He was not only involved, but he was also leading the research in some way, even if it was just funding, and probably with this other person, who I think is Grant Lyons,'

Sean turned to the screen. 'This is the ultimate future, Ivan.'

His bulbous eyes flicked from Ivan's face back to the screen. Ivan felt a little bemused.

'What do you mean?' 'The future without oil. Your father and all the others in the photograph would have been part of what we could achieve over the next couple of years.'

Sean flicked to the next slide.

'This slide shows an impossible reaction; it is an active compound of two metals. This compound or something similar will be created,' he paused significantly, 'I don't know, in a couple years and then we will have an environment of totally renewable energy.'

Ivan was speechless and it took him some time before he could speak again.

When he did, he whispered, 'That is an incredibly significant advancement. How did no one come up with this idea sooner?'

Sean cackled. 'No money, no research and utterly vested interests who just don't care. They will soon though.'

Sean paused and passed over a copy of The Economist open at the editorial.

Ivan scanned the article and listened with interest.

'Recently I have been reading more and more reports suggesting that Saudi Arabia will cease to be an oil exporter by approximately 2030. This is far sooner than previously thought. Part of the reason is due to rocketing internal consumption. A recent report by Heidy Rehman (Director at Citi-Group) has stated that a quarter of the 11.1m barrels they produce are used domestically, with residential use making up to 50% of this demand; two thirds of that goes to air-conditioning?! Mind-blowing stuff! With Iranian sanctions cutting supply and that situation not likely to be resolved anytime soon; Japan's increased reliance on oil since switching off most of its nuclear reactors on top of the fall in output from the North Sea and the Gulf of Mexico and the escalating cost of extraction from deep sea fields, we are seeing the beginning of the end of oil as the fuel which drives the world (forgive the pun).'

Sean waited for a few seconds for the information to sink in and then led into his own research.

'On top of all that, despite all the climate change deniers, the environment surrounding us will deteriorate far quicker than the most extreme predictions. Global warming has reached an absolutely critical stage and, unless something is done in months, not years, the polar ice caps will melt. He paused 'What does that mean, you might ask; well for a start 50% of central London would be under water including this building, Buckingham Palace and the entire financial district.'

Sean paused. 'Now you know why you are here,' he said emphatically.

Ivan mumbled 'I just thought you agreed to see me because you felt sorry for me?'

Sean leant forward slowly so he was barely a foot away from Ivan's face. He opened his mouth, his lips curled back from crooked teeth that had not been corrected in his childhood, 'Well, part of it is to continue this research when we can, but also we need to get to the bottom of what happened in Canada. I became very disillusioned while I was there. I know that a couple of my colleagues, in particular Tom Dingwall and maybe Dougie Fields had found a catalyst, but I was not part of it. I am pretty sure that's why someone tried to burn the evidence. Not Tom or Dougie, but maybe someone else linked to Abdul.' He took a breath.

'First of all, we should try and get to the bottom of your father's death.'

'I know that's really important, but what about continuing this research.' Ivan stammered.

Sean leant forward, 'It's too dangerous, your friend is dead; you cannot believe that was suicide. Can you?'

Sean laughed; it was a laugh tinged with a touch of hysteria. 'We need to try to get to Abdul first; he may have the answers. Only then will it be safe to continue the research.'

'OK!' Ivan said under his breath.

He knew that he had to link up with this slightly eccentric man.

'I will introduce you to Dougie Fields when I get an opportunity. I know he is desperate for additional funding and ideas, and we may be able to help him.'

'What, the same Dougie in the photograph?' said Ivan. 'Are you still in touch?'

'Of course, it was an amazing few weeks that bonded us all, and now there are just the three of us. You were aware of the fire that engulfed the camp?' Sean said sadly. 'Well, we were incredibly lucky to escape. It was just us and the management team. I have a quick question—well, a request really—for you.'

He continued more calmly, 'Tom and Dougie are working together on different lines of research into the oil alternatives, but it's costing a lot of cash. I cannot be bothered with all that corporate mumbo jumbo.' He tailed off into a whisper. 'However, first things first, let's get hold of some information and try and try to get to the bottom of your father's death.'

Sean paused and looked very thoughtful.

'So, what I need is your help in researching this catalyst; I am sure I can get the management to pay for you as a graduate entry, and while you are here, we can look into the circumstances around your father's death.'

There was a deathly silence, then suddenly it was all over.

Ivan grabbed Sean's outstretched proffered hand and shook it hard.

'We have a deal,' said Ivan emphatically, 'I cannot start immediately but can be back here in the next three months.'

Ivan stood, preparing to depart, but was quickly gestured to stay in his seat.

'I would like to introduce you to someone else. She used to work with Jock in the shipping industry and also shared concerns about the incidents in Canada and the suspicious circumstances surrounding his death.'

Sean stuck his head around the door and spoke quietly.

'Gerta, can you come in for a second.'

A long-legged brunette appeared at the doorway and gave a brief smile to Ivan.

Sean spoke again, 'I can't join you, but maybe you two can go to the local bar and catch up on everything.'

As they left, Ivan wondered if Gerta knew anything about his father's death.

CHAPTER – 33

LATER THAT EVENING

Farina's Wine Bar Mayfair

Ivan was in a bit of a daze as the two of them made their way to the wine bar. Gerta explained that she knew Jock from the shipping days when she was just a teenager and had been horrified to learn of his death. Ivan looked at her more closely. She had large brown eyes framed by a ruddy oval face. Her black straight hair was pulled back in an untidy ponytail that flopped over the upturned collar of her padded red ski jacket. Ivan felt comfortable with her immediately and could not wait to exchange stories.

After a brief chat, they decided to have a drink. He followed Gerta down to the best and least well-known wine bar in London. The wine bar was quite tatty, with shreds of white paper peeling from the ceiling and the dim lighting.

Ivan looked at Gerta and started blurting out his life story. Gerta raised her finger to his mouth.

'Don't worry, I know everything,' she said.

'You can't.'

'Oh, indeed I do. It's amazing what you can find on the internet.'

Gerta's eyes opened wide. Ivan looked into pools of dark sadness, with just a shimmer of brightness.

Over several drinks, it turned out that, while Gerta knew about his father's death and George's fate, she didn't know about his mother's illness. She also cared deeply about the environment and had been fascinated by the story of the Canada camp. After sympathising with him about his mother, she stated quite calmly, 'Yes I believe that your father's death was not completely an accident, and certainly George's death was not suicide.'

'Even worse,' Gerta whispered furtively 'I know that one of the other men at that camp was murdered.'

'Who?' asked Ivan.

'James White,' stated Gerta.

'But I thought that he was killed in a boating accident?'

'It was no accident Ivan, at least that's what my sources say.'

'But I thought that the body was never recovered?'

'It wasn't but that is what my sources have told me.'

Ivan looked at her in utter disbelief. 'We must still continue the research, though, even though it seems to be like issuing your own death warrant.'

Gerta interrupted: 'It is really far too dangerous; first we must destroy the roots of this evil.'

They talked through the night and were the very last of the clientele as they staggered up the stairs into the quiet street above the bar. After finishing several bottles of the house Chianti, they both felt quite tired and worn out. They were so engrossed in each other's company that they didn't notice the black Ford transit that mounted the curb on the corner of Berkeley Square. Gerta caught it from the corner of her eye and instinctively pushed Ivan towards the black railings leading to the steps to the fashionable nightclub Annabel's. The black van hit her full on. She died instantly.

Ivan was hit with only a glancing blow, but his head struck the railing, and he was unconscious within moments. The ambulance raced across London in response to the distressed call from a passer-by who had seen the whole incident.

On arriving at the scene, the paramedics checked Gerta's pulse, confirming her death and then turned their attention to Ivan. Though still alive, he was severely injured with a broken arm and multiple fractured ribs. There were also worries about a potential head injury as he remained unconscious. The lead paramedic radioed the hospital for assistance before they rushed back for immediate medical attention.

'We have one fatality and one critical head injury. Returning to the hospital now,' he reported over the radio.

As luck would have it, the hospital where Ivan was taken was the City of London University Hospital, the same one as his mother. Ivan was rushed to A&E emergency ward. In the meantime, the hospital staff tried to find out who was the next of kin and were astonished it was Natalia.

Down the hall, on the third floor of the hospital, Natalia was recovering from a powerful round of chemotherapy and an equally strong dose of morphine. The nurses decided not to disturb her; she was in no condition to handle any updates or inquiries. In fact, over the past day, her health had declined significantly. Just as the nurses were about to leave her room, all of the alarms started blaring. They quickly returned to find that Natalia had suffered a massive heart attack and was unresponsive. They made repeated attempts to resuscitate her, but it was no use; after 20 minutes they declared her to be dead.

CHAPTER – 34

FOUR WEEKS LATER

Sally Nichols, a Staff Nurse, was having one of those days where everything that could go wrong, did. It started off with the coffee machine malfunctioning and spilling hot liquid all over her uniform. Then she received a call from her colleague, Dermot McIntyre, asking her to cover for him as he had injured himself playing rugby. Despite her reluctance, she agreed to help out.

When she arrived at Dermot's ward, she immediately noticed the commotion among the nurses and two police officers. Sally approached Elspeth, one of the nurses, and asked what was going on. Elspeth whispered in Sally's ear about a patient with a head injury who had recently woken up and needed to be informed about some things before speaking with the police. Sally grumbled about her bad luck, especially since she wasn't even supposed to be working that afternoon. She looked around for guidance and spotted the duty doctor engrossed in some papers.

Wandering over, she tapped him on his shoulder. He whirled round.

'Ah Sally, just who I needed to talk to; I gather you have been handed the poison chalice?'

Sally nodded glumly again.

Dr Tripton pulled out the medical records from the middle of the large pile in front of him.

'In the room behind me, we have Ivan O'Neill. As you know, he was brought in about three or four weeks ago with a serious head injury after a hit and run. In that hit and run his, we are presuming, girlfriend was killed instantly.' He drew breath.

'That is why the two police officers are here – to try and get the facts. What you may not know is that his mother was also being treated here. This is where it has become very difficult. She passed away by some horrific coincidence on the same day that Ivan was admitted. He, therefore, knows nothing of this. We believe he knew she was ill but not that it was so serious.' Dr Tripton paused again.

'Unfortunately, Sally, you have been designated as the person to tell him this news. Also, you will have to let him know his girlfriend is also dead. We have tried to find some relatives, but it really is a tragic story. His father also died in a tragic accident in an oilfield barely six months ago. On top of that his best friend committed suicide just a few weeks ago.'

Sally became very still taking it all in – and there was lot to take in. It seemed he had lost everything. 'OK I will do it, just give me a few minutes to gather my thoughts.'

Sally walked into the room.

It was modern hospital room with a Smart TV, nicely decorated and with plenty of space around the bed for visitors. Ivan was sitting up in bed, looking a little bemused, sipping what looked like a watery orange squash. He smiled politely at Sally who sat next to his bed and was silent for a few moments.

She coughed and then started, though she wasn't quite sure how should she begin. She grasped his hand tightly.

'Ivan, you know why you were bought in here?' Ivan nodded sagely.

'I was involved in a car accident, but not sure how and why it happened. I remember I was with a girl I had not seen for years.'

He sucked in breath, 'Do you know if she is alright, I think the car hit her first.'

Sally looked into his eyes and sensed sadness, as if he already knew.

'I am really sorry, but I am afraid that Gerta was killed instantly. The vehicle struck her full on before hitting you.'

Ivan's eyes glistened with tears.

'I hardly knew her really, but I was really fond of her even though we only had that night together.'

Sally gulped in air and then told Ivan that his mother had also passed away, almost at the same time. The scream of despair could be heard over the entire floor. Then there was an eerie silence.

CHAPTER - 35

REVENGE

After spending a week in the hospital, Ivan was interviewed several times by the police. He cooperated and provided all the information he could remember. He was informed by the police that the van that had hit them was stolen earlier in the day. The authorities later found the burnt-out van in a secluded forest located south of the Thames River in northwest Kent.

As Ivan spoke with the investigators, he could tell they were eager to solve Gerta's murder but had no solid leads. They seemed content to put it on hold until new evidence surfaced. But Ivan was determined to find justice for his friend. As he lay in his hospital bed on his last night before being discharged, he plotted his revenge. He knew he needed to start by revisiting Sean and getting answers from him.

Six weeks had passed since their fateful meeting in Sean's office. Lost in thought, Ivan stroked his chin and absentmindedly gazed at the picture on his wall in his new penthouse flat on Munster Road. So much information had been revealed to him that day by Sean, but Ivan struggled to make sense of it all in light of recent events. He was still in shock and couldn't fully process everything he had learned. As he thought about Gerta, a tear rolled down his cheek. Then he thought about Dougie Fields, one of Sean's Canadian colleagues. And Paul Carruthers, son of George Carruthers who Gerta had mentioned during their conversation. Apparently, Paul was working with Dougie as a PhD student assistant at Clerkenwell University. It was all quite confusing. Before diving back into the details with Sean, Ivan decided to do some research on George Carruthers' background.

The first search didn't yield much worthwhile information, but typing in Professor George Carruthers revealed a whole different story. George Carruthers had a very tragic tale. His daughter had died in a boating accident, though there was mystery about that too. It then got into the more interesting stuff. Carruthers was renowned for his expertise in finding alternatives to hydrocarbons. Utilising a specialised catalyst, he had theoretically created these compounds and was on the verge of a major breakthrough before his sudden death. Ivan was taken aback by this revelation and tried to piece together the puzzle. *Was this discovery the reason behind so many mysterious deaths?* There were countless tasks to be done, including pursuing further information on his friend's passing and attempting to reopen the inquest. He had followed up on his father's death. This was indeed interesting.

A series of coincidences and incompetence had hinted at the possibility that there was more to this than just a simple accident. It wasn't enough to prove malicious intent, but there was a glimmer of corruption at the highest level. Abdul seemed to be involved in all paths, along with some of the investors who funded the Canadian students. Ivan had only been focusing on Abdul, but now he realised that it could be much more complex than he originally thought. Everything hinged on this mysterious catalyst, and he was determined to uncover the truth behind it.

After travelling home from hospital , Ivan scanned his flat once more, letting the memories of his loss wash over him.

While waiting to sell his mother's house he rented a flat in Fulham Road. It seemed like the perfect place for him and a future partner, perhaps even Gerta, whom he had considered as a potential mate. But fate had other plans. As tears welled up in his eyes again, Ivan scolded himself for dwelling on the past and resolved to focus on moving forward. He turned on his phone and dialled Sean's number, eager to get things in place for the next chapter of his life. He was greeted by a groggy voice on the other end.

"Is this Sean?' Ivan asked.

'Yes, who is it?' Sean's tone was more alert now.

'It's Ivan, Sean. I need to see you again. I want a more detailed explanation of this catalyst and its role in all these deaths.'

There was a brief pause before Sean replied in a cryptic manner, 'I'm currently in Dubai but will be flying back to Heathrow tomorrow morning. Let's meet outside the office. I'll send you a text with the location later; perhaps somewhere in Hammersmith or Fulham would be convenient?' 'That works for me,' said Ivan.

'We'll leave it at that then.' The line went quiet, and Ivan stared at his phone screen in silence for a moment.

CHAPTER – 36

THE NEXT DAY

Sean had chosen a small pub around the back of Fulham Broadway tube station for their meeting. Ivan walked slowly up the North End Road, looking at all the bustling shops concluding the last deals of the day. It was a wet evening and Ivan struggled to keep his umbrella up in the strong wind. Swirling newspaper pages and a few odd leaves only made things a bit worse. It was just past 7 pm when a very wet Ivan reached the Fulham Arms. He opened the door to the pub, shook his umbrella dry and glanced around. The pub was full of Chelsea fans, presumably ahead of a game on that evening. He spotted Sean in the corner of the pub, also looking very bedraggled. He squeezed between a couple of supporters who were discussing potential outcomes of the night's game in loud voices. Ivan didn't share the peculiar fascination that England had with football, but it was hard to ignore the banter.

Sean stood up as he approached Sean. For some reason, rather than just shaking hands he gave him an enormous bear hug before gesturing towards a beer-stained cloth bench next to him. They sat in silence for a while before Sean opened the conversation.

'I thought it best to meet outside the offices; it just doesn't feel safe at the moment.'

Ivan nodded his head and watched as the football supporters started to disperse.

Sean glanced over his shoulder and mumbled, 'Yes, I guess the game has almost started. That's good, we can talk in peace.'

Sean began, 'Let me start at the very beginning, as I think that will help to explain things much more easily.'

Sean proceeded to explain his childhood and how he had become entangled with the 'Canada group', as he called it. When he got to the discussions about the catalyst, his tones became hushed, almost secretive.

'You cannot believe how it was out there in Canada, we were stuck in the middle of huge forest. Every day was the same, trying to find this catalyst. I had made friends with Tom Dingwall; he was in that picture you showed me. He was actually the one that introduced me to the consortium that were funding the whole operation.

'So, it was Abdul who was the frontman to fund me, while the other two had their own separate arrangements. Tom was being funded by an American corporation, while Dougie Fields was being funded by an English organisation, Shetland Oil. Anyway, after we arrived, Tom and Dougie got together, and I felt more and more excluded.'

Sean paused and looked around the pub, which was now almost empty except for a couple of small after work groups in the corner trying to put the world to rights in very loud voices.

'Can I ask you a question, Sean?'

'Sure, fire away.'

'What is this catalyst, why does everyone want it and most of all why is it causing so many deaths; I just don't know who to blame.'

Sean leaned forward and took a piece of paper out of his back pocket before placing it on the table.

'Before I tell you what it is, let me tell you the background, which may help explain some of these things.' He took a deep breath and gulped down a large portion of his lager.

'Climate change is obviously the huge problem of this age.'

Ivan nodded in appreciation.

"Well, what if, overnight, we were able to reverse all the effects, live in a carbon negative society and also overcome our dependency on the oil-producing countries... all in one big, monumental, big bang.'

Sean paused, 'I can see the disbelief in your eyes, but let me continue. Climate change and global warming are here to stay; within your lifetime there will be a huge environmental crisis. I believe that consortium led by Abdul, the US and the UK came together and decided to invest in the best chemists and set up a research centre in Canada.'

Sean stopped.

'Have I got you interested now?'

Again, Ivan nodded.

'Their research wasn't making any progress, so they reached out to the leading expert on climate change and its solutions, who happened to be George Carruthers. George is, or I should say was the pre-eminent force behind the team in Canada; he personally selected at least half of the contingent. Unfortunately, he passed away last year; otherwise, we would get to the bottom of this much more quickly. His son Paul is working with Dougie Fields at Clerkenwell University, still searching for the holy grail of this catalyst.'

Ivan managed to get a word in edgeways.

'So, Sean, tell me what is so damn important about this catalyst that all these people had to die for it? If it is so simple, I really don't understand why it hasn't been thought of before.'

Sean took out the paper from his back pocket and spread it out in front of Ivan.

'So here we have the two most common compounds known to man.'

He drew H_2O and CO_2 in pencil. 'One is essential to life and the other is the root of all evil and the primary cause of global warming. So, what if we could break these up into their relative elements and then combine them into something less harmful and incredibly useful.'

Ivan scratched his head.

Sean smiled.

'Well, there are two separate things we could do. One is to pump billions of tons of oxygen into the atmosphere a day. The other is that we could create a really clean fuel like ethanol, but even cleaner. If we do that then great, we won't need to burn any more petrol and can solve the climate crisis in one fell swoop. Global warming could be stopped and reversed overnight.'

Ivan interrupted, 'But surely burning ethanol would create more CO_2?'

'Yes, fundamentally that is correct, but to create the ethanol would take in over twice as much CO_2 as emitted.'

Sean scrawled a few basic chemical equations on the piece of paper and suddenly everything made sense. 'The thing is that this catalyst does not exist and, even if it did, it would be unstable and incredibly expensive. That's where the Canadian group came in, we needed to create a stable catalyst that could be used millions of times without degrading. It needed to be safe to deploy and was relatively inexpensive because it could be used so many times. I believe that one of the groups found out how to make it and that's where all of this started.' Sean came to a sudden stop and gazed at his half-consumed drink.

'Can you imagine Ivan, Gas power stations powered by water and air, cars running on water and air and all the time the atmosphere being rebuilt with huge amounts of oxygen. No more global warming and a wonderful future for the next generation.'

Ivan stroked his chin once more. 'So why is everyone desperate to stop this happening?'

'We are discussing large oil companies, so it's not surprising that they are all trying to be the first one to take advantage of a new technology. An alliance was formed between Abdul, who has support from Russia and Saudi Arabia, as well as the US and a company in England. They all needed to ensure that none of them got ahead of the others. However, greed took over and one or more groups tried to steal the technology for themselves. It's possible that one group actually found the catalyst, which led to the arson at the Canadian camp and subsequent murders. I don't believe that Abdul is necessarily responsible for everything, despite what you may have assumed.'

'So, what should I do next?'

'Well firstly, you need to get to see Dougie Fields and Paul Carruthers; they will be able to give you more answers. After that if you want to come to work alongside me that would be great.'

The pub was starting to fill with Chelsea supporters again; their team had obviously won as they were all in an ebullient mood arguing which goal was the best and engaging in loud, barely comprehensible singing.

Sean stood up as if he had said enough, glanced at Ivan, and said nothing except a brief, 'See you soon and good luck,' and then he was gone.

Ivan had a lot to think about as he strolled home through a much more pleasant warm evening. One thing was clear; Abdul was no longer the prime suspect; it went far deeper than that. It involved industrial espionage not on a corporate level but potentially much higher than that.

CHAPTER - 37

ABDUL REHMANN AND THE OILFIELD SCAM

Abdul's once simple life as a liaison between Saudi Arabia and Russia had become complicated upon his return from Canada. The death of his colleague, Jock, made him fear for his own safety as well. He went about his day-to-day tasks with little enthusiasm until he received a call from investors about a promising oil bed off the coast of Egypt. They claimed it could yield 10 million barrels per day, similar to a neighbouring field. For just 5% investment, Abdul could secure a lifetime of wealth. After some cautious questioning, he agreed to attend presentations about the opportunity.

John D. Davis Junior was well into his 70s but still a very shrewd grifter who was always ready to take on any new challenge. It was nevertheless an interesting day when he received an overseas phone call offering to pay him and his team £5m to discredit Abdul.

The next day he got the team together and assigned roles to everyone.

Henri Maguire – Surveyor

David Thomas – Lead person

Sally Junkett – Receptionist

Simon Lambert – Researcher

Jenny - PA

Once the roles had been decided, the plan was put into action.

Since the death of Jock, Abdul had moved to palatial offices in Frankfurt. This was also where the investors had their main location.

To start the project, the team needed to deceive Abdul and his investors at their offices. Luckily, Jenny had connections that allowed her to secure a position as a temporary PA in the office next to Abdul's. Using this cover, she intercepted the regular paper delivery and swapped out a fake copy of the Financial Times. The plan was for David Thomas to visit the offices the next day and persuade Abdul to buy a majority share in the field they were discussing. This would require convincing him through false information in the FT article about adjacent fields and seemingly positive preliminary results from their own site. It was a brilliant tactic, agreed upon by the team.

The fabricated FT report made vague references to inaccurate estimates and exaggerated success rates. The article featured quotes from a renowned surveyor, which was crucial to David's plan. He knew that Abdul would reach out to the surveyor for verification, giving David an opportunity to negotiate for a higher price. He and John spent hours strategising and by the end of the night, they had a solid plan in place. Now they just needed to execute it successfully.

John and David were jolted awake as the undercarriage thumped down on the tarmac at Frankfurt Airport. A dull, unpleasant mist was hanging in the air, quite typical of the country, particularly in the north.

They listened to the familiar tones of the airplane staff: 'Wait until the plane comes to a complete stop.'

They smiled to each other at the thought of the meeting at Abdul's office in about two hours' time. Clutching their bags, they stepped onto the gangway.

'God, it really is cold.' John said with a grimace on his face.

They passed through passport control and stepped out to the waiting ranks of Mercedes.

'The Central Frankfurt Marriott please,' John instructed.

They were due to meet up with Simon, who had flown in the night before.

The taxi whisked up the rank onto the newly built Autobahn which would take them to the Marriott on the outskirts of Frankfurt town centre. They drew up outside the entrance, stepped out into the biting cold wind and looked around at the surroundings. The doorman, wearing a bulky leather jacket with fur lining and a black cap with ear flaps, stepped aside as they made their way towards the main lobby. They strode confidently across the lobby to reach the Champions Bar where Simon was waiting for them.

Simon was already perched on a bar stool, sipping from a glass of beer.

He looked a bit forlorn. As they approached, he acknowledged their presence with a slight nod and gestured to the two stools on either side of him.

John was the first to speak.

'Why do you seem so down, Simon?'

'I can't quite put my finger on it, John. The plan seems sound, but I have a nagging feeling about it all. Something just doesn't feel right. Maybe it's because we're handling such a large sum of money and our client is still unknown to us. It's all very unusual.

And now he wants to meet at a hotel instead of his office. It's not making sense,' Simon paused thoughtfully.

David looked across at John and signalled that he should offer some reassurance.

John gave a big hug to Simon and whispered into his ear.

'I know it's an unusual situation Simon, but I have promised this will be my last job and all of you will have enough cash to never do a job again. So, let's make the most of it and see if we can pull it off.'

Simon smiled wanly and nodded in hesitant agreement. 'Right let's get on with it then.'

John raised his glass and the others followed suit. 'To us.'

'Yes, to us!' echoed David and Simon.

The three of them made their way next door, rapped on the door, which almost immediately opened, and there he was: their target, Abdul. He stood quite still staring at them with passionless eyes. Abdul didn't extend his hand for a handshake, instead gesturing towards some chairs on the other side of the large desk. Two of Abdul's colleagues sat across from them. They all settled into their seats and waited for Abdul to speak. He began with a polite introduction and offered them coffee. John placed his red attaché case on the desk, opened it, and pulled out a beige envelope folder.

He looked directly at Abdul and his two associates and asked, 'Shall we begin?'

'Please do.' Abdul replied.

'However, you must realise that I am extremely sceptical of anything you are about to say to me. For a start, I have not ever heard of Middle Eastern Oil, and I have lived in that region for most of my life.' he concluded.

'We thought you may say that, if I may, can I link to your screen?'

David fired up an app on his phone, and after a couple of minutes, some images appeared on the screen. It seemed to be a corporate event of some sort. The camera flicked around the room and rested on a few banners, all exhibiting the logo of the fictitious company Middle Eastern Oil. David let the group on the other side of the table rest their eyes for a moment before turning to them.

'The images you are seeing are of the 5th birthday party of Middle Eastern Oil and the people you see on stage are the very people you see before you right now.' David smiled and looked at John and Simon, who both nodded their heads vigorously.

'OK, even if I believe that MEO exists, why are you so willing to sell some of your prize asset to a potential competitor?' asked Abdul.

It was Simon's turn to speak. 'That's easy to explain. It all comes down to taxation; unless we sell now, we stand to lose millions in tax and there are other reasons which I will come to in a minute. We now have over 50% of the field and it is making us a ludicrous amount of money.'

Abdul waved his bejewelled fingers and Simon looked at John who nodded and continued.

'What you do not know, and there is no reason why you should know, is that through a number of other partners we have now acquired a controlling interest in the field. In fact, nearly 70% of the field is in our hands.'

Simon paused to judge the effect of these words and then went on, 'Why do we want to sell ? Well, the simple answer is we don't. It is only because of the reasons I have already indicated and because of this document I am about to show you.'

Simon reached down into the case next to him and rummaged around for a few seconds.

'You should read this.'

Simon handed a large buff envelope to Abdul.

It had a broken seal on it, making it look as it was from a government department. Abdul opened the top flap and removed the contents. The headed paper was from the Monopolies and Mergers Commission. Abdul scanned the document. It was very detailed. It showed the ownership very clearly with the expected yield of some 10 million barrels a day. There was a clear geological survey, again indicating the same detail. The document was some 40 pages long, but it was only towards the end that it became really interesting. He read the last paragraphs over and over again. Here it was in black and white. MEO had to sell a majority holding in the field, as it had acquired the assets by deception, and the only remedy was a partial sale.

Abdul looked over the top of the paper; he could hardly control his excitement. Not only was he getting a bargain, but he was also getting the bargain from a supposed large competitor.

He spoke softly 'If you want this to go ahead, then I need to arrange an independent survey to verify the potential yield.'

Simon and John nodded their heads vigorously and in unison. David smiled warmly at Abdul and his two colleagues.

Simon said, 'We thought that would be the case, so we have arranged for one of our surveyors to fly out tomorrow.'

'We will all fly out to Cairo and then out by charter boat to the site of the field.'

Abdul thought rapidly, he had to get hold of his own surveyor quickly. How was he going to do that?

Then it struck him.

'There was a surveyor named in the FT article,' he said, 'Perhaps I can use him?'

'She is tied to another company out in the Middle East and will almost certainly be on site as we speak.'

Finally, after a few moments, he spoke again. 'Alright but you need to give me an hour or so.'

'We will wait in the Champions Bar.' Simon said.

Abdul gestured towards the door.

As they left the suite, they knew they had to move quickly. This was the complex part of the elaborate deception. The survey company in the FT article, existed, but the person named did not exist.

Simon, John, and David were gambling that Abdul would choose him for the independent survey. It was the only logical choice. John fired his mobile phone into life.

He spoke tersely: 'Jenny, are all the interceptions in place? Is Sally ready to take the call?'

He smiled to himself when he received the affirmative to both questions.

He nodded to the barman. 'A small lager please.' Simon and David looked at him with their eyebrows raised.

'Alright, guys, agreed, we don't want to get too overconfident,' he looked at the barman again.

'Three small glasses of lager,'

They appeared almost immediately.

'Danke,' John said to the barman; he put the ice-cold glass to his lips and took a small sip looking at both his colleagues.

'To success.' he clinked his glass with the other two in deep satisfaction.

CHAPTER – 38

BARANTA OILFIELD

After nearly two days of travelling, the group finally reached the Baranta Oilfield in Egypt. The flight had taken seven hours, and it took a whole day for Abdul to locate Henri. (Henri was the planted surveyor and played a crucial role in their plan; John had spoken to him at length before departing from Frankfurt.)

Unfortunately, the first boat they tried to use turned out to be unusable, delaying their arrival until late in the day. At the site, Henri greeted Abdul warmly and escorted them all to a reception area where he explained the necessary procedures. Although everyone present was familiar with the procedures, John and his team had taken all the necessary precautions to make the survey appear as legitimate as possible. Abdul was told that three separate surveys would be conducted to confirm the sediment contained oil and determine the expected pressure from the top layer. This pressure reading was crucial, as it would indicate the thickness of the layer and the estimated amount of oil that could potentially be extracted. A reading above 1.1 mm/m2 indicated an expected yield of over 10 million barrels per day.

John broke the tense silence by addressing Abdul, 'Shall we begin?'

Abdul's response was a guttural, 'Yes.'

Both John and Abdul had their own concerns; Abdul needed to ensure that Henri was on his side and would underestimate the results, while John's biggest worry was that Henri wouldn't lose his nerve while playing double agent.

John was positive that Abdul would get to Henri before the first survey results, this indeed proved to be the case.

Abdul was so confident that Henri would play cards for him, having met him and bribed him before the meeting, he felt he's already won the deal.

Henri led the party to the laboratory hub, where the surveys would take place. He indicated for them all to sit. He then began.

'There would be a calibration period lasting one hour and then the small drilling probe would start sending back initial readings.'

Henri quickly went through the routine, making sure Abdul did not notice. Behind the scenes, John's team was manipulating the readings on screen to appear as if they were from a highly productive oil field in Saudi Arabia instead of locally in Egypt. It would take at least an hour for the results to show up, so Henri suggested taking a break until then. He gathered his stuff and left the room, followed by curious looks.

After waiting ten minutes, John made his way to the designated meeting spot in the small resident's coffee area at the back of Drill Derrick One.

Sure enough, Henri was there, but he appeared anxious and was shaking slightly. 'I cannot go through with it, John.'

'Of course, you can. It will take only twenty minutes, and for that, you will be paid $20K.'

'I am getting double the amount from Abdul.'

'I know, but remember that when the deal is signed, you will get a much bigger share of the pot.'

'Yes, yes, I know, I know. I guess I can do it.'

John glanced at his watch 'You better go now; you need to be with Abdul in ten minutes.'

Henri shook his head. 'I just hope you know what you are doing.'

John gripped Henri's head with both his hands. 'I have waited all my life for a payout like this; it will be fine.'

John turned, pushed aside the grey steel door and was gone.

Henri looked at his watch and made his way to his berth to wait for his visitor.

CHAPTER – 39

ONE HOUR LATER

Henri was dozing in his cabin when there was rapid series of knocks at his door.

Henri blinked his eyes open.

There was incessant shouting outside: "Henri Henri, HENRI."

'Yes, yes I am coming.'

'Well hurry up," insisted the disembodied voice.

'Is that you, Abdul?'

'Yes, open up open up, we only have a few minutes.' Henri stumbled towards the door.

As soon as the latch was unfastened Abdul strode in flanked by his two henchmen. They took up a position opposite him. Henri felt intimidated.

'Are you clear what you must do?' Abdul spoke firmly.

'Yes, very clear.' Henri stuttered.

'I must ensure that whatever the results are, they agree with the figures agreed in the pre-survey,' Henri spoke clearly and very precisely.

'How will you ensure this?' Abdul spoke in clipped monosyllables.'

'Easy, I will use the pre-prepared print out from these sheets from an adjacent field.'

'Good, very good.' Abdul seemed satisfied. He abruptly turned and left without speaking another word.

'Two hours later, Henri was addressing his audience. 'This has been a relatively uninteresting survey.' Henri paused and looked around the room making sure he had everyone's attention.

'The results convey a high-yielding productive field, meeting almost exactly pre-survey expectations. We have an expected output of in excess of one million barrels a day with a total expected yield of 36 billion barrels. At today's price this equates to a total value of 100 billion dollars, with an expected profit of some 10 billion dollars throughout the life of the field. This I believe to be to the satisfaction of both parties.'

Abdul could hardly contain his glee. Henri had already tipped him off that the field was so vast it would probably exceed the adjoining field which was currently tipping the scales at almost tenfold this amount. This would treble his company's value. All he had to pay John and the team was 10 billion dollars. He could hardly wait.

John almost imperceptibly nodded at Andrew. 'Gentlemen I must get on my helicopter now. I think the deal is done.'

CHAPTER – 40

FRANKFURT, THREE DAYS LATER

John cautiously approached the abandoned manor house on the outskirts of Frankfurt. He had been given a secret task that he had not revealed to the team when they met to discuss their main objective. The bitter wind relentlessly blew through the vacant property, causing the fir trees to sway and their branches to tap against the windows upstairs. This was an unusual job for someone with his level of expertise; he was neither a thief nor a lawbreaker, and he couldn't shake off the unease he felt about the entire situation. As he stood outside the looming structure, starkly silhouetted against the dark sky, John wondered how he had ended up here. Their primary goal had been to discredit Abdul, which they had achieved with great success.

A few weeks before, he had been unwinding with some fellow mates at The Dappled Cat in Neasden, North London. This particular pub was known for its late-night brawls and predominantly male clientele. Situated in the middle of a council estate, it had seen better days and only a handful of patrons bothered to show up before 10 pm. That's what made it odd when, on this particular night at 10:30 pm, John noticed a stunning blonde sitting alone at the bar, winking at him. He rubbed at the stubble on his face from a less than satisfactory shave that morning, but there was no mistaking her intent. She winked again, directly at him. Looking around, he saw that all of his friends were too drunk to notice. He approached her cautiously. She wasted no time in getting straight to the point.

'Don't ask for my name. I have £1000 pounds in this envelope, and I know you are going to be in Germany, well Frankfurt to be specific in the next few weeks.'

John looked incredulous for the moment. 'How do you know that?'

'I said no questions. When you get there via this airline ticket, I would like you to get some documents for me. These documents are locked in a safe in a house just outside Frankfurt. Once you have these documents safely in your possession, you will ring this number.' She handed him a card with a UK mobile number. 'You will then be picked up approximately an hour later.'

'Any question so far?' 'How do I get there?'

The blonde's glib reply was, 'That's easy. 'The instructions are in the envelope. If you complete the job satisfactorily, you'll get a further £40,000.'

John tried to sound firm, but it came out as a small squeak.

'Is that all £40,000 to break into a secure house?'

He paused. 'It has to be worth more than that, I mean I could end up getting killed.'

The blonde sounded exasperated.

'The house has been made insecure and there is no one in residence. If you do not want to do it there are plenty of others available.'

She turned to go.

'No no wait.' John pulled her up.

'£40,000 you say,' he stared at her fixedly. 'Alright, let me look.'

He took the envelope. He peeled open the seal to look at the notes and glanced up again. She was gone. Inside the envelope was exactly £1,000, with a note detailing the arrangements. There was a first-class ticket to Frankfurt from Heathrow plus accommodation vouchers for Frankfurt and open tickets from the oilfield to Frankfurt. There was a note of the taxi number to pick him up whenever it was required. Also, there was the number he was to call after the job was completed.

There were also clear details of where John should collect the remaining £39,000. His victim was to be Abdul Rehmann, a rich industrialist currently living just outside the Frankfurt suburbs. John paused and thought to himself. Why was he stealing off someone that they were trying to fix up in an elaborate scam? He read on. He was to not to steal any cash or jewels.

His specific task was to look for papers relating to several oilfields and specific holdings in various companies. It seemed almost too simple. Finally, there was an acceptance instruction. The single word 'yes' was to be left with a specific newsagent in Kilburn, North London. He did not know the newsagent, but he recognised the road.

Standing in front of the manor, John checked his instructions once more and approached the back patio windows. She was right. Not only was there no security on the gates, but there was also no-one in the house, and best of all the patio doors were unlocked. John pushed them open and stepped inside. He flicked on a small pencil torch and glanced around the room. There were several paintings of old masters. Surely not. This really cannot be that easy. He looked at the instructions again. As indicated, heavy curtains hung snug to the windows and across the room, his pencil light picked out a copy of 'The Sunflowers' by Van Gogh. He strode over to the picture; a sharp tap opened the frame to expose the safe. John opened the safe; with a memory stick easily.

Inside the safe, there were a number of documents. John glanced briefly at each one. There were many oil-related papers and also some filled with chemical formulae. John thrust them all into his bag. He glanced once more into the beech-panelled room and then, without a second thought, padded across the lawn to his strategically placed rope on the outside wall. It only took a minute, and then he was outside again.

John did not feel the thud of iron as it caved his skull in. He was dead as he hit the ground. The driver pulled out the papers from John's bag. He grunted with satisfaction. It all seemed OK.

A cloud of pallid dust hung over the dawn scene as he sped away.

CHAPTER - 41

SAN FRANCISCO AND EGYPT,
ONE DAY LATER

Claude had arrived back from the office exhausted. He had been dealing with the grifter bunch for many years and had financed them on several occasions, but this had proved to be the most complex and, at times, the most infuriating. His family had no idea what he had been involved in for the last few weeks, only that he had come into a considerable sum of money.

The grifters' team had been paid off, and now it was just the loose ends. He needed to call Marianne straight away. They had spoken before the team made the journey to the oil rig. She had found exactly the right person for the job in Frankfurt. The phone rang three times and then went to the answerphone. Claude was frustrated and slammed the receiver down. He dialled her mobile.

'Yes,' a tentative voice said.

'Marianne?' There was a sharp intake of breath.

'Yes, who is this?'

'It's Claude, where have you been?' Marianne drew breath.

'Don't worry everything has been concluded satisfactorily '

'I can't reach our housebreaker,' Claude said impatiently, 'so, it is not satisfactory at all my end. He should have called and claimed his remaining cash.' 'You've tried everywhere Claude? Well, don't worry, I have a couple of other ways of getting in touch,' Marianne paused. 'I will get back to you shortly.'

With that, she cut Claude off. She smiled to herself; she was aware of what had happened to the greedy grifter, and she had the papers and documents in her hand; now, she could get in touch with her contact to check on the next steps. She looked around and eased herself onto the down pillows in the luxurious room. The Cairo Renaissance was quite stupendous. Gold leaves decorated the carved oak stairwells. Wonderful marble statues stood on black plinths outside every lift.

There were two bathrooms, each with a choice of multi-jetted showers or a whirlpool Jacuzzi. The furniture was antique walnut and oak, and the bed had to be at least eight feet across. Draped over the bed were some silk fabrics and a white goose-down duvet.

Marianne stretched out. She knew she had a lot of things to do, but many of those could wait until morning. Intoxicated by her surroundings, she fell into a deep sleep. Weird dreams floated in and out of her subconscious. She did not hear the suite door open. She did not feel the prick in her arm as a lethal dose of potassium carbonate was injected into her body. Her last thought was how wonderful life was and how easy everything had become.

The masked intruder felt her pulse and, confident that his job was done, left as silently as he had entered.

In San Francisco, Claude was growing increasingly anxious. Marianne had promised to deposit the cash into his account by the next morning, but he couldn't shake off his nerves. Despite this, he wasn't going to let it ruin his plans for the evening. He checked his watch and realised he was already running late for his appointment. He looked out of the window on the top floor and saw that, as usual, the Golden Gate Bridge was obscured by swirling mists as evening descended. He quickly combed over his thinning hair and applied some cream to his overly tanned face before heading out for what promised to be an exciting night.

The evening passed without any great excitement.

She was a typical San Francisco socialite - wealthy and busy, with no time for someone like him. Despite this, their date went better than some of his previous blind dates; she didn't walk out within the first five minutes like so many others had before. As he left in his car hours later, he couldn't help but feel a small sense of success.

As he drove up the steep incline towards the small village where he lived, he was too lost in his own thoughts to notice the black SUV pulling up behind him. He felt a slight bump against his rear bumper and then it was all over in an instant. With one forceful push on the next sharp turn, his car went careening off the edge of the cliff. It tumbled uncontrollably several times before finally landing upside down about 100 feet below. The impact caused it to burst into flames almost immediately, followed by a massive explosion. The driver of the SUV stopped and peered over the edge of the cliff, satisfied that his work had been done successfully. He calmly returned to his vehicle, made a U-turn, and drove back to the city without attracting any attention. On the way, he placed a call to an unlisted number in New Jersey as instructed. After it went to voicemail, he uttered just two words as previously arranged: 'Job done.'

CHAPTER - 42

FRANKFURT - A DAY LATER

Abdul touched down in Frankfurt, his nerves increasingly unsettled during the flight. The saying "if it's too good to be true, it probably isn't" kept repeating in his mind. He had done thorough research on John and his team but found nothing substantial. He also couldn't determine where Henri's loyalties lay; he was a convicted criminal after all. Abdul knew he needed to uncover the truth before making any decisions about investing the company's money. As he went through customs, thoughts of all the possible outcomes swirled in his head.

Frankfurt was experiencing a warm snap. He glanced both ways as he looked along the line of taxis and hire cars stretched end to end. There was some relief as his chauffeur gestured towards him. Abdul took in a deep breath, well at least the car was here. Whether that was a good sign or not, he couldn't decide.

As the car approached the house, his suspicions were immediately raised as, just outside the gate were the vehicles of the Bundespolizei, the federal police of Germany. The chauffeur pulled alongside and wound the window down. Abdul leaned out and, in broken German, asked what the issue was. Both officers got out of the car and a tall female officer asked. 'Are you Abdul Rehmann?'

'Yes, why do you need to know?'

Officer Werner looked sternly at Abdul. 'I think we better talk inside, sir.'

'I presume you have been away?'

Abdul nodded.

'I am sorry to tell you that you have had a break-in. However, that is not the main issue, we also found a dead person in the grounds.'

She consulted her notes.

'A John D. Davies, on his possession he had a mobile phone, and you were one of the contacts.'

'Oh, but I knew him,' Abdul stammered.

'But I am not sure how I can help you as I have been out of the country for the last few days.'

Officer Werner continued.

'We just need a bit of background of your business association and why he might have broken into your house.'

Abdul tried not to smile, as now he was starting to put all the pieces together.

Although he knew, he hid the truth. 'I was away, he replied nonchalantly, 'I have no idea. It seemed like he had been planning something while I was away. Now, I have to investigate and see if anything was missing.'

'Thank you, sir.'

Both officers got up and moved to the door.

As they left, Officer Werner turned towards him.

'If you think of anything, please could you let us know immediately? This is also a murder investigation and is now top priority.'

Abdul closed the door on them, and his immediate thought was that the Baranta oil deal had been a hoax all along. He wandered back to his office and was shocked to see the safe door open. It had clearly been expertly opened by an experienced safe-cracker or by someone who knew the combination.

He cautiously looked inside. The jewellery was still there, as well as a significant amount of euros. He flipped through the papers at the bottom and realised that all the documents from Canada, along with a memory stick, were missing. Unfortunately, he hadn't had a chance to thoroughly examine the contents of the memory stick., He sat down at his desk and jotted down some notes on the notepad that was lying near the safe. There were so many unanswered questions: Why did John Davies risk breaking into his home just to take some papers? What led to him losing his life, and who has the papers now? It was clear that the Baranta oil deal was a sham, but why was it even established in the first place? And most importantly, was his own life in danger? As he wrote down this last question, he glanced around his room and quickly closed the curtains. Not that it would make much of a difference if someone tried to enter.

He pulled out his cell phone and scrolled through the contacts until he found the right one. After dialling the number, he waited patiently for someone to answer. Finally, after half an hour, Abdul received an answer from his investigator that confirmed his suspicions.

It was clear that whoever had arranged the Baranta Oil deal not only wanted to ruin his reputation but also gain access to his property to steal the papers. And to make matters worse, Abdul's contact had discovered that John Davies was a well-known fraudster. Now he knew that there is a mastermind behind this oil deal and perhaps a sinister motive to kill him.

Abdul sat down in his armchair, feeling relieved for now that he had confirmation of what he had suspected all along.

But he never got up; the following day, his daughter found him with his head tilted back in the chair. He had been dead for several hours. There was a bullet hole in the centre of his forehead, and pieces of bone were embedded in the white satin cushion behind him. His eyes were closed, and it was clear that he had no idea what happened.

His daughter let out a piercing scream that reverberated throughout the entire house.

CHAPTER – 43

THE NEXT DAY

Back in England, things were bit calm. Ivan awoke, stretched his legs and decided to take a short walk to the local shop. He walked into a nearby shop, filled with all sorts of items that you often didn't need. A young woman from Eastern Europe greeted him at the counter with a kind smile, but he decided to forgo conversation in favour of getting some extra sleep. He quickly grabbed a newspaper from the morning delivery, along with a bottle of milk and a jar of instant coffee. As he left the shop, he smiled at the girl again, feeling bad that her name had slipped his mind. When he returned home a few minutes later, he went straight to the kitchen and was reminded of the mess from the previous night. With a sigh, he loaded the dishwasher and then sat down with a large cup of coffee and opened the newspaper. After skimming through the main headlines and sports section, he was about to put the paper down when a short article caught his attention in a small column on one of the inside pages. It reported that Abdul Rehmann, a well-known oil industrialist, had been found dead in his home in an apparent suicide. Ivan briefly felt sorry for him before remembering his own father's death years ago.

After finally feeling satisfied with the outcome, justice had been served. It was time to move forward. He poured himself another cup of coffee and returned to his newspaper, flipping to the page with the latest commodity prices. Oil had hit a record high, most likely due to ongoing conflicts disrupting supplies. The demand from rapidly developing countries like India and China also contributed to the increase. 'Ah well, leave it,' Ivan said to himself, deciding he would worry about it another day.

He settled back in his chair and soon felt his eyes droop as he dozed off. It only felt like a few moments before he was rudely awakened by his loud mobile ringtone - one that he accidentally set up just a few days ago. There was no caller ID. A disembodied voice came through sounding quite anxious.

'Hello, is that Ivan O'Neill,'

'Yes, this is him, who wants to know please?'

'This is Detective Sergeant Damien Course from the Metropolitan Police. I am phoning you about Sean O'Paul. I understand that you met him in the last couple of days?'

'Yes, that's right. How do you know that?'

'It doesn't really matter at this moment, but your details and the appointment he had with you was on his mobile phone. Anyway, I am really sorry to inform you that he was found dead this morning and we suspect foul play.'

'Oh my God, that's truly awful; who on earth would want him dead?' 'We don't know sir; all we are doing is going through his contacts and approaching them all.'

'How can I help?' Ivan asked anxiously.

'I am not sure you can sir, it is a really difficult situation, and we really don't know who to contact. He doesn't seem to have any close relatives here in London. He did have a girlfriend, but she is travelling somewhere in Asia and totally unreachable. Also, both his parents died a few months ago after a long illness.'

DS Course paused.

'I don't suppose you would be able to come to the hospital mortuary to identify him though?'

'Of course, of course; that's no problem. What's the address?

Ivan scrawled down the address on his notepad. 'OK, I will see you in about an hour.'

He ended the call and sat down again in total shock. Why was it that everyone he touched was now dead. His father, his mother, his best friend, Abdul Rehmann, Gerta and now Sean O'Paul. Surely, they weren't all connected. Or maybe they were. He wondered how Sean had met his fate.

Ivan grabbed his coat, glanced around the apartment to make sure all was secure; steam was still circling skywards from a yet to be drunk cup of coffee. He closed the door as quietly as possible, not wanting to disturb his neighbours. He stumbled down the stairs and hailed a passing black cab. He gave the driver the address of the hospital. 'Got it, boss, said the cabbie. In just 15 minutes, they arrived at St. Matthew's Hospital on Euston Road.

As they approached, a chill ran down his spine. DS Course was standing by the side of the road, waiting patiently for him.

'You must be DS Course.' Said Ivan.

'Yes, sir. I wish we could have met under better circumstances.'

'Do you have any idea what happened?'

'It's hard to say for sure, sir. What we do know is that after your last meeting with him, he went back to his office to retrieve something. Along the way, he stopped at the bar across the street and grabbed a cappuccino before continuing to his office.'

DS Course paused to take a deep breath before continuing.

'His personal assistant, Veronica, was also working late. We're not exactly sure why, but it seems she had some urgent calls to make to the USA. According to our information, Sean asked her earlier in the day to stay late and finalise some papers for him and contact a few clients for the following week's meetings. She should be here soon, and we'll need to question her further. If you'll follow me, sir, we can go identify the body before she arrives.'

CHAPTER – 44

THE EVENING BEFORE

Sean had really enjoyed the conversation with Ivan earlier that evening and cursed to himself about forgetting the file he had left open on the desk and the laptop, which still had several open documents. He approached the office and noticed the coffee shop was still open even though, as he glanced at his watch, he saw it was 10.30.

He felt a sudden urge for some caffeine, so he strolled up to the counter and asked for his usual large cappuccino. As he took a sip of the rich, dark liquid, he glanced at his office building across the street and noticed that the light was still on. This meant Veronica was probably still working. After grabbing the coffee, Sean entered his office building and stepped inside, just then the light upstairs went out. He heard footsteps coming down the stairs and soon enough, Veronica appeared in front of him.

'Hi Sean, there was no need for you to come back. I found the documents you were looking for earlier and they are on a neat pile on your desk. Also, I have shut down your computer.'

'Thank you, Veronica, I will take a quick look in any case.'

Once he reached his desk, he started to scrutinise the documents that were in a neat pile on the desk. His eyebrows furrowed in a perplexed frown. 'These figures in the main document still didn't make sense at all; I have to get a couple of associates in tomorrow morning to see if they could interpret them. 'Sean sighed and leaned back into his office chair rocking back and forward.

The sound of a ringing phone echoed in the room, coming from the jacket he had hung over the back of his chair earlier. The mobile device was now disrupting the peaceful atmosphere on his desk.

Retrieving the phone, he looked at the caller ID, swallowed a deep breath, sighed out loud and accepted the call.

'Yes, what do you want?'

There was a moment's silence then the whisper came.

'Can you come downstairs to the back alley; I have some fascinating information that could interest us both.'

Sean's curiosity was piqued. He strolled over to the door but suddenly remembered the recycling box that needed to be taken out. He grabbed the box with one hand and made his way down the stairs to the back fire exit. The door swung open; Sean glanced both ways and spotted a shadowy figure halfway down the alleyway. He deposited the recycling box to the container and continued down the pathway towards the figure. He felt a little trepidation as he approached, could this be the key to what he had been explaining to Ivan earlier that evening.

He thrust his hand forward, and the hand opposite met it with a firm grasp. The other hand placed a stack of papers into his open palm. He crouched beneath the light, quickly flipping through the first few pages. It didn't take long for him to realise that he had been tricked - these papers were completely irrelevant and had nothing to do with his research. He turned to face the person who had given him the papers, but before he could fully turn around, he heard the soft padding of footsteps approaching from behind. He tried to turn back around, but then felt a strong forearm wrap around his neck, cutting off his air supply. A sharp pain shot through his back as the knife pierced into his lung, causing instant damage. As he collapsed, he caught a glimpse of his assailant; he recognised him even though his face was partially covered.

PART-5

THE END GAME

CHAPTER – 45

MORTUARY

With every step down to the basement where the mortuary was located, Ivan's nerves grew more and more frayed. He couldn't shake the feeling that he was in grave danger. Finally, they reached the drawer, and the nurse carefully removed the white sheet. Ivan nodded, confirming that the lifeless body in front of him was indeed Sean. His mind was still reeling as he left the hospital and searched through his contacts for Dougie's information. He dialled the number, and a sleepy voice answered on the other end.

'Hello Dougie, I know this is sudden, but I desperately needed to talk to someone. My name is Ivan O'Neill, Jock O'Neill's son. You met my father before, right?'

There was a pause before Dougie responded in a reserved tone, 'Yes, that's me. Why are you calling?'

Ivan took a deep breath and explained the situation, 'I met with Sean O'Paul yesterday and now I've had to identify his dead body.'

The line went quiet for a moment before Dougie spoke again, 'Oh my god Ivan, I had heard about Abdul but had no idea about Sean. How did he die? Was it natural causes or something more sinister?

Ivan replied, 'The police haven't confirmed yet but from what I gather, they believe he was murdered.'

Ivan paused, waiting for Dougie to respond.

'We need to meet, Ivan, and as soon as possible, I am off to the US in a few days; thankfully, I delayed my flight because there were issues with my visa. I need to explain a lot to you.'

'OK, tomorrow at 12. Would that suit you?' Ivan enquired politely. 'Yes, that's fine Ivan, let's meet at my flat in Clerkenwell.'

Ivan had a restless night and woke up several times. In an attempt to clear his head before the meeting, he decided to walk to the tube station at Parsons Green. It was no longer rush hour by the time he arrived, but the train was still crowded. He got off at Blackfriars and aimlessly strolled towards Fleet Street before turning onto Clerkenwell Road. Eventually, he found himself on a road adjacent to Smithfield Market - where he finally spotted the entrance to Clerkenwell University on his left. As he approached the building, Ivan noticed a few converted houses on the left that had been turned into flats. After double-checking the number on his mobile, he pressed the corresponding button with anticipation.

Dougie opened the door cautiously and let Ivan into a surprisingly cavernous living area. On the walls were documents showing off Dougie's academic prowess with some framed pictures, which Ivan assumed were of his family. He was somewhat surprised to see a boy, probably only a little younger than himself, sitting in a leather armchair in the corner.

As Ivan walked into the centre of the room the youth rather awkwardly rose to his feet. Dougie looked at Ivan. 'Ah, you two haven't been introduced, this is Paul Carruthers; his father was also in Canada with us where it all began.'

Paul nervously nodded towards Ivan before taking a seat once again. Dougie took a good look at Ivan, noting his jet-black hair and piercing blue eyes. However, it was evident that his troubled mind lay behind those eyes.

In an attempt to make Ivan feel more comfortable, Dougie offered him a cup of coffee, which he gratefully accepted. Once everyone was settled, Dougie began to recount his lengthy tale while looking at both of them in the eye.

He shared how he had been fascinated with Chemistry since he was a young child, and how his parents had high expectations for his success. He then delved into the story of his friendship with Paul and the tragic events involving his father. Paul chimed in intermittently when necessary. Dougie continued to explain how he became involved in financing research on a "wonder" catalyst and the chaos it caused. It all sounded grim and familiar to Ivan. Dougie continued, 'It was during our time in Canada when things became more complicated, and our paths converged. And the research to find the catalyst commenced. Before going to Canada, I was asked by George Carruthers, my professor, to mentor his son,' Dougie said, gesturing toward Paul, who had been quietly listening to the unfamiliar parts of the story. 'So, Paul and I formed a partnership to continue our research for the catalyst; he was doing the donkey work, while I was giving him guidance and really not getting very far.' Dougie paused for breath.

'There was also a young Irish American student, Alicia O'Garra who also was seconded to help me. I know Paul was fond of her,' Paul nodded again. 'But to be frank, I did not really trust her at all. There were some emails I glimpsed which seemed to show her involvement in several pots.'

Paul spoke for the first time. 'My father was so special, and I am really keen to help everybody here. After all you all are trying to fulfil my father's dream of creating a catalyst and finding the culprits who destroyed everything! God knows why?' A tear ran down his left cheek and trickled into the coffee mug in front of him. 'I just need some sort of closure.'

'I know Paul,' Dougie leant behind him and gave him a hug. 'We all do, and that's why we are all here.'

Paul smiled wanly.

'But let's get to the heart of the story, where it all began. Right before George passed away, he helped me secure a spot on a project in Canada that was offering an astronomical amount of money for finding a specific catalyst. This immense pay was due to the hazardous nature of the chemicals involved and their high flammability. It was during this project that I met not only your father, Jock, but also Sean and Abdul.'

Ivan raised his eyebrows.

'So, that's why you were all in the same picture?'

'Yes, that's right, Ivan. Now virtually everyone who has touched this chemical or come close to it is dead. It's not only your father and Sean, but also there were two other project leaders, one who disappeared very strangely and the other who was killed in a boating accident in Australia.'

Dougie paused for breath again.

'So, you see, it's not only impacted you, but there have also been repercussions everywhere.'

Ivan and Paul were about to jump in, but Dougie raised his hand to stop them.

'Let me finish. Before the massive fire at the camp, which I'm sure you both are aware of, there was a significant breakthrough. I think one of my close friends had found the key to the catalyst.

Thankfully, he is still alive and the main reason I was heading to the States was to meet with him and discuss his findings.'

Dougie continued.

'You have most likely heard from various sources that this breakthrough will prevent the world from facing extinction and reverse the effects of climate change to pre-industrial levels.'

Ivan and Paul both nodded in agreement.

'What you may not know is that this discovery could potentially hold more value than the combined GDP of the UK, and possibly even a significant portion of the G7 nations. '

Dougie paused and looked in both Paul's and Ivan's eyes.

'There are trillions of pounds at stake. And my dilemma is, I am not certain if my colleague Tom in the US really did discover this catalyst. That's all the information I have, so the pressing question is : what do we do next?'

There was a stunned silence before Ivan spoke first.

'I have a list of people who I knew died because of this research? Hear it out:

'Dad – of course

'Mum – though not necessarily linked

'Gerta – my potential first girlfriend

'Sean O' Neill – definitely linked

'Abdul Rehmann – definitely linked

'George – my best friend.

'The list goes on and on.'

Paul spoke up: 'Well, there is my father, of course, and my sister and also my mother subsequently. She survived the accident but died of complications afterwards.'

Dougie nodded sagely.

'Well to add to that sad list is James White, who died in a boating accident, Graham Southwell, who allegedly left Canada early but never turned up, so is presumed dead, and at least 20 workers killed in the fire. Also, I forgot to mention the death of Paul's father's colleague in Paris that I witnessed when I was on a holiday with a friend after the end of my first term at university . The list goes on and on.'

Everyone sat glumly for a few minutes. Eventually, Paul spoke.

'Well, instead of dwelling on it, why don't we convene at a local pub and discuss the next steps?'

Dougie smiled. 'That's the best suggestion I have heard all day – there are a really pleasant two or three in Smithfield's. Let's make our way down there.'

Sitting around a round table in The Kings Crown, all nursing a pint of the local ale, felt much more comfortable than all the talk of death.

It was a typical English pub, with dark wooden beams in the low ceiling and cream-painted walls with pictures of scenes of London interspersed with anecdotal posters of various past events. It was very comforting.

'Well let's be positive,' Dougie murmured, as he supped his first beer. When I spoke to Tom just before I had to delay the flight, he was very excited about something, he wouldn't tell me on the phone, but it sounded really important.'

'Why are you telling us this,' said Ivan as he too took his first sip of the beer.

Dougie looked at him steadily.

'Well, I want both of you to come with me to the US. I am pretty sure that I can get Rhys to fund it.'

Paul looked sceptical but decided not to argue. A trip to the US would be great.

'Where are we meeting Tom?'

'He lives in Richmond, Virginia, I have no idea how and why he went there from Texas. Anyway, it is extremely warm this time of year so dress lightly.'

A few pints later, all three of them started to embrace the idea with more enthusiasm.

'What do we tell Alicia?' asked Paul when the joviality had calmed down a little bit.

'I suggest it's best she knows nothing. Anyway, she goes back to the US in a couple of weeks, so we don't need to worry about her after that. It's going to take that long to get visas sorted and all the other various bits of paperwork.' Dougie spoke firmly, 'Well, now we have a plan.

'OK let's go for it.' Ivan and Paul said in unison.

'Right, I will be in touch in a day or two. Paul, do you want to stay with me tonight? I think it's dangerous now. Ivan, will you be ok to make your way home?'

Ivan nodded. 'Yep, I'm fine.'

They left the pub, the warmth of the day giving way to a cool and refreshing evening. The walk back to Blackfriars tube station was enjoyable, and for once, Ivan felt a sense of excitement. His thoughts were tangled as he wondered if he would finally receive answers about all the death and suffering in his life. The journey back was filled with happiness and anticipation, a rare feeling for Ivan.

CHAPTER - 46

WASHINGTON DC

After two weeks, three travellers gathered at the taxi stand in Dulles airport, patiently waiting for their cab. Luckily, their visas had been processed quickly and Dougie had arranged to meet Tom in Georgetown, Washington where he was already on another project. On the way to the hotel, the taxi driver tried to engage them in conversation, but they were all too exhausted and opted for a quick nap instead. By the time they arrived at their hotel on the outskirts of Georgetown, it was well past 8pm. The Old Bell hotel boasted over 150 years of history and supposedly had hosted several former presidents during its tenure. Despite being eager to retire to their rooms, Dougie insisted on one final drink to discuss their plans for the next day. The bar at the Old Bell was like many others found in American hotels - complete with screens displaying current news or various live sports games. The trio was enthralled by the grandeur and spectacle of America, a country they had never visited before. After taking a few moments to process everything, they each requested a coffee instead of beer and found seats in front of the giant screen. They sat in silence, savouring their drinks and taking in the vibrant atmosphere around them.

Ivan spoke first. 'Dougie, what do you think we are going to find out tomorrow and please don't say, I don't know.'

Dougie smiled and after a long pause 'Well I am really hoping that we will receive some final information on this catalyst. After all that's why we are all here. Each of us has a vested interest in one way or the other.'

Paul and Ivan both nodded.

Paul whispered under his breath. 'So, this is what my dad was working on for all those years and the dangerous chemicals that ultimately killed him and indirectly responsible for all these other deaths. Has it really been worth it?'

Ivan looked at him steadily, 'I damn well hope so, Paul, I honestly do.'

Dougie just nodded, raising his cup of coffee, 'To tomorrow guys, to tomorrow.'

It was not long after at about 10pm that the three of them found their way to their respective rooms and fell asleep almost instantly.

Ivan was the first to wake up, surprised to see that it was already 10 in the morning. He glanced at his watch and calculated that back in the UK, it was 3pm. Not sure what to do with himself until their planned meeting time of 5pm in the hotel lobby, he decided to explore the city on foot.

As he made his way past the White House towards the Washington Monument, he couldn't help but admire the perfectly constructed roads that intersected at right angles with alphabetically named streets. He had figured out that the NW quadrant, where their hotel was located, seemed to be the most affluent area. On his walk, Ivan stopped at a charming coffee shop and ordered a cappuccino before sitting outside and watching the bustling scene around him. At 11am, he continued his journey and eventually reached a vast expanse of playing fields leading down to the mall. Climbing up a small incline towards the monument, Ivan couldn't contain his awe as he gazed upon its towering structure. From there he could see the Capitol Building in front of him, the reflecting pool behind him, and just to his right, hidden from view by trees, was the Jefferson Memorial. He contemplated waiting in line to go up inside the Washington Monument, but ultimately decided against it. Instead of consulting his guidebook, he wandered down towards the Smithsonian - a collection of museums that stood tall amongst the Washington skyline like a beacon. One museum in particular caught Ivan's interest: the Air and Space Museum. It took several hours to fully explore it; by late afternoon, Ivan realised he needed to grab some lunch before heading back to the hotel for their meeting at 5 pm. But before leaving downtown DC, there was just enough time for a quick stroll around the captivating Capitol Building.

As planned, the three of them gathered at the hotel bar and checked the location for their meeting with Tom at 7 pm. It appeared to be tucked away by the canal, far from any bustling areas.

WASHINGTON TUG BAR, 7.00 PM

After some searching, they finally found the bar nestled along the canal at a mooring point. It was bustling with people, but Tom was nowhere to be seen. Dougie spotted him on the far side of the bar, surrounded by five individuals, mostly women. Tom noticed them and waved enthusiastically as they approached.

Three of them joined the large table, the group parted ways to greet them, and Tom stood up to shake their hands.

'You must be Paul,' he said, then turning to Ivan, 'and you must be Ivan.' He paused before acknowledging Dougie's earlier conversation about their father's passing.

'I am so sorry for your loss. Dougie told me all about it over the phone when he booked for you guys to join me.

Tom suggested they all have a drink and offered his condolences once again. Ivan couldn't help but feel overwhelmed by the surrounding crowd, but Tom reassured him with a laugh.

'Don't worry about them,' he said, gesturing towards the group.

'This is Jeanette,' he introduced her with a nod. 'And this is Henry, Charlotte, April, and Veronica.'

The group smiled back at them, and it seemed like it was going to be a long evening ahead.

WASHINGTON TUG BAR, 10.00 PM

As the night progressed, their acquaintances slowly trickled out until only the four of them remained. Tom narrowed his gaze and leaned in closer.

'Let's go in the corner over there; it's too noisy here and I don't want anyone to overhear what I am about to show and tell you.'

All four retreated to the corner table.

At the new table, Tom had a smug smile on his face as he pulled out a small tablet from a brown bag that he hugged closely to his chest. As he switched on the device, Ivan, Dougie and Paul crowded around the small screen.

On the tablet screen, they saw a scene that was far from extraordinary. A car pulled up to a gas station and selected its fuel before driving off. It was a mundane occurrence, one that happened every day in gas stations across the country. Tom looked at the others, who simply shrugged in response.

But then, he grinned and said, 'Let me show you something.'

He switched to another memory stick and the screen changed once again. This time, it showed a tanker filling up the garage's tank. At first glance, it seemed like a normal refuelling process. However, upon closer inspection, it became clear that the tank was being emptied and cleaned with water. And after this was done, a water tanker arrived to fill up the tank - not with gasoline, but with water.

As the tank filled up, the person in charge took a moment to grab a glass and take a sip from the incoming liquid. The rest of the group watched in amazement as he drank. No one could find the words to express their shock and excitement. Tom looked at each of them knowingly, waiting for someone to speak up.

'You've found it,' Dougie finally exclaimed with a huge grin on his face.

Tom played coy and innocently asked, 'What did I find?'

Ivan chimed in, 'It's the catalyst, isn't it?'

Tom looked at Ivan with a smile and replied, 'You got it on your first try, Ivan. But let's keep this top secret for now; even the people who worked on the video thought it was just some kind of magic trick using a fake tank.'

He continued to smile at their grinning faces before explaining further.

'Right before filling the tank with water, we added just one ounce of catalyst. And voila! All the water immediately turned into ethanol while also absorbing a significant amount of CO_2.

And when we burn this fuel, only 30% of the CO_2 is released compared to what was absorbed during its creation.'

'It's revolutionary,' Ivan marvelled.

'It sure is,' Tom agreed.

'This discovery has the power to reverse centuries of human-caused damage to our planet overnight,' Paul said.

'How did you find this Tom? I thought that all the records were lost in the fire and so were any results from the catalyst experiments,' asked Dougie.

Tom smiled again and touched the side of his nose. 'Dougie, you'll remember I showed you a flash drive after the fire.' He turned to the others. 'A couple of days before the fire I was called into the weathering hut where we tested the catalysts after they had been produced. Graham was extremely excited when I met him there.

He recounted his recent discovery, his excitement barely contained. Apparently, the catalyst he created had been remarkably successful, producing pure ethanol. He admitted he initially didn't believe it but kept a copy of the formula safe on a separate memory stick. He patted his jacket pocket to reassure himself of its presence.

The others - Dougie, Ivan, and Paul - sat in stunned silence. Eventually, Dougie spoke up. 'How did you get your hands on this? And more importantly, how was it funded?'

Tom paused before responding. 'Honestly, I have no idea.' He continued, explaining that he had been receiving funds but couldn't trace the source. He had originally thought it was from his Saudi contacts, but they had all met their untimely deaths. He stopped mid-sentence, remembering Ivan's father's tragic passing.

'Sorry, Ivan,' he apologised.

'Anyway,' Tom continued, 'I know it couldn't have come from the Saudis since Abdul Rehmann - who both you, Ivan, and you, Dougie, knew well - is also dead.'

Moreover, I also know that Grant Lyons, Sean's benefactor, has shown no interest in carrying the research further. I also thought that maybe it had come from Rhys Giles, your funding source, Dougie. That made no sense either. Why would he start funding both ends?

Tom looked again at the three of them and all had rather glazed looks in their eyes.

'I suspect it's someone associated with a connection from my father's side. Out of the blue a few months ago I received a call from a woman, claiming to be a close associate of my departed father, offering funding to continue my research here in Washington.

'Before I knew it, I was in a secluded laboratory and had successfully reproduced the catalyst in a remarkably short time. Trials were conducted soon after, and that brings us to this video.

Dougie spoke in a hushed tone. 'Well, what happens now, Tom?'

'I am eagerly anticipating the offer that is sure to come. This opportunity is truly invaluable and has the potential to revolutionise our world overnight, cutting energy expenses by a staggering 90%. Not only can it replace gasoline, but with some minor adjustments, it can also be utilised in gas-powered generators and as fuel for household appliances. Its value could easily reach trillions of dollars.'

Ivan's voice was serious as he spoke: 'So this is the cause of all the deaths and murders.'

Tom nodded, his expression grim. 'Yes, it's hard to believe but it's true. And despite the losses we've faced, I believe it was worth it to save future generations.'

He paused before continuing. 'Money doesn't matter to me, and I hope it doesn't matter to any of you either. This is about something bigger than us, and we need to ensure it stays in the right hands.'

Leaning in closer, Tom stressed the importance of keeping their discovery safe. 'It has already caused so much suffering, so we have a responsibility to protect it. And most importantly, we need to protect ourselves too.'

He looked at three of them. 'I trust all of you, which is why I'm giving you one of the only two copies of the formula and the accompanying video.' He let out a chuckle, breaking the tense atmosphere for a moment and slid the memory stick across the table to Paul.

'Paul, you take this, after all, it all started with your father all those years ago. He was the one who truly believed in it from the start.'

Tom's hands trembled slightly as he gave a nervous smile. 'I don't want to alarm anyone, but I have a feeling I've been followed for the past few days,' he said with a hint of anxiety in his voice. 'Just to be on the safe side, let's all be extra cautious.'

Tom took another sip of his drink before addressing the group. 'I plan on staying for a couple more drinks, but you all look exhausted. How about we meet tomorrow morning and discuss our game plan?'

Dougie and Ivan nodded in agreement.

It took some time for the three of them to navigate through the dense crowd near the entrance. It was quite a relief to be outside in the sultry late evening air.

'Let's go then' said Ivan, and they began walking down the canal towards central Georgetown.

CHAPTER – 47

GEORGETOWN CANAL, 11.00 PM

They had barely taken thirty or forty steps when a deafening noise erupted from behind them, resembling the roar of a jet engine or the rush of a speeding train. They quickly turned around to see a massive explosion engulfing the bar they had just left. The force of the blast knocked all three of them to the ground, narrowly avoiding shards of glass and debris flying in their direction. Then, an eerie silence settled over the area. Dougie cautiously looked over at Ivan and Paul, who were still lying motionless on the ground. He could taste the acrid combination of dust and smoke in his mouth as he carefully crawled towards them, not wanting to disrupt the peace.

'Are you OK?'

Ivan mumbled, 'I think so.'

Paul remained motionless for a few moments before answering. 'I think so, but my ankle hurts a bit, I must have twisted it.'

Dougie turned to look at the bar, where smoke still billowed from the rubble that had once been the front of the building. Pushing himself into a squatting position, he cautiously made his way towards the bar. In the distance, he could hear sirens approaching, the arrival of police and paramedics. Taking a closer look inside the bar, or what was left of it, he was hit with a repulsive odour later identified as burning flesh by investigators. He quickly tried to piece together what had happened and came to the conclusion that no one could have survived the explosion. Unable to hear any signs of life inside, he assumed the worst. Just as he was about to move closer, two burly law enforcement officers stopped him from doing so.

They just glared at him before grunting, 'Get away, it's not safe.'

Dougie moved back to Ivan and Paul and brought them into a close huddle. They looked shaken and white as sheets.

Dougie quickly processed the situation.

'You two will return to the hotel, and I'll face the interrogation. Remember to stay out of sight once you're there. It seems this attack was carefully orchestrated to eliminate anyone who may still be associated with the catalyst.'

Ivan's expression twisted into a frown, clearly showing his desire to stay. He seemed like he wanted to say something but changed his mind.

Dougie fixed his eyes on Paul, who was still shaking.

'Listen Paul, Tom is dead; there is no way anyone could survive that blast which leaves only the three of us and Tom's unknown benefactor or benefactors with the knowledge of the catalyst. We must preserve that for Tom's sake and stay safe.'

'OK,' stuttered Paul. 'I will go along with what you think best.'

It felt like an eternity, but they eventually arrived back at the hotel. Exhausted, they both fell asleep in the same large suite they had been in just the day before, but under very different circumstances.

Dougie got back to the suite at about 4 am. It had been a frantic night, and he was totally exhausted after being questioned by both the local enforcement agencies and the FBI. The FBI clearly thought it was a terror-related incident, but Dougie knew if he explained the real reason, they would think he was insane.

The night was filled with unease, and when they finally woke up, Dougie knew they needed to come up with a plan. It was likely that whoever was responsible for causing the chaos would try to contact them soon. With that in mind, he immediately called Rhys in the UK and briefed him on the situation. He also sought his advice on their next course of action.

There was a pause at the other end of the line.

'We have to get Paul and Ivan on a flight home right away. I'll have my PA take care of that for us. Wait for my call; I'll be in touch shortly.'

As expected, Pam, Rhys's personal assistant, called back within minutes.

She got straight to the point. 'Ivan and Paul are booked on the 5 pm flight from Dulles to London. A car will pick them up shortly. They can take you to a place of safety prior to the airport lounge opening.'

Dougie looked at Paul and Ivan, who were both pale and physically shaking. He hugged them both.

'Don't worry; it's all over now, guys, you can relax. I just need to wait to see if there is any follow-up.'

Later that day, Dougie checked his laptop and saw that the flight had taken off on time.

Hearing from Ivan while waiting in line at the gate eased his nerves, and he finally allowed himself to relax. He lounged on the couch and grabbed a beer from the fridge in the corner of his suite. It didn't quite taste as good as the previous day, but it still helped him unwind as he tried to make sense of everything that had happened in the past 24 hours. He began scribbling notes on the hotel notepad but couldn't get far as he kept writing the word "catalyst" over and over again. Was the video clip of the catalyst real? He was sure it was; why would Tom lie about something like that? If that was true, then the memory stick in his hand was more valuable than anything else on Earth.

As he drifted off to sleep, his mind filled with frightening scenarios and endless possibilities. He was abruptly awakened by the loud ringtone of his phone, set to a classic rock song by Guns 'n' Roses. A smile formed on his lips as he answered the call.

'Is that Dougie Fields?' A gruff voice said.

'Yes, that's me, who wants to know?'

'Don't ask stupid questions, we need to meet. You have something we need.'

Dougie felt a lump sink to the bottom of his stomach, but he managed to keep calm.

'What might that be then?' Dougie said innocently.

'Again, don't ask stupid questions, just be downstairs in the lobby in 15 minutes.'

'OK but...' the phone went dead.

Dougie sat on the edge of the bed and contemplated his approach before the meeting. He ultimately decided to adopt a calm and collected demeanour.

CHAPTER - 48

THE MEETING

Dougie's heart was pounding as he made his way to the elevator, unsure of what awaited him. Upon arriving at the lobby, he found it deserted except for a young boy who glanced up at him. The boy walked over and asked for Dougie's name before handing him a crumpled piece of paper with handwritten words on it. There were only four words on it.

'Ratcatcher Bar M Street'

After a brief pause, Dougie gathered his courage and adjusted his jacket. He then inquired with the concierge about the location of the bar.

It was a five-minute walk.

He walked into a fairly empty bar, apart from the far end, which was busy with some sort of celebration party. A lone man sat at a nearby table, his nose buried in a newspaper, making it difficult to recognise him. However, he didn't have time to dwell on it as a woman in a black gown waved for his attention from a discreetly placed small table in the far corner. Dougie approached cautiously, carefully navigating through the tables. She greeted him with a welcoming gesture, and they shook hands briefly before he took a seat across from her.

'It's really good to finally meet you, Dougie. Let me get to the point.'

Dougie interrupted her with a sharp comment. 'You could at least tell me your name?'

She looked impatient. 'You can call me Sheila Black. You know why you are here?'

Dougie nodded, feeling quite intimidated by her presence. Sheila took out an envelope and placed it between them.

'Inside the envelope, you will find a round-trip ticket to the Maldives from the UK and a Swiss bank account under your name, along with accounts for your colleagues. Once I receive what I'm after, I will deposit $20 million into each of these accounts. All I ask for in return is the memory stick you have. '

Dougie had been expecting this, but maybe not so directly. 'Do you really think I would bring the memory stick with me?'

'OK!' Sheila said firmly. 'We will go back to your hotel and get it, unless you are not interested in the money and,' she shifted to a more sinister tone, 'the welfare of your friends?'

Dougie got up slowly; as he did so, he finally recognised the person sitting on the corner table. It was James White. But it couldn't be him, he had been killed in a boating accident, unless that was all part of the game. He thought.

As he walked out of the bar with Sheila Black by his side, he couldn't help but reflect on how they had ended up in this situation.

CHAPTER – 49

SHEILA BLACK

As they walked out of the bar, Sheila Black by his side, Dougie couldn't shake the feeling of how everything had spiralled out of control. How did he even get here? The night felt heavy, and he had this nagging sense and started thinking back, trying to piece it all together. He realised that the woman walking next to him had some resemblance to someone he knew closely. She had the same sharp features and dark hair as Alicia. Alicia, who had been working with Paul Carruthers on his project in the UK. Dougie tried to connect the dots and came up with a plan in his mind.

'Let me give it a last try and see if I can get some answers from so-called Sheila,' he said to himself.

Dougie started a friendly conversation and made Sheila believe that he is after money, he doesn't bother what people do with the catalyst and he is worried about his life and would do anything to save himself. He opened up the conversation, 'I feel I know you! You are Alicia's sister. Aren't you?' At first, Sheila refused but later, she opened up and shared her story.

'Yes, you're right! I am Alicia's sister. And I am trapped in this chaos. At first, it seemed like a harmless job, but it had turned into something much darker. I used to work as Grant Lyon's trustworthy personal assistant, which gave me access to all sorts of insider information about the secret project in Canada. Recently, things between me and Grant had been strained, so I started snooping around. One morning, while clearing Grant's desk, I stumbled on some documents about a supposed miracle cure for climate change. I didn't understand all the technical details, but I knew my sister Alicia, with her chemistry background, could figure it out.

'It didn't take long for me to connect the dots. I tracked down a lab in London that I knew are still carrying out their secret research on the catalyst after Canada's mishap. I further delved into those documents and managed to get Alicia a job in your lab. Then I came to know about the value of the catalyst. And I wanted to get hold of this invaluable product. But what I hadn't expected was how messy things would get. It wasn't just about navigating tricky situations anymore—I had to start eliminating obstacles, even if it meant dealing with people in a more...permanent way.

'At one point, I thought about backing out. But then, out of nowhere, I started getting these mysterious messages, promising me a huge pay out if I could get her hands on catalyst. At first, to be honest, I didn't take it seriously, but when £250,000 showed up in my bank account, I got greedy. That's when I started researching further and met Tom, and started to fund him. Later on he became a dear friend. He told me everything about everyone who was involved in this project. So together, we decided that we all would form a consortium secretly and would not let this catalyst fall into foul hands. With that intention, Tom reached out to you and set up a meeting in the US. Just when I thought I had things under control, this disaster happened, and I lost Tom. Now, I am not worried about where this catalyst goes. I want to save my life, get money and lead a peaceful life, and I suggest you do the same.

Dougie nodded in agreement.

As they neared the hotel, Sheila couldn't help but smile to herself. She looked at Dougie, wondering if maybe things were coming together a bit too easily. She felt a mix of excitement and unease, knowing that the real danger might still be lurking around the corner, waiting to catch them off guard.

CHAPTER – 50

THE FINAL SHOWDOWN

Dougie grinned as he boarded the plane at Dulles airport, holding tightly to the tickets to the Maldives and the promise of $20 million. He had also stocked up on new beachwear during his stay in Washington. He was confident that Sheila and her accomplices would not stop until they had eliminated him, so keeping a low profile was crucial. Of course, he also had the added security of having the true catalyst formula safely stored in his pocket while he handed over a fake version on a memory disc. The fake formula would only work for a limited number of uses before needing to be replaced, making it an expensive affair compared to Tom's version which could be used countless times. Dougie chuckled to himself as he thought about how easy it had been to deceive Sheila by giving her the fake formula. It wasn't long before his mind drifted back to the last few years and all that had led up to this moment. In his pocket lay the solution to reverse years of climate change - a simple formula that would make all the difference. He had already made arrangements with Paul and Ivan to meet them in the Maldives, where they would put their plans into action. Dougie settled into his seat, preparing for a long flight ahead.

Meanwhile Siobhan had worked quickly and had verified that the catalyst did indeed produce the correct initial results at her laboratory in Virginia. Now, they would move on to the repeat and longevity tests.

Delighted with the results, she called James White.

'One last job, James. We are following Dougie Fields, I will text you, his location as soon as I trace his whereabouts.'

James read the text and then decided what he would do. He dialled another number and spoke clearly.

Hearing the response, he was satisfied and put the phone down.

Two days later Male airport was its normal incredibly busy place, and it took a while for Dougie to find Ivan and Paul. Dougie brought them up to date with all the events from the previous 48 hours, looking very pleased with himself.

Ivan looked at them. 'Something is not right here, Dougie. I cannot believe that Sheila has been responsible for all these killings. It doesn't make any sense at all. The connection to her sister, yes, that makes sense, but where did she get the funds, and what is she going to do with the catalyst information now?'

Dougie's smile disappeared.

'Well, what about the James White connection?' Ivan paused for a moment.

'Well, that makes more sense, but again, I don't understand how he got involved. Anyway, let's get to this Tilumba place, and we can discuss it a bit further. Let's enjoy it while we can.'

Tilumba was extremely hot, so none of them slept well that night. Dougie, in particular, was mulling things over, wondering if Ivan was right about everything.

Breakfast was a sombre affair, which was a pity as the setting was so idyllic. Palm trees fluttered in the light breeze, and the native wildlife buzzed faintly. None of them could eat much of the lovely array of fruits on display in the buffet.

After breakfast, they decided to take a walk around the island to the remote side away from the hotel. As they did so, Paul kept glancing behind them, in case they were chased by someone. Finally, they reached the beach on the far side of the island. It looked deserted, but as they moved across to a rocky alcove. Ivan's breath caught in his throat. There was a figure lying on the shore that looked like a dead body. As they approached, it became clear that it was indeed a white man in his late 40s, and he had been shot recently. Already, tiny crabs were crawling over him, drawn to the wound on his forehead. Paul stood frozen in shock while Dougie gasped audibly. Ivan tried to speak but couldn't find the words.

A rustle from behind them caused them to turn around. They could not believe their eyes to see James White walking towards them with a big grin on his face and a pistol in his hand. He waved it playfully and gestured for them to sit down.

'Are you planning to kill us, James?' Dougie asked in a flat tone, almost accepting.

James chuckled. "'You really don't understand, do you? I'm not here to kill you. I'm here to save you.'

Ivan's heart flickered with a mix of hope and confusion. How could James possibly save them while pointing a gun at them?

'The person lying here is the assassin," James continued, "Not me. I managed to kill him before he got to you.'

Ivan walked over to the body and turned it over, revealing the full face. He gasped in horror.

'It's Dave,' he said, shocked. 'He was my father's best friend in Saudi and helped my family through the trauma of my father's funeral.'

James looked unsurprised by this revelation.

'Why don't I start from the beginning?' he said, taking a deep breath. 'Long time ago, there were three incredibly rich oil companies whose entire existence depended on producing more and more oil. You all know the main players: Abdul Rehmann," he looked at Ivan, "Rhys Giles, and Grant Lyons,' he glanced at Dougie.

'All of them had a vested interest in maintaining the status quo. None of them wanted this new catalyst to come to market, so they did everything in their power to stop it. Paul, your father first discovered the potential of this catalyst and shared it with you, Dougie. At that time, he probably didn't have a clue about the foul play that these big oil industrialists were planning. Your father helped them bring all the experts together to develop it. Unfortunately, as soon as he got to know the truth, he died from cancer. He couldn't save his daughter, but he saved you. Sadly, he also lost a colleague in France, which I believe you, Dougie, knew about."

After that, they came up with this strange scheme to bring us all together and pay us huge sums for finding the catalyst. Even though they believed it was impossible, they wanted to make us believe it too. Dougie, Tom, and Sean were seen as the biggest threats, so it worked out well to keep you all in one place. You weren't trying to save the planet like you thought; you were actually helping them destroy it.

Once the catalyst was successfully created, they had to act fast. They were caught off guard and had to clean up the chaos before it destroyed them. The first person they targeted was my friend Graham Southwell. I'm not sure who they hired to kill him, but Dave here may have been involved. After he disappeared, I was afraid that I would be next. That's why, after the incident in Canada, I faked my own death and went undercover to uncover the truth.

'Next, they went after your father Ivan. I'm not entirely sure of the order of events, but then your best friend was killed in police custody, and another friend of yours died in a hit-and-run.

'I am certain that Dave was responsible for your father's death and probably your friend's as well. By then, I had managed to gain connections with both Grants and Rhys' chain of command and earn their trust.

'I had also been in communication with the UK police and law enforcement agencies in the US to gather evidence. I was almost finished with that task.' Ivan interrupted James abruptly.

'What about Abdul? Why was he murdered?' James nodded his head slowly, thinking through all the possibilities.

'My guess is he became too greedy and threatened to expose the entire operation, so they got rid of him as well. He probably had some documents on the catalyst, but those were stolen too. Then it was just Sean left.' He paused before adding, 'I think Dave was responsible for his death as well. 'The room fell silent as everyone processed this information. Sheila's name came up next, and I explained that I believed she was working with Dave and had become consumed by greed and distanced herself from Grant while being kept away from the main activities. However, I feel she tried to be a double agent.'

They all looked shell-shocked. It was Dougie who finally broke the silence with a question: 'What do we do now?' Paul and Ivan echoed his sentiment simultaneously.

James took a moment before responding, 'I am going to clean up this mess, I want them to be convinced that you all are murdered as per their plan, meanwhile, you should lay low for a few days while I handle things. I have arranged for you to stay on an island nearby. Once Grant and Rhys are arrested, you can go back to your normal lives as if nothing ever happened.'

This time all three of them piped up.

'What about the catalyst, has it been a complete waste of time?' No, I don't think so, let's wait and see, just wait and see.'

Dougie smiled. 'Ah well,' he said. 'We can wait until the world is ready to be saved, we have waited 300 years, so another few months won't matter.

THE END

EPILOGUE

James was true to his word.

Grant and Rhys were arrested and are now in prison.

James had managed to persuade the authorities to act and was now pursuing his dream of living in Noosa.

Ivan came back to London and was content having found his true love.

Dougie and Paul are already working together on another project, this time relating to plastic regeneration.

What about the catalyst? Dougie also wondered if he had actually looked at that residue that Paul had accidentally created all those months ago and realised that maybe that was also a catalyst. Anyway, the real catalyst is in a safe in Dougie's office, and that is another story which is to be continued...

ABOUT THE AUTHOR

Born in London's East End and now residing in Buckinghamshire, Stephen brings a lifetime of rich experiences to his writing. Married for 28 years, blessed with three children and a grandchild, his personal life is as fulfilling as his professional journey.

He studied Industrial Chemistry at university, graduating with honours. His university years were marked by an awakening to the profound implications of chemical research, inspired by a mentor's passion for discovering new chemical compounds.

Post-university, he travelled the globe, deepening his concerns about environmental issues. It was during a significant stint in the USA that he became acutely aware of the detrimental effects of fossil fuels on our planet. This revelation planted the seeds for his debut book, which resonates more than ever in today's environmentally conscious society.

An avid sports enthusiast, Stephen is a keen sportsman and a certified rugby and football coach.